Dear Reader,

A day of shop[...]
candlelight din[...]
what better w[...] to spend a day set aside to
thank her for the many gifts she gives to her family? In
celebration of motherhood, we've put together this new
collection, featuring some very special single mothers as
they meet and marry some very special heroes.

In "Nobody's Child," a classic story from Emilie Richards,
foster mother Gemma Hancock gets the surprise of her
life when she falls in love with the handsome police officer
who brings home her latest charge. There's just something
about the way rugged Officer Farrell Riley cares for the
little orphan girl that makes Gemma long for his loving
touch.

The "Baby on the Way" is what brings J. T. Walker
and Madeline Reed together in Marie Ferrarella's
heartwarming new story. Just imagine how *you* would feel
if you went into labor on the side of the road, only to be
rescued by a handsome stranger! Now that J.T. and Maddy
have shared the miracle of bringing Maddy's baby into the
world, will love follow?

In Elizabeth Bevarly's wonderful new romance,
"A Daddy for Her Daughters" is what Naomi Carmichael
gets when she finds herself sharing parent duty with
dashing Sloan Sullivan. Now if Naomi could just figure
out how to make the sexy bachelor say "I do," she'd
be a happy mom, indeed!

We hope you enjoy these wonderful stories, and that
you'll take a day to relax, enjoy and celebrate someone
very special—you!

Happy reading!

The Editors of Silhouette Books

EMILIE RICHARDS

Award-winning author Emilie Richards believes opposites attract, and her marriage is vivid proof. "When we met," the author says, "the only thing my husband and I could agree on was that we were very much in love." The couple has lived in eight states and briefly abroad, and now resides in Virginia. Emilie loves creating complex characters who make positive changes in their lives. And she's a sucker for happy endings.

MARIE FERRARELLA

earned a master's degree in Shakespearean comedy and, perhaps as a result, her writing is distinguished by humor and natural dialogue. This RITA Award-winning author's goal is to entertain and to make people laugh and feel good. She has written over 100 books for Silhouette, some under the name Marie Nicole. Her romances are beloved by fans worldwide and have been translated into Spanish, Italian, German, Russian, Polish, Japanese and Korean.

ELIZABETH BEVARLY

was born and raised in Louisville, Kentucky, and earned her B.A. with honors in English from the University of Louisville in 1983. When she's not writing, Elizabeth enjoys old movies, old houses, good books, whimsical antiques, hot jazz and even hotter salsa (the music, not the sauce). She resides with her husband and young son back home in Kentucky.

EMILIE RICHARDS
MARIE FERRARELLA
ELIZABETH BEVARLY

A Mother's Day

Silhouette Books

Published by Silhouette Books

America's Publisher of Contemporary Romance

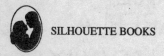

SILHOUETTE BOOKS

A MOTHER'S DAY

Copyright © 2002 by Harlequin Books S.A.

ISBN 0-373-48461-5

The publisher acknowledges the copyright holders of the individual works as follows:

NOBODY'S CHILD
Copyright © 1998 by Emilie Richards McGee

BABY ON THE WAY
Copyright © 2002 by Marie Rydzynski-Ferrarella

A DADDY FOR HER DAUGHTERS
Copyright © 2002 by Elizabeth Bevarly

Visit Silhouette at www.eHarlequin.com

Printed in U.S.A.

CONTENTS

NOBODY'S CHILD   9
Emilie Richards

BABY ON THE WAY   141
Marie Ferrarella

A DADDY FOR HER DAUGHTERS   243
Elizabeth Bevarly

NOBODY'S CHILD
Emilie Richards

Dear Reader,

All of us have issues that are particularly dear to our hearts, and one of mine is adoption. I absolutely believe that each and every child deserves a home where he or she is loved and valued, and adoption is just one of the ways we, as a society, can make that happen.

My husband and I are adoptive parents. Our daughter came to us from Calcutta many years ago, a six-year-old fascinated by the extravagance of our American home and by the flickering picture on our television set, which carried the image of Mother Teresa, whom she had last seen in an orphanage so far away.

But when I think about adoption, I also think about the other families I met on our own adoption journey. The friends who had their health benefits canceled when they tried to adopt a child with severe medical problems. (They went ahead with the adoption anyway.) The friends who took children with fatal illnesses, with mental handicaps, with severe emotional problems. None of them were saints or martyrs. They were simply people who believed they could make a positive difference in the life of a child. And they did.

I'm delighted to be part of this collection of stories. I'm thankful to be the mother of four children who bring joy into my heart every day. And I'm particularly happy that my own experience with adoption brought me into contact with so many wonderful people who change the world one child at a time in beautiful and extraordinary ways.

My warmest wishes for a happy Mother's Day.

Emilie Richards

Chapter 1

"**N**obody's here, damn it. Something tipped them off!"

Farrell Riley gave his partner, Cal, a curt nod as he tried not to breathe in more air than he needed to sustain life. The house smelled the way it looked, fetid and filthy. Months of garbage had been carelessly shoved to the borders of most of the rooms to make walkways, and even now, with a dozen of Hazleton's finest plowing through the house, a rat feasted contentedly not more than ten feet from his shoe.

"They must have gotten out just seconds before we surrounded the house," Cal said. He sounded the way Farrell felt. Disgusted, tired. Pissed. The house on Keller had been watched for days, the raid carefully planned. The small city of Hazleton, Ohio, had its share of drug problems, but not enough that losing to dealers was a ho-hum experience. Nearby, the slamming of doors and angry shouts testified to the frustrations of his brothers in blue.

"It doesn't look like they need us anymore." Farrell gave a halfhearted kick at the rat, which had moved closer, like a friendly puppy expecting a treat. Farrell and Cal had been called in as backup, but clearly, the unit in charge could handle the remains of the unsuccessful raid on their own.

"I'll get the word." Cal holstered his gun and left Farrell and the rat alone in what passed for a bedroom.

While he waited, Farrell did another visual survey, although by now he knew exactly what he would see. A bare mattress spilled its guts in a corner, and a frayed sleeping bag lay crumpled at its foot. A chest of drawers, with only two of its three drawers intact, was covered with bottles and vials. The kitchen was a makeshift drug lab, but this room had been used for storage as well as sleeping. Boxes of chemicals were stacked in the corner opposite the mattress, and Cal's cursory search of the closet had revealed more of the same.

Farrell shoved a hand through his unruly dark hair and wondered, as he always did, about the choices people made. Some undetermined number of people had made a conscious decision to live, eat and sleep in this hellhole. They had chosen to make and sell illegal, mind-and-soul-destroying drugs. And what had they gotten in return for this pathetic example of the Puritan work ethic? Filth and rats and, at the moment, cops crawling all over their humble home.

Farrell was an orderly man. Everything he owned had its own special place and could be found in a matter of seconds. Clutter made him uneasy, and this house would have made him crazy if he'd been forced to stay overnight. Now, with no way to bring order out of chaos, he did the only thing he could think of. He closed the closet door with an angry shove and turned to go in search of Cal.

"No!"

For a moment Farrell stood very still and wondered if his imagination was running away with him. He thought he'd heard a child's cry. But no one else was in the room.

The bedroom was silent again, except for the noise of cops rummaging through the adjacent hallway. Farrell did another quick exam, but the closet was the only possible source of the sound. He turned the doorknob and pulled the door toward him until it was wide open; then he shone his flashlight inside.

And he saw what Cal, who had examined the closet first, had not.

"Oh, sweetheart…" Farrell squatted on the floor so that he could peer between two tall stacks of boxes. Two very blue eyes peered back at him, tear-filled eyes over a streaming nose and a mouth that trembled inconsolably.

The little girl—at least, he thought by the length of the hair the child was female—tried to wiggle farther away from him. But she was literally boxed in, with no place to go.

"I didn't know you were here. You must be scared to death," he said as softly as his baritone could manage.

She didn't even blink. She stared at him as if she were waiting for him to raise his fist, as if that was what she expected.

Some emotion as dark as the closet shuddered through him. "It must be lonely in there." He sat back a little to show her he had no intention of hurting her. "I'd be scared, if I were you."

Her lip wobbled, and her nose ran. But she still didn't blink.

"And I think I'd be hungry," he continued. "Are you hungry?"

She didn't nod, but something changed behind her eyes, as if she were reassessing him.

Farrell wished that he had something to give her, some offering that would convince her he could be trusted. Cal had a package of cupcakes in their patrol car, but Farrell knew he couldn't leave her long enough to go for them. "If you come with me, I have a surprise." He smiled at her, something he didn't do often. His cheeks and lips felt rusty from disuse.

She didn't move. She watched him, her blue eyes taking in everything from the unflinching gray of his eyes to the tips of his highly polished shoes.

He didn't know which of them would have given in first if it hadn't been for the rat. With the bravado of a domestic pet, it came closer to investigate this new turn of events. The child's eyes flicked in its direction; then, with a small cry, she launched herself at Farrell.

He hardly had time to catch her. She was sobbing in his arms, babbling incoherently, with her arms wrapped in a death hold around his neck. He got to his feet and shooed the rat with his foot. Then, with the too-thin body plastered against his, he went to report what he'd found.

The child was filthy and almost naked. Despite the cool spring evening and the unheated house, she had been dressed in nothing more than thin cotton underpants when she had jumped into Farrell's arms. The house had yielded no clothes for her to wear, but Cal had produced a Police Athletic League sweatshirt from the squad car trunk, and Farrell had slipped that over her head to keep her warm. The sweatshirt fell well past her feet.

Right now she was sitting on his lap, a position she absolutely refused to relinquish, and nibbling on a cupcake. He had expected her to wolf it down, but her response was sadder. She nibbled, as if she had to make this unexpected treat last for hours. She nibbled as if she was uncertain another meal would ever turn up.

Farrell leaned against the back seat with his legs

over the side while he and Cal waited for Child Welfare to come and claim her. Red-haired Cal, who at twenty-four was admirably broad shouldered but fast gaining a pot belly, rested his back against the car. "How old do you think she is?"

Farrell shrugged. "I don't know anything about kids."

"I'm guessing about two. I have nieces and nephews."

Cal's wife was expecting their first child, so Farrell knew his partner took an interest in all things family. "I bet none of them look like this one, do they?"

"Sometimes..." Cal cleared his throat. "Sometimes I wish we could make the laws, not enforce 'em."

"That's why we vote." But Farrell's voice conveyed his own anger at a system that didn't always protect children.

"Yeah. Well, I didn't vote for any law that lets parents hurt their own kids."

Farrell shot him a warning glance. The child was young, but there was no telling how much she understood. "She'll be taken care of tonight. That's something."

"Yeah. Something."

A beefy officer who was still wearing a protective vest came over to join them. Sergeant Archie Weatherstone had been on the Hazleton police force for twenty years, and he had seen everything, including plenty of abortive drug raids. But now even Archie shook his head at the sight of the little girl. "Got some bad news."

"You ever got any other kind?" Cal said.

Archie's voice had a permanent rasp from too many cigarettes. "Child Welfare's emergency team is otherwise occupied. They can't come for another hour, at least."

"So what do we do? Take her to the station?" Farrell looked down at the child in his lap. She was still trembling, and he couldn't imagine putting the little girl through more hours of terror. "I don't like this."

"Don't worry. They gave me an address. They have emergency foster homes set up for situations like this one. You can take her to this one yourself. That's where she'll spend the night, anyway. Then, as soon as the team's free, they'll go there and do the intake exam."

"A home?"

"Yeah. The woman in charge is expecting you."

"A home with a bed? Food?"

"No bars on the windows. No maniac juvenile offenders. A home."

Farrell nodded, and the knot in his stomach unclenched a little. "Yeah. Okay."

"Think you can pry her loose long enough to hook her into a seat belt?"

Farrell made a stab at trying to extricate the little girl from his lap. She went rigid as a barn beam, and her lip began to tremble again.

"It's the law," Archie reminded him.

"How far's this house?"

"Galeon." The section of Hazleton Archie named was fifteen minutes away from Keller Avenue, a residential area on the way up, but still best known for its old houses in need of renovation.

Farrell wrapped his arms around the little girl. "Galeon, huh? We can take the back roads."

"I won't arrest you. Do what you want." Archie gave him the address and walked away.

"I'll drive slow and careful," Cal said. "You know, you look pretty good with a kid on your lap."

Farrell covered the little girl's feet with the hem of the sweatshirt. "Take a picture. It's the last time you'll see it."

"Nah, Sheila and I are making you a godfather. Remember?"

Farrell slid off the seat, still gently holding the child, who was spilling cupcake crumbs on his perfectly pressed pants. "Let's go."

Gemma Hancock checked all her preparations for the third time. A child. She was getting a child. She couldn't really smile. Any child who came to her in the middle of the night was a child who had undergone trauma. She grieved for all neglected children. In a perfect world a foster home would never be needed. But although her fondest wish was that her own services would someday become obsolete, she was glad that tonight she had a home and love and good sense to offer a child in crisis.

A child. A little girl.

The telephone rang and she almost yanked it off the kitchen wall. "Hello?"

She listened as Marge Tremaine, the caseworker who had first called to ask if she could take the abandoned child, explained that things weren't going well with the emergency team. Marge sounded rattled, an unusual condition for a woman with multiple years in a job that most people left after a short stint.

Gemma saw headlights as a car pulled in to her driveway. "I'll evaluate the situation. If I need to have someone come and take a look at her tonight, I'll let you know."

Marge was grateful and perfunctory, in a hurry to get back to her crisis. She promised that if all was well, she would see the child first thing in the morning. Gemma hung up just as the doorbell rang.

She straightened her sweater as she headed for the front of the house, and wished she'd had time to brush her hair.

The police officer standing on the other side of the door was tall and lean. She had a brief impression of hair the color of bittersweet chocolate and a face as stern as the Old Testament Jehovah.

"Gemma Hancock?"

She smiled, but she had already lowered her gaze to the tiny bundle in his arms. "Right." The little girl had been sleeping, but now, as if she felt a stranger staring at her, her eyelids parted.

Gemma's heart thudded against her breastbone. "Hi, there," she said softly. "You look comfortable."

The little girl began to cry silently, gigantic tears that slid down dirt-streaked cheeks. Gemma's smile didn't waver, although her heart beat double time in sympathy. "Well, of course you're feeling sad."

"She hasn't said a word," the police officer said. "Not since I found her. No, that's not quite true," he added, as if telling the story exactly the way it had happened was important to him. "She said something, but I couldn't understand her."

Gemma nodded. She looked back up at the man with the child in his arms. He was taller than she was by six inches, at least, and his sober expression reminded her of old "Dragnet" reruns. But this man was the looker that Jack Webb had never been. He was, in fact, as ruggedly masculine and appealing as any man she had ever seen.

"She seems to like where she is," Gemma said. "But you're going to have to turn her over to me eventually."

"Is anyone else here? In case you have a problem?"

She knew exactly what he was asking. At first glance she didn't necessarily inspire confidence. She was small-boned and deceptively fragile in appearance. She had wide pale green eyes that always made her seem a little lost, and fine shoulder-length blond hair that looked as if it should be tied up in ribbons.

"I'll be fine," she assured him. "I'm trained for this."

He hesitated for a moment, then held out his arms. The little girl began to shriek. Gemma had taken in his skeptical expression as he'd tentatively offered the child. Now he snatched her back as if Gemma was planning to roast her for supper.

"No!" The little girl clung to him, refusing to let Gemma take her.

"Well, she knows one word," Gemma said.

"She doesn't like you."

Gemma couldn't be angry at him. He probably had children of his own. He was probably an exceptional father. "Officer...?"

"Riley." He balanced the little girl against his chest.

"Does she have a name, too?"

"Not one we know."

"It's not that she doesn't like me," she explained patiently. "It's just that she's comfortable with you. She feels safe."

"I don't know anything about kids."

She suspected he knew a lot more than he thought he did. "Were you the one to find her?"

He gave a gruff nod.

"I'll bet she sees you as her rescuer." She brushed the little girl's lank brown hair off her filthy forehead. The child flinched.

"What are you going to do?"

"The question is, what are *you* going to do? If you have to leave immediately, I'll have to take her and that will be that. But if you have a few minutes to help calm her, that would be better." *For both of you,* she added silently.

"I guess I can stay."

She tried not to smile. She knew that, deep down inside, he had absolutely no intention of relinquishing the child until he was sure she was okay.

A second cop came up the walkway to stand behind Officer Riley. He grinned at Gemma appreciatively. "You a foster kid or a foster mom?"

Since there had been nothing provocative about the comment, she gave a friendly nod. "We're going to take the transfer slowly. Could you use a cup of coffee?"

The man clapped his hand on Officer Riley's shoulder. "I've got to run back to the station before we sign off."

Officer Riley looked pained. "Go ahead. Just stop and pick me up when you're finished."

The other man nodded and took off again.

"Come on in." Gemma stepped aside. "I have a rocker in the living room. Let's try that."

"Is anyone else home? Will we wake up your husband? Kids?"

"No, I live alone." She didn't add that this child was her first placement. He was edgy enough about leaving the little girl.

She watched him do a covert examination of the house as he followed her into the living room. She had moved into the house one year after her husband's death. She still had more work to do on the old shingled colonial, but she was proud of what she had accomplished so far.

The week she moved in, she had stripped 1970s orange shag carpeting, and sanded and varnished the oak floors underneath. She had removed four layers of wallpaper and painted all the walls with indestructible paint made especially for children's rooms. She had decorated with attic finds and garage sale specials, but the overall effect was warm and homey. Better yet, there was nothing here that was more important than a child who might accidentally damage it. It was a house designed for children, and even though she had lived in it for only a year, it was home.

She settled Officer Riley and his bundle in an old wicker rocker that had once graced someone's front porch. She had painted it white and sewed a colorful red-and-blue-checked cushion for the seat. Now it sat beside her front window, where she could watch the world go by as she rocked a progression of children to sleep.

She was more than ready for that experience.

Officer Riley looked incongruous against the lacy wicker. She wished that she hadn't randomly tied red and blue ribbons through the canes. It was too hard not to smile at the sight of a large-boned, six-foot cop in a sober black uniform framed by two dozen perky little bows.

"I made her a snack," Gemma said.

"I already fed her a cupcake."

"Oh. And it stayed down?"

He looked uncomfortable, as if that was something he hadn't considered. "Yeah."

"That's a bonus." She left and returned with a plate of crackers, cheese and grapes, and a glass of milk. She set them on a table beside him, then went to the sofa for an afghan, which she carefully tucked over the child on his lap.

She realized Officer Riley's face was just inches from hers. He seemed to realize it, too, although he didn't shift in the seat. "She wasn't dressed when we found her. My partner loaned her this sweatshirt."

He had eyes of such a dark gray they were nearly black, hooded, guarded eyes that told her as much about the man as a six-page biography. She straightened. "I'll be sure he gets it back. I have clothes of all sizes here. I'll find her something comfortable to wear after she's had a bath."

"You're going to give her a bath tonight?"

"We'll see how she does. I'm going to take my cues from her."

He seemed to relax a little. "Good." He directed his attention to the child on his lap. "Are you still hungry? The nice lady's made you something to eat."

"She can call me Gemma." Gemma reached for the plate and squatted beside the chair, holding out a cracker to the child. The little girl considered it, then lifted it from Gemma's fingers.

"She eats slowly, like she's not sure where her next meal is coming from."

"She'll have plenty to eat here. But probably nothing as good as a cupcake from her personal hero, Officer Riley."

She got to her feet and started to move away, and she was surprised when he touched her hand. She did not believe in electricity between men and women. She had never experienced it, despite having a satisfactory sexual relationship with her husband in the years before their marriage began to disintegrate. But she felt the oddest sensation when Officer Riley touched her. A stirring inside her. A restless fluttering of her senses.

After Jimmy's death, she had sworn off men, and she hadn't yet regretted that decision. But now she wondered how easy it was going to be to keep that vow.

"My name's Farrell," he said.

"Farrell Riley. Born to be a cop?"

His lips twisted into a wry, humorless smile. "Not even close."

She wanted to probe, but not as much as she wanted to move away. She already knew that this man, with his steel gray eyes and his roughly chiseled features, was complicated right down to his soul. She didn't need a man, and she didn't need complications.

She just needed the child sitting on his lap, and the other children who would pass through her life.

"I'll leave you two alone." She took a step backward, then another, before she squared her shoulders. "I'll be in to check on you in a few minutes."

"We'll be here."

She went back into her kitchen, with its sunny yellow walls and red tile floor. But when she got there, she leaned against a counter and wondered why Farrell Riley had made her feel things she had given up believing in a long time ago.

Chapter 2

Farrell always had his morning coffee at the kitchen table where he read the headlines, the sports section and the comics. He wasn't a slave to routine, but the simple morning ritual gave him pleasure. He liked good Colombian coffee, the way sunlight freckled the walls and floor of the old duplex, the sounds of his neighbor's children playing in the backyard. He liked waking up slowly in his own apartment, with no one to answer to except the landlord.

This morning the paper still lay on the front porch, and the coffee remained in the can. He shrugged into a sweater and slid his feet into loafers, grabbing his car keys off the hallway table on his way out the front door.

Farrell had been sure it wasn't a good idea to give

Gemma Hancock his telephone number. He still
didn't know what had possessed him. Last night he
had rocked the little girl to sleep and tucked her into
a warm, clean bed in a cheery pink room, and he
should have been done with her then. The child was
in good hands. He couldn't have asked for a kinder,
more conscientious foster mother. Almost anyone else
would have pried her from his arms and scrubbed her
within an inch of her life. Gemma had been more
concerned about the child's spirit.

Gemma Hancock.

He started the engine and backed carefully out of
his driveway. Gemma Hancock had been a real surprise. At first glance she had reminded him of dan-
delion fluff: one good puff and she would scatter in
a thousand different directions. She was delicate in
appearance, one of those women some men wanted
to spend their lives protecting from reality.

She wasn't fragile or scatterbrained, of course. She
was filled with good sense and goodwill, and she
seemed to know acres about kids. What she didn't
know was that Farrell Riley didn't get involved. He
had left his phone number on a whim, that was all.
She wouldn't have called him if she had figured that
out. But she *had* called him.

The phone had been ringing as he stepped out of
the shower. He had dripped water on his bedroom
carpet as he answered it.

"Officer Riley?"

He had recognized her immediately. She had a soft,

sweet voice that would soothe any child in crisis. "Mrs. Hancock?"

"Gemma. Right. Our little one is inconsolable this morning. I don't know if it will help or hurt things more, but if you'd like to stop by sometime in the next couple of hours, I think she'd be awfully happy to see you."

Our little one.

He almost hung up the phone at that point. Did he really want to know what happened to this child? Did he really want to go back to the house with the cheerful cream-colored walls, the polished woodwork, the kitchen with its red tile floor, its slate blue cabinets, its cheerful yellow wallpaper?

He hesitated long enough to make her contrite. "Oh, I'm sorry," she said. "You probably have a family of your own that keeps you busy. It's just that—"

He wasn't sure why he answered that. "No, I don't. I'll come over in a little while. Just as soon as I'm dressed."

There was a short pause, then an audible intake of breath. "You're sure you don't mind?"

"I'm sure."

"Then we'll look forward to seeing you."

Now, as he pulled up in front of the old shingled colonial with its wide porch and Easter bunny wreath on the front door, he wondered again exactly what he was getting into. He didn't know anything about kids or women so maternal they were willing to nurture somebody else's children.

But even as he told himself this made no sense, he knew why he had come.

He had come because he couldn't make himself stay away.

At the front door, he heard the little girl's wailing before he could raise his hand to knock. A moment later Gemma answered with the screaming toddler resting on her hip.

Gemma had a beautiful smile, a Madonna, earth mother, the - world - works - exactly - the - way - it's - supposed - to smile, and she used it now. "She doesn't like baths."

"I suspect she's had very few."

At the sound of his voice, the little girl raised her head from Gemma's shoulder and stared at him.

Something clenched inside him as her tears forgot to fall. "Hi, sweetheart."

She pitched her little body toward him, and he took her from Gemma's arms. "Do you mind?"

"Except for ten minutes in the bathtub, she's spent the last four hours welded to that very hip. No, I don't mind."

"Has she been screaming since she woke up?"

"No. We made friends over breakfast. But in her eyes, the bath was not a plus."

He examined the child. Her newly washed brown hair was clipped back from her face with pink poodle barrettes, exposing a skin so pale, she looked as if she'd never seen the sun. And even though her face was clean, there were still dark circles beneath her eyes, circles that didn't belong on a child's face. "You washed away a month of dirt."

A shadow crossed Gemma's face. "I almost wish I hadn't."

He cocked his head. He didn't understand.

"She's got some nasty bruises," Gemma said.

The fury that had simmered since he had found the child in the closet threatened to erupt. He swallowed. The child rested her head against his chest and sniffed and shuddered.

"I have an appointment with the pediatrician this afternoon for a good checkup." Gemma stepped aside so he could enter the house.

He followed her to the kitchen. The house smelled like cinnamon and yeast, and as they neared the kitchen, the smell of coffee joined the others with mouthwatering intensity. His stomach rumbled.

Gemma stopped at a restaurant-sized stove and motioned him to a seat at the table. "We were up early, so I baked fresh cinnamon rolls. Our little friend helped me. She can shake a cinnamon can like nobody's business."

Our little friend. Farrell settled the child against his chest. She had burrowed her fingers into the yarn of his sweater with fierce possessiveness. Obviously the sweater would go before she did.

"How do you like your coffee?" Gemma asked.

Farrell looked up. Gemma, in a leaf green dress the

color of her eyes, was standing in front of him with a plate heaped with fragrant rolls.

For a moment he could think only about how he liked his women. Not warm, soft-spoken and infinitely feminine, like this one. He liked his women remote, casual and ready to move on at a moment's notice. He didn't encourage relationships. He dated, and sometimes he dated long enough to have sex. But he carefully chose women who didn't want more, women who for their own reasons wanted no ties and no heartaches.

This woman was one big heartache waiting to happen.

"Maybe you'd rather have juice. Or tea?" She wrinkled her forehead. "No, you're definitely not the tea type. A cop who drinks tea?" She laughed.

"I like my coffee black."

"Easy to please."

He watched her search for the perfect mug, then pour coffee right up to the rim. He did not want to notice the way she moved, as if she was slow dancing to music that no one else could hear.

She didn't hover. She set the mug far enough from him that the child couldn't grab it; then she settled herself across the round oak table, which was set with place mats shaped like brightly colored pieces of fruit. His coffee sat on an apple, hers on an orange. A half-eaten bowl of cereal with a child-sized spoon beside it rested on a banana.

"I hope we discover her name." Gemma sipped her coffee with unconscious grace.

"Has she said anything today?"

Gemma looked at the little girl. "No, but she understands what we say to her, don't you, honey? I've told her that's what I'll call her, because her hair is the color of honey."

"Does she know what honey is?"

"She does now. I showed her, and she dipped her fingers in the jar. That kept her busy for a little while."

"How did she sleep last night?"

"Sporadically."

"I'll make it my business to follow up on this."

Gemma didn't ask him to elaborate. Both of them knew he was talking about finding the little girl's parents. "Well..." She smiled. "So, Officer Riley..." She appeared to make a decision. "Farrell. Does this happen to you often?"

"Does what happen to me?"

"Do you find yourself in strange kitchens providing support and counseling?"

"Is that what I'm doing?"

"Well, I appreciate your coming, and so does she."

"How do you handle everything when you have a whole bunch of needy kids at the same time?"

"I don't know. This is my first placement."

For a moment he didn't comprehend. "Your first...?"

Her eyes twinkled. "Yes. I just finished the training

last week. That shows you how desperate the county
is for good homes.''

"Then you've never—"

She stopped him with a wide grin. "Don't worry.
I've been training all my life to do this. I have a
degree in child development, and I taught preschool
for three years before—" She halted abruptly.

He never probed. He did now. "Before?"

The grin disappeared. "Before my husband died."

"Oh."

She sat back, taking her coffee with her. "I taught
middle-class children who went straight from their
mornings with me to music classes and gymnastics.
They saw their pediatricians and dentists every six
months, wore designer clothing with matching hair
ribbons or baseball caps, and read *me* stories. I wanted
to do something more personal and challenging. So
here I am."

"If you wanted challenging, you picked the right
job."

"I know."

The cinnamon roll melted in his mouth. He tore off
a hunk and held it out in front of him. The little girl
took it and repeated the behavior he remembered from
last night. She nibbled.

"She'll gain weight quickly," Gemma said. "She
has a good appetite."

Farrell wondered what he was doing sitting in the
coziest kitchen he'd ever seen with a girlchild in pink-
footed pajamas on his lap and a woman with a smile

as warm as summer sitting across the table. A woman who defined the word.

"So do you," Gemma added.

For a moment he didn't know what she meant; then he looked down and realized both cinnamon rolls were gone and his coffee cup was empty. He didn't know when he'd had anything as good as the rolls. He couldn't help himself. He grinned.

Gemma smiled, too, then took his dishes to the sink and refilled his coffee cup. "I really shouldn't have asked you to come. You have the kind of job you probably want to forget about in your off hours. I wouldn't have called except that, well..."

"It's okay. You were just thinking of her."

She brushed his arm as she leaned over to set the cup in front of him again. He inhaled the scent of steaming coffee and something new, something sweet and feminine that emanated from her and reminded him of lilacs. He remembered that he'd felt this same surge of unadulterated longing when he had touched her hand last night, and now, like then, he stiffened in denial. "I have to get out of here in a few minutes."

"I'm sure you do."

He found himself picking up the coffee cup, though he'd already had his fill. "Will she stay here long, do you know? Or will they move her as soon as a place in another home opens up?"

"No, she'll stay right here."

So the child would stay with Gemma, who had

probably taken better care of her in the past twelve hours than anyone else ever had in her whole sad lifetime. The child would stay until the parents were found, and possibly, a reunion was attempted. Or the child would stay until the parents' rights were terminated—a process that might take years—and she was placed for adoption.

Farrell knew that even though this solution was faulty, the child was more than lucky to have landed with Gemma for the time being. "She'll be happy here as soon as she settles in."

"Would you like to see the backyard?" Gemma looked startled at her own question, as if it had just popped out. "It's probably silly, but I'm proud of what I've done with it."

"You're a gardener?"

"Not much of one. No, bring your coffee and come see. Let's find out if our friend will come with us if you're not carrying her."

Our friend. He set the child down, and although she whimpered, she was not nearly as upset as he'd feared she might be. He stood and stretched, then extended his hand. She slipped her tiny one inside and padded beside him toward the door on the other side of the kitchen.

Gemma led them out to a small deck. "I bought the house because of the yard. It's a double lot. Apparently the previous owners never went outside, so it had grown into a jungle. I had to hire professionals to prune everything down to size. But see what you think.''

Farrell realized he was in a child's paradise. He stood beside Gemma with the little girl clinging to his hand and looked over the storybook creation. A weeping willow tree sat in front of a tall wooden fence, with a tire swing hanging from one massive branch. Beside it was climbing equipment consisting of timbers, posts and thick rope net stretching over what appeared to be the hull of a ship.

Closer to the deck was a wooden playhouse, complete with tiny window boxes under windows just tall enough for a child to see out. Curving even closer— right up to the steps, in fact—was a free-form sandbox large enough for four or five children to play in without endangering each other.

A picnic table sat off to one side, with a barbecue not more than a few yards away. Forsythia in full bloom bordered one fence, and an apple tree stood in front of the other. Brick pathways ran from one piece of play equipment to another, and flower beds just waiting for summer annuals circled the playhouse and deck.

''One of my brothers-in-law built the playhouse and the deck.'' Her voice dropped a notch. ''The other one put together the climbing ship. They're good guys right down to the bone.''

He suspected they adored this ethereal sister-in-law with her serene expression and her soft blond hair

curving to her shoulders. He doubted she'd even had
to ask for their help.

She gazed up at him. "I just wanted you to see it.
So you'd know…"

"So I'd know she's in good hands?"

"Exactly."

"I didn't doubt it."

"You did last night."

His voice sounded like steel against steel. "Look,
it doesn't matter what I think." He tried to soften his
words. "I'm just the cop who brought her here. But
for the record, I'm glad this is where she landed."

She hesitated just long enough that he knew she
was scrambling for an answer. He hadn't meant to
sound so harsh. But he was suffocating on the intimacy of standing beside this woman with a small
child clinging trustingly to his hand. Both of them
thought he was more than he was. Both of them
thought he was somebody who gave a damn.

And right now, he was afraid they might be right.

"Well, I know you have to be getting back."
Gemma rested her hand on the little girl's arm. Farrell
looked down and saw the child weave her fingers
through Gemma's.

The child was going to be fine. She didn't need
him anymore.

The relief he should have felt didn't materialize.
"I'd better get going."

"Thanks again for coming. It did the trick."

He squatted to say goodbye to the child. "Hey, sweetheart, I have to go now. Be a good girl, okay?"

She wrinkled her forehead, as if she were going to cry. Before the tears could fail he stood and faced Gemma. "I hope the doctor's visit goes well."

"Would you like to know what he says?"

He was out of this now. Done. If he had a place in this case, it was to find the scum who had abandoned this child. But what could he say? That no, he wasn't interested in how the little girl was? He was many things, but never a liar.

"I'd like to know." He met Gemma's eyes and saw questions she was too polite to ask. "Will you call me?"

"I'd be happy to. But not this early in the morning, I promise."

"Call me any time you want." He turned away before he could take back the words. But, of course, he'd already said them and wouldn't retract them, anyway. Worse, much worse, he'd meant every one of them.

Chapter 3

The report room of the Hazleton police station was a wasteland of battered metal desks and ringing telephones. Farrell sat at one of them, tackling what seemed like a bottomless stack of paperwork. Usually he tolerated filling out forms in triplicate better than most of his colleagues did. He understood the need for record keeping, but today it seemed like a huge waste of time. He didn't want to write up his part in finding the little girl in the closet. He wanted to search for her parents.

"You got a minute?"

Farrell looked up to find Archie standing in front of him with an open folder. "You have something?"

"I sent Brady and Scanlon out to question the neighbors last night after you left. Most of them didn't want to talk."

Farrell wasn't surprised. People protected themselves and their families in the only ways they could. "Did you discover anything about the little girl?"

"An old lady who lives next door claims that the kid's name is Mary. She said the kid's mother used to come and go at the drug house a lot, and one day a couple of months ago she caught the old lady out on her back porch and demanded that she baby-sit. The poor woman was afraid to say no, and the kid ended up staying at her house for most of a week until the mother finally came back to get her."

"And she didn't tell anybody?" Farrell shook his head.

"She was scared. I don't think she would have talked to us last night, either, but she's moving to Detroit in a few days to live with her son. I guess she thinks she'll be safe."

"What does she remember about the mother?"

"She never got a name, but she gave a pretty good description." Archie looked down at his folder. "Long dark hair. Short. Overweight. She said the woman was missing a tooth or two in front. The description matches one a neighbor across the street gave us. They both guessed her age at somewhere around twenty-two or twenty-three. Most of the time she was seen with a man, and they were pretty sure he lived at the house."

"Anything else?"

Archie closed the folder. "Nothing. They could be in California by now. Who knows? We'll run what we came up with last night, but we're probably never going to catch up with them. They'll find another house somewhere, set up business…'' He shrugged.

Farrell knew the answer to the next question already. ''So what about little Mary?''

''She'll be better off with the state than with a mother who abandons her whenever it's convenient. After a while—a long while, probably—some judge will admit she's been deserted and terminate the parents' rights. Then, if she's not too badly damaged by what she's been through, they'll place her somewhere more or less permanent. But at least nobody will drop her off with strangers for days at a time.''

''Some consolation.''

Archie dropped the folder on Farrell's desk. ''She's a cute little thing. It's too bad we probably won't find the mother. She might agree to give up the kid. It's happened before.''

Farrell didn't tell Archie that if he had his way, it was going to happen again. He did his job, and he did it well. He didn't take on personal missions, and he didn't become obsessed with crimes he couldn't solve.

Not usually.

Archie leaned over so his face was closer to Farrell's. ''Heard the foster mother at that home you took her to was something else.''

Farrell looked up and saw the speculative expression in Archie's eyes. He knew where Archie had gotten his information. "Cal never knows when to shut up."

"He tells me you stayed with the kid until she fell asleep."

"She was sobbing her heart out."

"This foster mom, she live by herself?"

Farrell heard the interest in his superior's voice. "Does it make a difference?"

"Could. It sure could. She might need some home security. A regular patrol, you know?" Archie winked.

Farrell arched a brow, but Archie just laughed. He was still laughing as he strolled away.

"She'll need vitamins. Lots of good things to eat. I want to do some blood work before you leave." Anna Choi, a pediatrician who worked with Child Welfare's clients, looked down at her chart. "I think she's not quite two. I want you to make an appointment for developmental testing. We have a psychologist in this building who understands cases like this and knows what we're looking for."

Gemma balanced her new charge on her knee. "Can she settle in a little first? I don't think anything we'd learn right now would be completely accurate."

"Oh, he'll take everything she's been through into consideration. But we need some results now, so we'll have a baseline for comparison."

Anna stepped into the hallway and signaled for her

nurse. "Will you take our patient down the hall and get her a toy from the basket?"

The nurse, an older woman with a friendly smile and superior child management skills, coaxed the little girl off Gemma's lap and out of the room. Dr. Choi turned to Gemma. "I didn't want to discuss this in front of her. We don't know how much she understands."

Gemma nodded.

"She's got some serious bruises."

"I know."

"They're consistent with what I've seen in other cases like this one. Somebody got angry and took it out on her. That's why I got some pictures. We may have to use them if the mother returns and wants her daughter back." Dr. Choi sighed and blew a strand of hair off her forehead. "Believe me, I've seen much worse. She's almost healed, and I didn't see anything to indicate broken bones, either recent or prior. But I'm going to order some X rays, just to be sure we know what we're dealing with."

"Whatever you need."

"This might be hard for you to believe, but this kid might be one of the lucky ones."

Gemma made a sound of disbelief.

"I know," the doctor said. "She's been slapped around, not so badly that she'll have any lasting physical effects, but badly enough that we can use the evidence in court. She's survived and come this far. If we can intervene and keep her from going back to a bad situation, then she has a chance to grow up more or less normally. Not all kids get that chance.''

''I want to protect her.'' Gemma's voice cracked with emotion.

''Don't get too involved,'' Dr. Choi warned. ''All you can do right now is take this one step at a time.''

''Just as long as the next step is making sure she doesn't go back into an abusive situation.''

Dr. Choi folded her arms and leaned against her examining table. ''You know we can't always prevent that, don't you?''

Gemma did know, and she'd thought she was prepared. But even after one night with the little girl, she felt fiercely maternal.

''Take good care of her while you have her,'' Dr. Choi said. ''Right now, that's the one thing you can do for sure.''

By the time Gemma made arrangements for X rays and shepherded the little girl through the process, both of them were starving. Gemma knew a deli that cut peanut butter and jelly sandwiches into stars and moons for their pint-size customers, and it was only after they were sitting at a window table looking over a busy street that she realized the police station was directly across the street.

Two stars, a moon and one turkey sandwich later, Gemma found herself choosing a giant slice of cheesecake to go. ''You don't have a bow, do you?'' she asked the proprietor.

He didn't, but he cut loops of string and fastened a carnation from one of the tables in the center of the plastic foam container. With the cheesecake tucked under one arm and the child tucked under the other, Gemma crossed the street.

Inside the station, she approached the woman in uniform sitting behind the reception window. "Hi, is Officer Riley in?"

Gemma hadn't had time to think about what she was doing. But by the time the question left her lips, regret was already taking the place of impulsive good-will. What had convinced her to bring Farrell the cheesecake? For that matter, what had possessed her to choose a restaurant directly across from the police station? She had wanted to say thank-you, but there were less personal ways to do it. She set the bag on the counter between them. "I can just leave this with you if he isn't."

The woman didn't lift her head. "I'll check. Take a seat."

Chastened, Gemma nearly told the woman to forget it, but her charge began to rub her eyes, as if either a nap or tears were imminent. Gemma took the bag and moved to the side of the room, murmuring sooth-ingly, "Hey, it's okay. We'll be going home in a few minutes."

Home. It wasn't the little girl's home, of course. She might stay with Gemma for years. She might stay only days. At any time, the woman who had aban-doned her might decide she wanted her daughter after all, and the courts might agree to give her a second chance. Then Gemma would be required to hand her over. She swayed to console the child, closing her eyes for a moment. When she opened them again, Farrell was standing in front of her.

"Oh…" She forgot everything she'd planned to say. She had only come to thank him again and to repeat what the pediatrician had said. But for moments she just stared up at him and wondered what it was about this man that made her feel safe and under seige at the very same time.

She already knew he was a man who didn't waste words. He didn't waste any now. "I have some news."

She nodded, as if that was the entire reason she had sought him out. "Do you?"

He bent his head to speak to the child. "Hi, sweetheart. I hear your name is Mary."

The little girl, who was no longer nameless, held up her arms so that Farrell would take her.

"Mary?" Gemma rolled the word on her tongue as she handed the child to him. "That's easy enough." She felt an unwanted connection to the woman who had given this child both life and a traditional name. "I don't suppose you have a last name to go with it?"

Farrell smiled down at Mary, who wrapped her arms around his neck. He didn't look at Gemma. "I'm afraid not. That's all we know for now."

Gemma admired the strong sweep of his jaw. His

dark hair was cut short, but it was thick and wavy enough to defy the closest supervision. She wondered if the man was the same way, if under the guarded exterior there was something inside him that couldn't quite be tamed.

She reached into the paper bag and pulled out the container. "We came to say thank you. We brought you something."

He turned his attention to her. She already knew that he hated emotion. He had probably been raised by a stern father who had taught him well. But now the expression in his gray eyes was not as remote as she had expected. It was, in fact, warm, maybe even probing. "You didn't have to do that."

"I know. And it's a silly present, really. I mean, you probably eat across the street all the time. It's their cheesecake. But it looked so good…" She realized she was babbling. He was smiling at her. A smile that made something inside her catch and hold. "If you don't take it, I'll eat it myself." She smiled back.

"It's a nice change from doughnuts."

She laughed, and his smile broadened in response. "We were in the neighborhood. I took…Mary to the doctor."

"What did he say?"

"*She* said Mary looks fine. She needs some extra weight and vitamins. Her throat's a little red, but Dr. Choi thought she's probably just coming down with a mild cold."

"That should be fun for you."

"Oh, we'll do fine."

"What will you do if you ever need help with her? Do you have...anyone who can lend a hand?"

She heard the hesitation over "anyone." With something akin to pleasure, she wondered if he was asking whether there was a man in her life. But before the pleasure could build, another possibility struck her. Perhaps he just wanted to know if she was going to continue to bother *him*. The thought horrified her.

She hastened to reassure him. "Oh, I have plenty of family nearby. In an emergency I can always call on them. We'll be fine. And I promise I won't bother you again. I still feel bad that I had to call you at home this morning."

"I don't."

For a moment his answer didn't register. Then she realized that he wasn't just being polite. He meant it. The pleasure began to build again. ".You're very kind."

"Not words I hear often."

"I don't know why. Maybe nobody else looks under the surface." She realized how presumptuous that sounded. "Look, I didn't mean that. Everything I say to you seems to come out funny."

"Everything you say comes out wonderful." He looked down at Mary again, as if he had revealed too much. "I have to get back to work. Shall I trade you a little girl for that cheesecake?"

She held out the bag. "Mocha chocolate chip.

Please ignore the carnation. It's probably wilted by now.''

He took the bag and leaned over, sliding Mary into her arms. They were tangled together for a moment, shoulders against shoulders, arms looped, as they made the transfer. Mary whimpered, but she settled against Gemma as Farrell edged away from them.

For just the briefest moment Gemma had felt his weight bearing down on her and his hip pressed against hers. Her heart was speeding faster; she could feel color suffusing her cheeks.

And that was when she knew what a dangerous game she was playing. She had not come to say a final thank-you. She had not even come to reassure him about Mary's health. She had come to see him once more, to watch the way his steel gray eyes soft-ened to pewter when he looked at the little girl, and the way they sometimes softened when he looked at her. She had come to see his smile, that rare but in-finitely rewarding smile that was already becoming an addiction. She was playing a dangerous game, playing with fire, in fact, because despite the fact that Farrell was fighting it, too, there was an attraction igniting between them that neither of them would be able to ignore if they were thrown together again.

"Well, we've definitely kept you long enough." She used Farrell's trick; she gazed down at Mary to avoid looking in his eyes. "And Mary's fading fast, aren't you, sweetheart? It's naptime.''

Farrell leaned over and ruffled the back of Mary's wispy hair. "Take care of her."

"Oh, I will."

"I'll let you know if I hear anything worth reporting."

She wondered if he would. Or would he just pass on his information to his sources at Child Welfare and count on them to get the news to her? She turned away. There was no point in speculation. She had asked more of this man in the past hours than she had asked of her husband in all the blighted years of their marriage. She couldn't ask for more.

"Thanks again." She looked over her shoulder and smiled a casual goodbye. "Hope you enjoy the cheesecake. It deserves a superior cup of coffee to wash it down."

"Believe me, nothing at this station compares with yours."

"My pot's always on." She wanted to yank her tongue out. "If you're ever in the neighborhood."

"I'll remember that."

She didn't trust herself to say another thing. She headed for the door, and, with Mary on her hip, she left the station without a backward glance.

Chapter 4

"Relax, Gemma. The doctor says Mary's ears are fine. Her temperature's just a little elevated. She's breathing, even if she doesn't sound too great. She has a cold." Gemma's oldest sister, Patty, settled back in the wicker rocker with Mary on her lap. Anyone who glanced at them would have taken them for mother and daughter. Patty's hair was the same light brown as the little girl's, her eyes the same vivid blue.

Gemma must not have looked convinced, because Patty added, "Honestly. You can stop worrying."

Gemma knew Patty was right. During Mary's exam, Dr. Choi had warned her that the little girl might be coming down with a cold. And now, three days later, the cold had been confirmed during a second appointment. Gemma knew better than to worry.

She had wiped a thousand little noses in her days as a preschool teacher. But in those days she'd sent the children back home after school for their mothers to take care of.

"I'll take her if you're tired," Gemma offered.

Patty waved Gemma to the love seat against the nearest wall. "I'm not tired. Sit and take a break. I'm used to this."

Patty had married young, and nine months later she had presented her graduate-student husband, John, with twin boys. Two years later the second set had come along. All the boys were rambunctious, and Gemma doubted that Patty had ever spent more than five minutes with one of them in her lap before he squirmed away to see what mischief the others had gotten into.

"This poor baby hasn't had a good night's sleep since she arrived." Gemma settled herself on the love seat, where she could observe her sister and Mary. Patty pretended to be thoroughly sick of her own children, but she never missed the chance to mother someone else's.

Patty smoothed Mary's hair back from her forehead. "I'm guessing this will be the worst day, then she'll start to feel better. How are you doing? Want me to send John over tonight to help you walk the floor? I'd come, but the last time I spent the night away from home, the dishwasher sprang a leak, Mark got the chicken pox, and Dillon fell and knocked out a tooth. John was beside himself."

"Baloney. John can handle the boys with a hand tied behind his back. You just hate being away from them for too long, and you want a good night's sleep."

Patty rolled her eyes, but she didn't deny it. Patty adored John, too. "You'll be all right? You look tired. Seriously, one of us can help if you need it."

For some reason Gemma pictured another man, not John, walking the floor with Mary that night. John was blond, and this man was not. John talked about everything. This man chose his words carefully and seemed most comfortable with silence.

Gemma shook her head. "No, I'll be fine. I had a lifetime of uninterrupted nights to rest up."

"You were always there when I needed you. Remember when the babies were cutting teeth?"

Gemma remembered, and she remembered how part of her had envied Patty during those months, both for her beautiful babies and the warmhearted husband who loved her.

"You handled everything without a fuss," she said. "And so did John."

"A little birdie tells me that the cop who brought Mary here is a total hunk and as single as John is married."

For a moment Gemma wasn't sure she'd heard her sister right. Since childhood, Patty had been good at suddenly changing the subject to throw her off guard. "A little birdie?"

Patty turned up one hand in defeat. "Okay. One of my neighbors is married to your cop's partner."

"Patty, he's not *my* cop."

"Sheila says that this guy...Farrell Riley, right? That he keeps to himself but everybody thinks he's terrific anyway. He's been cited for bravery twice. Her husband worships the ground he walks on. She says word is Farrell could be promoted, and Cal is afraid they won't be partners anymore."

Gemma realized her heart was beating faster. She remembered this feeling of anticipation and excitement from high school. She thought she'd outgrown it, along with training bras and rock star posters.

She tried to ignore it. "He was very nice. He took a real interest in Mary."

"I'm sure he'd like to know how she's doing. Maybe you ought to call him."

"Apparently I don't need to. I'm sure you'll tell this Sheila everything, and she'll tell her husband, and he'll tell Farrell."

"So you call him Farrell?"

"Patty..." Gemma's tone was warning enough. "I've sworn off men. You know I have. I have the life I want and need. I'm happy."

"Not every man is like Jimmy."

"Maybe not. But what makes you think I could tell the difference? I was fooled once. Why not twice? Or as many times as I take a risk?"

"Jimmy was a salesman. He could sell sand in the

Sahara, and probably did. All of us were fooled by
his charm, but we learned. You most of all.''

Gemma had learned things that Patty didn't even
suspect, but she wasn't about to go into them now.
''Look, I'm happy. I took control of my life. I'm doing exactly what I want. I don't need complications.''

''What about sex? Do you need sex?''

Gemma was used to Patty's direct approach, but
she could still feel her cheeks heating, not because of
what Patty had said, but because of a sudden new
image of Farrell.

And he wasn't walking the floor with a sick child.

''I thought so,'' Patty said triumphantly.

''I'm not going to get married just to have regular
sex! And I'm not going to sleep around. It's just not
my style.''

''Then why don't you get married for love? You
still believe in it, even if the prospect's a little tar-
nished right now. But pull it out and polish it up.
You're too young to be a monk.''

''Women can't be monks.''

''You know what I mean.''

''I *know* what you mean, and this conversation is
finished. Got it?''

''If the cop's not really your style, John has a client
who's—''

''Patty!'' John, an investment banker, had already
tried to promote romances for Gemma with several
of his clients. John's idea of a perfect match was a

healthy portfolio and an aversion to prenuptial agreements.

"You're such a prude." Patty wrinkled her patrician nose. "Well, I hate to do it to you, kiddo, but I've got to get out of here and make some dinner for the swarm. Give us a call if you're too tired to cope alone tonight. Better yet, give your cop friend a call. I bet he'd love to spend the night over here."

Gemma stood and gathered Mary into her arms so that Patty could rise. "Thanks for coming, if not for the conversation. Give my love to John and the boys."

"If I can shout above the din." Patty gave Gemma a hug. "Think about what I said."

"No."

"Oh, you will, no matter what you say."

Gemma's response was interrupted by the doorbell.

"Expecting someone? Someone...interesting?" Patty brightened considerably.

"No!"

"I think I'll go out the front door, just to be sure it's not a serial killer on the porch."

"Your car's parked on the side."

Patty smirked. "I feel a need for exercise."

The doorbell rang again. With Patty and Mary in tow, Gemma had no choice but to answer it.

Farrell didn't know why he was standing on Gemma's front porch. He'd had a long day, and just before going off duty he'd nearly had his head blown off by a teenager with a handgun. The kid had seemed almost as surprised as Farrell when the gun went off, and afterward, on the way to the station, he'd sworn that it wasn't supposed to be loaded. But who could believe a sixteen-year-old with a record as long as his daddy's latest prison sentence? The gun had been in the kid's possession, and the kid had made certain that the two men he robbed outside an automatic teller machine knew that he had it.

Hadn't there been a time when teenagers collected baseball cards instead of .44s and assault rifles?

The door opened, and Gemma stood on the threshold with Mary in her arms. Beside her was a woman who could only be Gemma's sister. The woman's coloring was different, but the features were much the same.

"Farrell…"

"I'm sorry. Did I come at a bad time?"

"Of course not. Patty was just leaving." Gemma turned toward the other woman. "Weren't you?" she asked pointedly.

"If I have to." Patty extended her hand. "I'm Patty Prescott, Gemma's sister."

He took her hand. "Farrell Riley."

"I figured."

"Patty…" Gemma sounded disapproving.

Patty grinned. "I live down the street from your partner. Sheila told me you and Cal were the ones to bring Mary here. I just put two and two together when I saw you."

Farrell thought that needed explanation. Did Gemma have so few men on her doorstep that the only possibility was the cop who'd dropped off Mary?

And if so, why?

"Come for dinner next Saturday, Gemma," Patty said. She turned to Farrell, and her eyes were dancing. "Since you like kids so much, Farrell, why don't you come, too? I have four little boys who'll change your mind. We'll invite Sheila and Cal, so they can see what they'll be getting into. Maybe Katy and her family can come, too. Katy's our little sister."

Farrell realized Patty had paused and was waiting for an answer. He avoided family get-togethers the way he avoided dark alleys and midnight strolls on Keller Avenue.

He found himself saying yes.

Patty patted his arm. "Oh, good. We'll do a barbecue if it's warm enough. I'll let Gemma know the time. We're always casual. Don't dress up."

Before anyone could say another word, Patty took off down the steps. At the bottom she waved before she disappeared around the side of the house.

"Well..." Gemma squared her shoulders and shook her hair back. "Hurricane Patty has blown over."

"How do you keep up with her?"

"She has to be that way. The boys are all under the age of nine. She's a Cub Scout den mother, and *she* wears the kids out." Gemma looked as if she didn't know what to say next.

"I don't know why I'm here. I just thought I'd check on Mary...and you."

"I'm glad you came. Come in. I promised you another cup of coffee, remember?"

He hadn't forgotten, although he'd tried.

He followed Gemma into the kitchen, trying not to notice the way her hips swayed gracefully in a blue dress that outlined her subtle curves.

"You must just have gotten off work. Have you had dinner?"

"No, but—"

"Good. Let me fix you something. Mary and I haven't eaten, either."

"I didn't come to beg a meal."

"Of course you didn't. You came to keep me company and hold Mary while I cook. She has a cold, and she hasn't been out of my arms for days."

"A cold? Are you sure that's all?"

"Absolutely. But on top of everything else that's happened to her, I guess she decided this was the last straw. She cries every time I put her down."

Gemma turned and held out the little girl to him. She had been dozing since his arrival; now she opened her pretty blue eyes, and they widened with pleasure. Before he could offer to leave, Mary pitched herself in his direction. All he could do was catch her.

"I hope she doesn't throw herself at men this way when she's a teenager," Gemma said.

Mary stroked Farrell's cheek. The exhaustion and frustrations of his job seemed to seep away with each childish touch. He was her captive. He couldn't make himself leave now.

Gemma opened the refrigerator. "What'll it be? Chicken? Fish? Are you a vegetarian?"

"I'll be a vegetarian when they sell soyburgers under the golden arches. Everything I eat comes straight off a fast-food grill or out of a can."

She peeked over the refrigerator door and made a face. "I'm going to make you something healthy, then, if you can stand it."

He tried to remember the last time anyone had worried about his diet. "Please don't go to any trouble."

"Trouble? This is sheer pleasure. Mary's appetite is good, but she's no gourmet. It'll be fun to cook for a grown-up."

"Anything will be fine."

"How about something to drink? Beer? Wine? I'm not much of a drinker. I don't have anything stronger."

"I'll take a beer." Farrell settled himself at the table and made Mary comfortable on his lap.

Gemma came over to the table with a bottle and a frosted mug. The beer wasn't something she'd picked up on sale at a convenience store. It was imported ale that was meant to be savored. He wondered what Cal and Archie would say.

"Here. Start on this." She returned with a plastic bag of fresh vegetables cut into thin strips. She arranged them on a plate and spooned something that smelled delicious into the center. "That's a spinach dip. You'll like it. Mary does."

As if to prove Gemma's point, Mary reached for a celery stick and lowered it into the spinach dip puddle. Farrell could do no less.

"Chicken breasts sound all right? I'll bake some potatoes in the microwave. I have fresh asparagus. Do you eat it?"

He didn't want to admit he'd never had the opportunity. "Sure. Thanks."

"Ummm… Good, I have mushrooms and red peppers. I'll do a sauce for the chicken. I know, I'll do pasta instead of potatoes. This is fun."

He had taught himself to remove frozen food from cardboard packages. Her plans were obviously on a different level. "You really don't have to go to so much trouble."

"Let me, please. I love to eat. Tell me about your day while I work. I'd like to know more about what you do."

He wondered what he could tell her. That until a sixteen-year-old tried to kill him, the rest of his day had consisted of traffic citations and faulty car alarms?

"There's nothing much to tell." He took a carrot stick from the plate. His stomach was rumbling, and he tried to remember if he and Cal had stopped for lunch.

Gemma filled a tall enamel pot with water and set it on the stove. "I'll bet you're good at defusing tough situations. You're so calm and reasonable. I bet you can talk people out of all kinds of crazy schemes.''

"Not today." He clenched his jaw the moment the words were out. He'd had no intention of telling her what had happened to him, but Gemma was too perceptive to let that go unchallenged.

"No? What happened?"

He was left with a choice. He could be rude and refuse to answer, or he could spill his guts. And neither solution was in character.

She seemed to sense his struggle. "I'm sorry. I didn't mean to be nosy. I'm sure that sometimes you'd rather forget what you do for a living."

"Today would be one of those days." He found he wanted to tell her what had happened to him, wanted it more than he wanted his highly valued privacy. He didn't know how to start, but he took a stab at it. "I had a kid take a shot at me today. He wasn't impressed with how calm and reasonable I was. He was more impressed that I was about to arrest him."

Gemma dropped her knife at the word *shot*. "Farrell...that's horrible. Awful. But you're all right?"

"Fine." But he wasn't, which was why he'd ended up on Gemma's doorstep.

"How about the kid?"

"He's in jail. And not for the first time."

She hadn't gone on with her preparations. She stared at him, her forehead wrinkled, her face a paler shade. "You must have been pretty shaken up. You can't possibly get used to that kind of thing."

"Yeah, you do." He paused, then he shook his head ruefully. "No, you don't. Thank God it doesn't happen often enough for me to get used to it."

"Tell me what happened."

He found himself doing just that. She resumed her preparations, but she was listening intently. He couldn't remember anyone listening to him that way before, head cocked, eyes focused on his. She nodded as he spoke, and her soft blond hair fell forward over her cheeks and caressed her collarbone. He couldn't take his eyes off her, and somehow, he couldn't stop talking.

"I arrested him once before, a couple of years ago," he finished. "He was fourteen then. He hadn't graduated to handguns and ATMs yet. That time he stole a box of candy to give his mother for Mother's Day. Not that there was any guarantee his mother would have been around to eat it. She and his father are in jail more than they're out."

"I want to say poor kid. But he could have killed you."

"They'll put him away for this one, but he won't get any help. I think there's still something good in this kid, but it won't be there by the time he's free again."

"I'm sorry."

He liked that. No suggestions. No easy answers. Just a sincere statement of regret. "Me, too."

"You must see a lot of situations like that one."

"More than I want to."

She was chopping vegetables now, with an easy, practiced motion that sent them flying into neat little piles on the cutting board. Garlic sizzled in oil on the stovetop, and as he watched, the vegetables joined it. Next she sliced chicken and added it strip by strip until the smells were mouthwatering.

The water in the enamel pot began to boil, and Gemma added pasta. "Well, it shouldn't be long now. I'll just do the asparagus, and we'll be ready to eat."

Mary stirred restlessly, and Farrell realized she was beginning to whimper.

"Uh-oh. I was afraid this was too good to be true." Gemma washed and dried her hands. "Shall I take her?"

"Why don't I try walking her a little?"

"She'd probably like that. But you must be dead on your feet."

"Believe me, this is exactly what I need."

She smiled her understanding. "Good. And maybe she'll feel better if I can just get her dinner on the table."

The equivalent of six blocks later, Mary reluctantly allowed him to set her in a booster seat at her very own place mat. Gemma served her plain chicken strips and canned fruit and one stalk of asparagus. The little girl sat stone-faced, staring at her plate.

"You know what? I suggest we eat quickly." Gemma took her own seat and motioned Farrell to his. "This may be the calm before the storm."

He didn't want to eat quickly. The food was delicious, even better than he had expected. And to his relief, the asparagus was edible, even if it looked like something Gemma had picked from an unmowed lawn. He was halfway through his meal when Mary began to cry in earnest.

Gemma was on her feet, sliding the little girl from her chair, before he could swallow. "You take your time," she said. "And that's an order. I'll entertain her a little, and when you're done, I'll finish my dinner."

He wondered if this was the way it was done in most families. Did mothers and fathers take turns comforting their children? Were there other women, like this one, who felt that a child's minor cold was enough of a reason to miss a meal? He couldn't imagine this kind of radiant goodwill, this attention to a child's needs. The world he had come from, the one he saw each day out on the streets, was a different one entirely. He felt as if he'd just been set down in the land of Oz.

And he realized he had no desire to find his way back to the land he was used to.

Gemma was murmuring softly to Mary, who was snuggled into her arms as if she'd been born into them. Something stirred restlessly inside Farrell, not for the mother or the child, but for the woman. She had strength that shone beyond the wide green eyes and delicate features. She believed in what she was doing. She wanted to make a difference in the lives of children like this one so that they didn't end up angry and desperate, like the teenager who had nearly killed him today. She was courage and wisdom packaged in a soft, shapely body that made his own ache with longing.

He wondered what it would be like to be loved by this woman, to lie with her in his arms, her body stretched the length of his. He knew better than to yearn for things he couldn't have. The lessons of his own childhood had taught him that.

But just for a moment, he wondered.

"Farrell?" She looked concerned. "Are you full already?"

Farrell knew he could never get enough of Gemma or anything she offered. He shook his head, and warnings flashed through his mind. He had a sixth sense that told him when he was in danger. Today he had dodged a bullet at exactly the right moment.

But somehow, he knew he was helpless to duck or dodge now.

Chapter 5

Gemma made potato salad for Patty's barbecue and a big chocolate cake with mocha icing. She had a feeling that Farrell liked chocolate. The night he'd stayed for dinner, he had eaten a bowl of chocolate chunk ice cream that was the equivalent of a week of desserts for her. She had shamelessly dragged out the meal that night because she had enjoyed having him there so much. If she could have followed up the meal with cheese and fruit in the European style, she would have. If she could have forced him to drink yet one more cup of coffee and followed it with brandy and cigars, she would have done that, too.

He had stayed for a while after the ice cream, anyway, patiently holding and walking Mary until the little girl finally gave in to sleep. Unfortunately, Farrell had put the little girl to bed, lovingly tucked covers around her sleeping body, then thanked Gemma for dinner and...left.

Gemma had been surprised at the disappointment she'd felt. She didn't want a relationship with Farrell Riley. But that night she had been sorry to see him go. She didn't know what she *had* wanted. But when he had walked out her door, she had felt a loneliness she couldn't pretend away. She had a full life, friends and more interests than she would ever have time to pursue. But the emptiness that had assaulted her after his departure wasn't something she could fill by sewing new curtains for the playroom or reading a novel by her favorite author. She had felt unwillingly connected to Farrell that night. She had been drawn in by his warm generosity with Mary and by his reluctant story of the day's events. She had been horrified to think that this man might have disappeared from her life before he had really entered it.

And, as before, she had felt the strong pull of sexual attraction between them.

She was almost surprised that he hadn't called to say he couldn't make today's barbecue. By leaving the moment Mary was in bed, he had made it clear that the child was their only tie. She thought that he felt the same physical tug that she did. Sometimes she found him looking at her with something close to desire. But clearly, Farrell didn't want a relationship any more than she did.

So why had he agreed to come to Patty's today,

even to pick her up first? And why, given the opportunity, hadn't he changed his mind?

Gemma realized she was staring into space. Since there were no answers to her questions, she busied herself by tucking the potato salad and cake into a picnic basket. Mary, who had been contentedly piling wooden blocks into rickety towers in the corner, came to investigate. Gemma was convinced that Farrell had worked some sort of magic the night he had lulled Mary to sleep, because the worst of her cold was gone the next morning, and now she was brighter and more cheerful than she had been since arriving on Gemma's doorstep.

Mary favored Gemma with a huge smile, and Gemma scooped her up for a hug. Mary hugged her back.

Gemma's breath caught. She wasn't sure if she had imagined the faint pressure. Mary was not unresponsive. She listened, she watched, and Gemma was sure that she processed everything around her. But she was a child who had learned that she was safest if she kept inside herself. Now she was discovering that people listened when she cried, and tried to help her. And little by little she was learning that no one would punish or ignore her if she had a statement of her own to make.

A statement like a tentative little hug.

"You're very special, Mary." Gemma hugged her again. "A very special little girl."

The doorbell rang, and Mary scrambled to get

down. Gemma's hands went to her own hair. Not that there was much she could do with it. Fine, straight hair did exactly what it pleased. Today she had pulled it back from her face with a headband that matched the soft gold of her skirt and blouse. But the age-old impulse to primp before confronting an attractive man won out over good sense.

Mary reached the door before Gemma did. She was in Farrell's arms the moment the door was unlocked. He lifted her and kissed her forehead. "How's my best girl today?"

Mary crowed with delight. "Yes!"

Farrell looked as startled as Gemma felt. Their gazes locked. "She's talking?" he said.

"A first." Gemma took a deep breath. She realized that in a matter of seconds she had nearly been reduced to tears.

"Well…" He looked down at Mary. "Definitely yes, sweetheart."

Gemma swallowed. "I bet she'd like to show you what she's been working on in the kitchen."

Farrell and Mary followed her inside. By the time they reached the kitchen, Gemma had her emotions under control.

Farrell set Mary on the floor, and Gemma watched the little girl run to the corner, making happy sounds. He made the appropriate fuss over her towers, insisting she was destined to become an architect. It was doubtful that she understood completely, but she beamed at the praise.

For those moments Gemma had the chance to watch Farrell undetected. He was dressed in dark jeans and a silver-gray sweater worn over a dark turtleneck. Men in uniform had a certain allure. This man still had it in casual clothing. The sweater stretched over shoulders broad enough to take on a thousand problems. The jeans hugged long, muscular legs and slim hips. No one looking at him could guess he was a cop, but even in civilian clothes he still retained a certain authority, a subtle unspoken announcement that here was a man to be reckoned with.

He looked up from Mary's blocks and found her watching him. For a moment their gazes locked, as they had when Mary had spoken. But this time something other than amazement passed between them. The air practically sizzled. His eyes drifted down her body, then up again.

"You look nice today." He didn't smile, but his eyes warmed.

"Actually, I was thinking that you do, too."

A few heartbeats passed, then a few more. Neither of them looked away.

"I'm glad you decided to come," she said at last. Not because she wanted to break the spell. She was not uncomfortable with Farrell, not even when neither of them knew what to say. She just wanted to be sure he knew she was glad he was there.

"I told you I would."

"And you never change your mind?"

"Not if I've made a promise."

She wondered if he knew how rare that was. Jimmy's promises had been worthless.

Her gaze dropped to Mary, and the spell was broken. "We have Mary and the picnic basket, and I packed a bag with Mary's toys, a change of clothes, a blanket..." She paused, trying to decide if she'd forgotten anything.

"I'd be glad to drive, but I don't have a car seat. Would you like me to move yours to my car?"

"I can drive. It'll be easier. Unless you're one of those men who can't stand having someone else behind the wheel."

"I have to put up with Cal's driving. I bet I can handle yours."

She flashed him a grin and found he was smiling back at her. The fluttery feeling inside her was becoming an old friend.

Farrell liked Gemma's family. Patty was a brassier, louder version of her sister, but every bit as devoted to making the people around her comfortable. Katy, their younger sister, was a grown-up tomboy with short blond hair and a tendency to get down on the ground to roughhouse with her rambunctious nephews and her three-year-old son. Their husbands, John and Michael, obviously adored them, and although chaos had reigned from the moment Gemma and Farrell arrived, everyone pitched in and got along.

"Feel like you're trapped in the middle of a 'Brady Bunch' rerun?" Cal leaned against a picnic table in the backyard and handed Farrell a beer. He and Sheila, his hugely pregnant wife, had immediately fit right in with everybody else, and now Sheila was lumbering after one of the little boys in an impromptu game of tag.

"'The Brady Bunch' was never this loud," Farrell said.

"My house was just like this. Lots of kids, lots of noise. We fought more, though. I figure we just yelled a lot to be sure we were heard." Cal took a swig of beer. "What about yours?"

He and Cal had been partners for two years, but Farrell had discouraged conversation about their respective pasts. He had come to terms with his life a long time ago, but he never thought of it as something to chat about.

"Nothing like this," he said.

"You're such a quiet guy. I always kind of thought you might be an only child."

"Good guess."

"I'm one of six, but I just want a couple of kids of my own. Sheila and I want to be able to spend a lot of time with them, you know?"

"You'll be a good dad."

"You think so?" Cal sounded pleased. "I get scared sometimes. What if I screw up?"

"Maybe you will. But kids are hardy, and you won't screw up often."

"Yeah? That's good to hear. What about you? You always say you don't want kids. Do you mean it?"

"I mean it."

"You're real good with Mary."

Farrell sought out the little girl with his eyes. She was safely ensconced in Gemma's arms. Mary seemed fascinated by the other children, but so far she had resisted all attempts to involve her in their play. Farrell couldn't blame her. Gemma's nephews were a high-speed, high-impact bunch.

"I'm not a family man," Farrell said.

"You'd have trouble convincing Mary of that. If she could talk, she'd tell you some stories about people who don't believe in family. The ones who had her, for starters."

Gemma must have seen them looking in Mary's direction. She smiled and started toward them.

"I'm going to make Sheila slow down. If this keeps up, I'll be a father before I'm ready." Cal strolled off and left Farrell to wait for Gemma alone.

"How are you doing?" Gemma settled herself and Mary at the picnic table beside where he was standing. "Is the noise getting to you yet?"

"I can take a lot of noise."

"Good thing. It's always like this, though. They aren't doing it for your benefit."

Farrell dropped to the bench beside her. Mary wiggled onto his lap and cuddled against him as if she was ready for a nap.

He stroked her hair. "She's pooped."

"I know, but she's enjoying this. I don't think she's seen many children."

Farrell was acutely aware of Gemma beside him. He hadn't purposely avoided her since their arrival at Patty's, but he hadn't sought her out, either. She had been busy with her family, and he had stayed on the sidelines.

Gemma lazily stretched her legs in front of her, shapely legs with trim ankles. The day was warm enough for sandals, and pink polished nails peeked out from crisscrossed leather straps. "John's just about to throw the burgers on the grill. Are you hungry?"

He turned to answer and found her face just inches from his. His heart slammed against his chest. He had thought about her constantly since the night he had stayed for dinner. And despite what he'd told her, he had strongly considered finding an excuse not to come today. In the end, he hadn't been able to lie to her or break his promise. But he had considered it, because he was fast getting in over his head.

"I am hungry," he said, but he didn't know which question he was answering. The one she had asked, or an unspoken one issuing from somewhere inside him.

"So am I."

Neither of them spoke. Neither of them looked away. He felt Mary sagging into sleep against him. He felt himself leaning toward Gemma. The space between them contracted. The air between them was charged with longing.

"Hey, Gemma," Patty called. "Come pour the

drinks, would you? The swarm is thirsty and I'm up to my elbows in ground beef.''

Farrell thought he saw disappointment in Gemma's eyes. He hesitated just an instant, then sat back against the table. ''Go ahead. Mary's comfortable where she is.''

Gemma's skirt swished against her legs as she went to join her sister. Farrell was powerless not to watch every step.

Farrell watched as Gemma pulled the door to Mary's room half-closed. She obviously wanted to be sure she would hear the little girl if Mary awoke during the night.

He spoke when she joined him on the stairs. ''Poor little thing. She'll probably sleep a week.''

''The boys wore her out, but she had fun. And she was holding her own there at the end. I think she really liked playing with Shawn.''

Shawn was Katy and Michael's son, the closest in age to Mary and a shade less aggressive than Patty's boys. By the end of the evening, he had coaxed Mary out of Farrell's lap to play with trucks in the sandbox. Farrell had kept close watch over them, but Shawn had been careful not to hurt or frighten her.

''I know you can't eat another bite,'' Gemma said when they reached the bottom of the stairs, ''but would you like some coffee before you go?''

This was where he had made his exit the last time. Then he had known that the intimacy of sitting quietly over coffee with Mary sleeping upstairs would lead places that it shouldn't. Tonight he knew the same thing, but he couldn't seem to summon up the good sense to refuse her.

"You're probably tired." At the bottom of the stairs, Gemma stopped and faced him as she spoke.

The man who answered her was someone whose good sense had fled entirely. "You probably are, too. Do you really feel like making coffee?"

"Sure. After Mary goes to bed, I always sit and unwind a little."

"I'll tell you what. I'll make the coffee. You supervise."

She started to protest, then she seemed to catch herself. "I'm not used to being waited on. Thank you."

"You're welcome."

She made herself comfortable in her chair at the kitchen table. He could feel her eyes on him as he lifted the glass decanter from the coffeemaker. "I don't cook much, but somewhere along the way I did learn to make a decent cup of coffee."

"Good for you. I was married to a man who would have thought that was beneath him."

"Did he expect you to do all the cooking?"

She was silent long enough that he guessed she regretted mentioning her husband. "Jimmy believed in a division of labor," she said at last. "He did the division, and I did the labor."

This was the first inkling he'd had that her marriage

hadn't been as happy as her sisters'. "Where do you keep the coffee and filters?"

"In the cabinet to the right of the coffeemaker."

He found what he needed without trouble. "The morning after I brought Mary here, you told me that you bought this house for the yard. Did you live here with your husband before he died?"

"No. We lived in Shore Haven, on the lake."

Shore Haven was an expensive housing development in the most exclusive suburb of the city. Farrell wondered if she regretted what was a noticeable move down in prestige. If so, the regret never showed.

"I like this better," she said, as if she'd read his mind.

"Do you?"

"We couldn't really afford that house. Jimmy worked on commission. I was never sure from one month to the next whether we could pay the mortgage. We had to have the right cars to go with the house, of course, and an interior that would impress anyone who made it through a security system sophisticated enough to protect Fort Knox." She smiled ruefully. "I don't have to keep up with anybody here. I can do what I please."

"And what you please is taking care of other people's kids."

"Yes."

Farrell switched on the coffeemaker, then leaned against the counter while the coffee brewed. "You must have had other options."

"I did. I could have kept my job at the preschool. And I'm certified to teach elementary school."

"I'm sure Mary's glad you made the choices you did."

She seemed pleased. "Do you think so?"

"She's happier every time I see her. And she seems more alert."

"I took her in for developmental testing on Thursday."

"Do they have results?"

"Not an official report, but the psychologist talked to me afterward. He says she's definitely behind. I knew that, of course, but I think she's already beginning to catch up. He's not as optimistic as I am that it's all environmental and that she'll make up for everything she's lost, but he seems to think that in the right kind of home, she'll continue to improve."

"A home like this one." It wasn't a question.

"Thank you."

"If she's too far behind, she'll be harder to place for adoption. That is, if the courts ever get around to making adoption a reality."

"I guess we have to take it one step at a time."

Farrell poured the coffee, which had just finished brewing. He heard the sound of Gemma's chair sliding across the floor, but he was still surprised when he turned and found her inches away.

"I was just getting the milk. I like…"

Her pupils grew larger and her cheeks stained slowly with color. He knew he should move away, that if he did, nothing would be altered between them. He could still come and see Mary, still have casual conversations with Gemma. Nothing he had done today had changed anything. He and Gemma were still practically strangers.

But she didn't feel like a stranger when he put his arms around her. And she didn't taste like a stranger when he kissed her.

Lord, she didn't taste like a stranger at all. She tasted like heaven.

Her arms crept around his back as he pulled her even closer. Her lips were soft, and they clung to his with honeyed sweetness. Her body pressed so firmly against his felt as real and as forbidden as the happy life that had always been just out of his reach. He knew, as he kissed her, that she was all the things he had ever longed for and all the things he had been denied until, one day, he had finally stopped reaching for them.

And still, he couldn't let her go.

"Farrell, I didn't mean for this to happen." She whispered the words against his lips, not a protest but a confession.

He heard her words, but he felt the heat of her flesh continue to fuse with his. She wanted reassurance. He had none to give, but still, she didn't move away.

He kissed her again, and her lips parted under his. He brushed his hands over her hips, then under her shirt. Her skin was smooth and warm beneath his palms, and she sighed as his hands moved higher.

His fingertips lingered at the edge of her bra, the softest lace against the rough calluses. He hooked an index finger under the catch and realized that with one twist, the bra would give way. He could feel her hips melting gently against his, her body seeking its rightful place. Desire flared like fireworks in a night sky, and for that moment he gave in to it and ignored the insistent voice warning him that he should move away.

A car door slammed on the street in front of the house, and somewhere nearby a dog began to bark in protest. The ordinary neighborhood noises accomplished what a lifetime of caution had not. Farrell lifted his head and stared down at this woman who wasn't ordinary at all. No, Gemma wasn't ordinary, but she expected the world to give her ordinary things like love and family and happily-ever-afters. And how could he be the one to disappoint her?

"I didn't mean for this to happen, either." He clasped her close rather than look into her eyes. Her head rested against his shoulder.

"We can still go back to what we were," she said.

He shook his head, because he knew that nothing would ever be the same for him again.

Her voice deepened with emotion. "I've been in love once. I couldn't survive it again."

"I've never wanted to try love at all."

"So what do we do?"

His body was telling him in no uncertain terms what they should do. He had never felt desire this compelling. And he had never felt anything this close to terror.

"We don't do anything." His voice was gruff. "I leave."

Her arms were still wrapped around him. They remained that way. "And when do you come back?"

"It would be easier if I didn't."

"Yes. But we've already passed 'easy.'" She let her arms fall to her sides. "I'll settle for 'difficult,' if that means you'll stay around until we sort this out."

"*Is* this something we can sort out?"

She smiled sadly. "Not a chance."

He pushed a lock of hair off her cheek, and his fingertips lingered against her skin.

She covered his hand and held it against her cheek. "Go home and think about this, Farrell." She dropped her hand. "I'll think, too."

He knew he would think about nothing else. He left her standing in the kitchen, beside the coffee he had brewed for them both.

Chapter 6

Archie strolled by Farrell's desk in the report room, then backed up like a show horse being put through its paces. "Jeffries tells me you're checking some leads on that little girl's parents."

Farrell dropped his pen and leaned back in his chair. "We talked it over. He's in charge of the Keller Avenue investigation, but as long as I report anything I find, he doesn't mind if I snoop a little."

"He wouldn't. You know he's been shorthanded since Canfield moved over to homicide."

The day had been long, and Farrell's patience was uncharacteristically short. "Look, I'm doing this on my own time. I'm not working on this while I'm on duty, okay?"

Archie didn't address that. "You know we'll be

promoting a patrol officer to detective to work in vice with Jeffries.''

"Relax. I'm not bucking for the job, Archie. I'm just trying to find Mary's parents so her case can be settled.''

"Isn't she doing okay where she is?''

"She's doing great.''

"So?''

"A kid deserves to know where she's going to wake up every morning.''

"What if you find her folks, they want her back, and the courts choose not to stand in their way?''

"I'm hoping that doesn't happen.''

Archie rubbed the back of his neck. Obviously it had been a long day for him, too. "You know you're top of the list to make detective, don't you?''

Farrell didn't answer. He'd heard rumors, but he wasn't a particularly ambitious man. He liked his job; he would also like the move up to detective. In his professional life, as in his personal life, he didn't hope for the things he might never have.

When Farrell didn't respond, Archie went on, "Some people are going to think you're doing this to increase your chances. It could work against you.''

"Then I'll take myself out of the running if I have to. But I'm not about to take myself off this case.''

Archie nodded. "Just do it on your own time.''

"I promise you'll get your usual pound of flesh.''

"With you, it's always been a pound and a half.''

Archie rapped his knuckles on the desk, then turned and continued across the room.

Cal, who had been on the telephone a few desks south of Farrell, came over to see what Archie had said. Farrell shook his head. "He just wanted to know about the Keller Avenue raid."

"I just got a tip from a guy who lives over on Keller. He says he remembers some things about the folks who set up shop in that house we raided. And he thinks he saw one of them last night at a Laundromat over on Fifth Street, but he's not sure."

Farrell regarded his partner. "Who's the guy who called? And why'd he call you?"

"Max is a schoolfriend of Sheila's. I'm the only cop he knows. He was probably afraid if he called and talked to just anyone, they might think he knows more than he does."

"You don't think he's involved?"

"No, he's a little eccentric, an artist or something, but he's a good guy. He lives about half a mile farther down Keller, but he used to see the people at that house when he walked his dog. Had a run-in with one of them once when they almost backed a car over him. He remembers a couple of faces, that's all."

The story seemed plausible enough, and it fit with the little Farrell had been able to discover on his own. If the man was really an artist, his description might be good enough to be helpful.

In the days since the picnic at Patty's, he had put in his time on patrol, then worked three or four hours each evening on Keller Avenue, trying to see if he could discover anything new. He had made a few contacts, and last night a guy in a bar had been able to tell him the street name of one of the men who had lived at the drug house. But this was the best break yet.

Cal looked eager to help. "Do you want to go talk to him? I'm done here."

"Yeah. I'll clear it with Jeffries."

"Hell, Jeffries would give you the case if he could. He's got a pile of files so high, he can't see over the top of his desk."

Farrell felt the thrill of the hunt, even though he schooled himself not to get his hopes up. "Let me finish my report, then we can get out of here."

Gemma heard the doorbell ring as she started down the stairs. She had just put Mary to bed for the night, and she was tired herself. She hadn't had a good night's sleep in a week, and she was beginning to feel the strain. For just a moment she was tempted to pretend she wasn't at home. Patty or Katy might be standing at her front door to start one more conversation about Farrell and her future, and she definitely wasn't in the mood.

The temptation waned. Marge Tremaine had planned to stop by earlier, and since she might be here now, despite the lateness of the hour, Gemma knew she couldn't really ignore the summons. She smoothed her hair behind her ears and opened the

front door, only belatedly realizing that to be safe,
she should have squinted through the peephole first.

"Do you open your door to just anybody?"

Farrell was standing on the front porch in civilian
clothes. He was scowling, which did nothing to di-
minish his appeal.

She was so surprised to see him that for a moment
she didn't speak. Then she pulled herself together.
"No lectures, okay? I realized I forgot to check as I
was opening the door. I usually do."

"This isn't Shore Haven."

"You're right. It's a neighborhood for people with
a whole lot less to steal." She opened the door wider
and gestured him inside. She didn't even want to
think about what she was feeling. "You just missed
Mary. She almost fell asleep during her bath. By the
time I tucked her in, she was out like a light."

"I didn't come to see Mary."

Gemma's heart beat a little faster. During the past
week she had tried not to think about what had passed
between them, about their mutual confusion and ret-
icence, and the attraction that blinded them both to
other things. But she had thought about those things
anyway, in the darkest hours of night, and now she
was paying the price.

"I came to talk to you about Mary's parents."

She lifted her chin. "I see." She didn't offer Farrell
a seat or a cup of coffee. Not being hospitable was
foreign to her, but Gemma was in no mood to pretend
she was glad to be discussing business with this man.

"Let's sit."

Her shoulders drooped. She couldn't politely resist his direct suggestion. She led him to the sofa and curled up against one end. "Have you heard something about Mary's parents? Have you found them?"

"No, but we're closing in. I just wanted you to know that I'm looking for them, Gemma. I didn't want you to find it out from somebody else."

"Is that your job?"

"No. But I've made it mine. I've been working on it in the evenings. And we're making some progress on the case."

"Why?" She crossed her arms in front of her. "Do you think she'll be better off with them than she is with me?" The words were out before she could withdraw them. She knew how stupid they were, but her exhaustion and insecurity were showing.

"That's what I was afraid you'd think." Farrell leaned forward. "You have to know that's not why I'm doing it."

"I'm sorry. Of course I do. It's been a long week, that's all."

The doorbell rang again before Farrell could reply. She shook her head in apology. "I don't know who that could be, unless it's Marge." At the blank look on his face she added, "Marge Tremaine. Mary's caseworker. She said she wanted to stop by at dinnertime, but she never made it."

This time she used the peephole and discovered that it was indeed Marge on the other side of the door.

She opened the door, and the caseworker, a middle-aged African-American woman whose tastes ran to bright colors that glowed against her dark skin, greeted her warmly. The two women were fast becoming friends.

"I bet she's in bed, isn't she?" Marge said.

"I'm afraid so. I'm sorry you missed her. She's growing and learning by leaps and bounds."

"I got the psychologist's report. He's not as optimistic as you are, but we pay him to be cautious." Marge seemed to sense someone else in the house and glanced toward the living room.

Gemma filled her in. "Farrell Riley is here. He's the policeman who brought Mary to me that night. Come meet him."

Farrell got to his feet. Gemma made the introductions, then waited until Marge made herself comfortable in the rocking chair. "Can I get you anything?"

Marge waved her to the sofa. "Sit down, Gemma. You look beat. In a few minutes I'm going home to a good stiff drink and a hot bath. I just wanted to catch up with you first."

"Farrell has been telling me that there are some leads in the search for Mary's parents." Gemma sat back, hoping that the conversational ball would roll on without her. She didn't know what to think about Farrell's bombshell. He knew how well Mary was doing with her, yet he'd made it his mission to find the little girl's parents. Why?

"What kind of leads?" Marge asked, as Gemma had hoped she would. "Can you talk about it?"

"We've got a couple of detailed descriptions we didn't have before, and a possible sighting in the area. And if I can get a couple of people to look through mug books, we might even get some names. Anyway, we're farther ahead than we were this morning."

Marge nodded. "I guess I ought to be glad, huh? But I'm not. The minute Mary's folks are found, we have to start working with them. I don't know about you, but a mommy and daddy who leave a baby like Mary in an empty house just to save their own skins aren't my top candidates for reform. Sometimes people change. Sometimes there are circumstances. But my gut tells me this is not one of those times."

Farrell leaned forward. "Are you saying you don't want me to find them? Mary needs a permanent home."

Marge gave a wan smile. "Mr. Riley, this is the best home that little girl's probably *ever* going to have. Even if we get her parents to give up their rights, our Mary's not going to be tops on anybody's adoption list. She's a special-needs child. We don't know if she'll ever be normal. And by the time she's available for adoption, she'll be older and even harder to place. Having contact with her biological parents will confuse her more. By then she'll be thinking of Gemma as her mother...." Marge shook her head. "I'm sorry. It's been a long day. You're a cop. But

I see stuff every day that would make even *your* hair curl.''

"I'll tell you what makes my hair curl—a system that keeps children like Mary in limbo."

"I'm just saying there are worse things than an excellent foster home."

"Let me tell you what it's like to grow up in foster homes, Miss Tremaine." Farrell leaned even farther forward, and his eyes were the gray of thunderclouds. "I have some personal experience with it."

Gemma had been trying to think of a way to intervene tactfully, but now she couldn't have spoken if her status as a foster parent had depended on it.

Farrell didn't look at her. His eyes were on Marge. "Most of the time if you're a foster kid nobody ever takes the time to show you what a real home looks like. Still, you have dreams. You walk through each strange new door with those dreams intact, until you find out that the new place you've landed isn't a real home, either. You know because you have to keep your suitcase packed all the time, in case the people who gave birth to you decide they want you back, or until the judge and the social workers decide you're getting too comfortable where you are, maybe too attached to your foster parents."

He paused a moment, and Gemma held her breath. She had never suspected that Farrell had been a foster child, or that his interest in Mary's case was anything more than his personal attachment to her. She heard him struggle to sound objective, and she heard him fail.

He shook his head, as if he were remembering something that even now had the power to hurt him. "One day you come home from school and somebody's waiting to move you to another home. Your third or your tenth, by then you've lost count. And this new home isn't real, either. These people are strangers, too, so you keep your bag packed again. You never enjoy the most basic feeling of security. You learn early that you can't even leave your toothbrush in the bathroom with everybody else's, because one time you were moved so suddenly you forgot to pack it. And the people at the new house punished you for not bringing a toothbrush with you."

Gemma felt tears stinging her eyes.

"I don't want Mary to grow up that way." He sat back, as if he were forcing his emotions to settle somewhere deep inside him again. "This may be the best home Mary will ever have, but unless we get her out of the foster care system, it may be the first of many. She deserves better."

Marge was silent for a few moments, and Gemma didn't know what to say. Finally Marge spoke. "It's different now than it was when you were a child, Mr. Riley. Mary can stay here until she's out of the system. We don't move children unless we absolutely have to."

"But the minute she's old enough to realize what's going on, Mary will figure out that her life could change in a heartbeat. Even if it never changes, some part of her will always wonder and worry.''

He turned to Gemma, and the expression in his eyes was still fierce. ''Gemma deserves this child. If she wants to adopt Mary, she should be able to. That can't happen if Mary's birth parents are still somewhere on the scene. And if they want her bad enough and prove they can take care of her, then they should have her back as soon as possible. Before Mary's torn apart.''

''Foster care is an imperfect solution, but it's the best we can offer in a lot of cases.''

''It's not the best solution in *this* case. Because at least two adults love this child and are willing to fight for her.''

Gemma was still so stunned by Farrell's revelations and the intensity of his response that she couldn't find the words she needed. But Marge didn't give her a chance to speak, anyway.

''Then she's already luckier than half the kids I see.'' Marge stood. ''I'll leave you two alone. Will you let me know when you find out anything, Mr. Riley?''

''I'll be sure you know.''

Gemma rose and walked Marge to the door. In the hallway Marge turned to her. ''You know, he's his own worst argument.''

Gemma didn't understand.

Marge smiled sadly. ''The foster care system may

not be perfect, but it produced one fine man when it chewed up and spit out Officer Farrell Riley.''

Farrell's eyes were closed, but he heard Gemma come back into the room after saying goodbye to Marge Tremaine. He felt sick inside, as if he had laid himself open for examination and now he couldn't put himself back together.

He felt the sofa sag beside him. Gemma wasn't sitting at her own end of it anymore. She was close enough that he could feel the heat from her body and smell the faint fragrance of lilac.

"Don't tell me you're sorry about my childhood," he said at last.

"I'm not sorry."

Her voice was low and musical. He could feel her leg pressed against the length of his. He had tried not to think about her this week. He had nearly worked himself into oblivion just so he wouldn't have to think about her. Now he knew that underneath that frantic activity he had longed for her with single-minded intensity.

He could feel her leaning closer as she spoke. "How can I be sorry when your past made you the man you are? I wish it had been accomplished some easier way, but I wouldn't want the results changed even one little bit."

He opened his eyes and turned his head, which was still resting against the back of the sofa. "The man I am is more flawed than you can imagine."

"Farrell…"

"I learned a long time ago that I'm better off alone. As a kid, I wanted a family so desperately, and every day that went by and I didn't get one, I discovered that taking care of myself was the only sure thing. But that knowledge came with a price, Gemma. I've been alone so long, I don't know how to be anything else. I have nothing to give, because I never learned how."

"Oh, Farrell, none of that is true." She touched his cheek with her fingertips, then laid her palm against it.

"You just don't want to believe it. But I'm not the man for you. You need someone who wants the things you do. You need a man who knows how to love you the way you deserve."

"I had a man like that, at least on the surface. I don't want another one."

He wanted to push her away. He knew he should leave and never come back. But the same longing that had compelled him to seek her out tonight kept him in his seat.

She kissed him this time. With measured calculation. The soft, womanly Gemma whom he had come to know changed subtly. Her lips were as ripe and sweet, but there was an insistence in her kiss he couldn't ignore. Before, she had been hesitant; now she was the aggressor.

He was lost from the moment her lips touched his. His good intentions vanished. In that moment it seemed to him that he had spent his whole life being good in hopes that someday someone would reward him. Now he knew that he wanted no reward other than this night. If this was all he was ever given, it would be enough.

He wound his arms around her and pulled her closer. She made a sound of pure pleasure and pressed her breasts against his chest. He was aware of everything between them, of his wool sweater and her denim jumper. He was aware that she had no curtains in this room so that the daylight would shine more brightly. He was aware that now, because it was dark outside, a lamp glowed in the corner and anyone who cared enough could see them in its reflection.

He was aware that all the bedrooms in the house were upstairs. And he was aware that she had not yet invited him to share one with her tonight.

"If this is only a kiss," he said, holding her just far enough away to see her face, "then we have to stop now."

"Is this my first warning, Officer Riley?"

"It's your only warning, Gemma."

"My bedroom's at the end of the hallway upstairs. If I stop kissing you, are you going to find your way upstairs or out the front door?"

She sounded faintly out of breath, and although she was trying to sound sure of herself, he heard the very real question behind her words.

"I'm going to find my way upstairs *while* you kiss me."

"It might take some time that way...."

"We have time, don't we?"

"We have all night."

They took a good portion of the night making their way upstairs. He could not imagine turning and moving away from her, not even with the prize that was waiting for him at the end of the journey. He couldn't seem to stop kissing her, or to stop holding her. He was hungry for the feel of her skin against his palms, for the swell of her breast in his hand, for the warmth of her breath mingled with his.

Her bedroom was large and comfortable, with heavy walnut furniture and filmy curtains billowing gently in the breeze. She took a moment to light three pastel candles sitting on a dressing table before she turned back to him. She rested her palms against his chest and lifted her head to kiss him again.

They took turns removing clothing. She tugged his sweater over his head and unbuttoned the shirt beneath it. He unzipped her jumper. She unbuckled his belt. He smoothed her panties over her hips.

Gemma was as beautiful as he had imagined. She did not have an athlete's body. She had a narrow waist, and full breasts and hips. It was a body meant to bear and suckle children, and he thought he had never seen anything quite so beautiful.

She turned back the covers as if they had always gone to bed together in this room, and he joined her under them. He felt no awkwardness; she didn't hesitate. She came into his arms as if she had done so every night for years. Her leg slid between his, her hand trailing over his chest and lower, until he was afraid he would explode with desire.

Her lips tormented his flesh. He explored her with the same relentless precision, with his hands and lips and the caress of his body. When he entered her, she moved against him as if she had been made for that alone.

He had not allowed himself to imagine the pleasure he might find. Only once did he break the silence that had fallen between them.

"If I had known that making love to you would feel like this, I would never have been able to stay away." He whispered the words against her neck, just before she arched against him in final fulfillment.

Later, as Gemma fell asleep in his arms, Farrell realized with a sinking heart what he had said. Worse, he knew that he had meant every word. He had never dared to imagine what loving and being loved by Gemma Hancock might mean. But now that he knew, he was sure he would never be able to walk away from her.

The lessons of his childhood had been hard won. But by falling in love with Gemma, he had failed his final test. He had not succeeded in locking himself away from dreams and hopes. Tonight he had given this woman the key to his heart.

Chapter 7

"This guy, he comes in with two, three others."
The old man who owned a grocery store on Orchard
Avenue gestured excitedly with his hands, as if he
could sculpt images in the air. "I watch him, always.
He looks at things, this way." The man narrowed his
eyes, then glanced back and forth between Farrell and
the counter, as if he was watching to see if his activities were detected. "He'd steal anything not..." His
voice trailed off.

"Nailed down," Farrell supplied. The old man's
English was excellent, but his command of the vernacular was less so, since he had left his native Kuwait only a few years before. Farrell put the photograph back in his folder. Nearly a month after his first
conversation with Sheila's friend Max, Farrell's per-

sistence had paid off. Max had finally been persuaded to come down to the station to pore over mug books. The photograph he had chosen was the one Farrell had just shown the store proprietor. Now, not only did the police have a name, the proprietor had seen the man in the photograph last night.

"And he came in about this time last night?" Farrell said.

"Little later. Maybe ten. Every night almost. Right before I close."

In the past two evenings Farrell had shown this photograph at every small grocery store and service station within a two-mile radius of the Laundromat where Max thought he had seen the man. "Does he ever come in with a woman?"

"All the time." The old man made a face. "Dirty woman. Dirty clothes. I watch her, too."

"Anything else you remember about her?"

"Dark hair. Tooth missing here." He opened his mouth to show a full white set of his own and pointed to a bicuspid.

"I'm glad you're so observant."

"You going to stay and see if they come back?"

"First I'm going to call the station and tell them what's going on. Can I use your phone?"

The old man took him into a back storeroom and left him to make the call by himself. Archie was still at the station, and he listened as Farrell told him what he'd learned.

"Don't do anything until we get you some

backup," Archie instructed. "I'll call Jeffries, then I'm on my way."

"Don't send anybody in uniform."

"You think I don't know how to do my job?"

Farrell hung up. He wondered if he was about to encounter Mary's mother at last. For a moment he tried to imagine what Gemma would think when she found out.

His thoughts these days were almost always of Gemma. Since the night they had become lovers, she had inhabited his thoughts, his dreams, his plans for the future. When he wasn't with her, he was planning what they would do when he was. They maintained the illusion of separate lives, but the time they spent apart was only preparation for the time they could spend together.

Farrell and Gemma had talked at length about his quest to find Mary's mother, as well as a million other details of their lives. He thought she understood his obsession with finding a permanent home for Mary, but he didn't know if she would ever forgive him if this turned out badly. If he had done this work only to have Mary taken from Gemma's loving care and returned to abusive parents, then he wasn't sure he would be able to forgive himself, either.

He returned to the front and spoke briefly to the proprietor, instructing him on how to act. Then he went to one of the outside aisles and began to methodically examine canned goods.

The door opened, and a large man in casual clothes

strolled in. Archie directed one quick gaze in Farrell's direction before he continued his stroll to the other side of the store and began to examine cereal boxes. Ten minutes later Jeffries, a thin man with less hair than savvy, entered the store and devoted himself to an intent study of the freezer case.

Farrell knew that impromptu stakeouts like this one rarely bore fruit, but he prayed that this one would prove the exception.

Half an hour passed, and ten o'clock drew nearer. Farrell had progressed to fresh vegetables and was weighing mushrooms in a hanging scale when the door opened again. He didn't investigate immediately, and when he did, only his head turned, as if in idle curiosity.

Two men and a woman sidled into the wide center aisle. The face of one man was familiar, although without a mug-shot scowl he was slightly better looking. The woman was overweight, with long unkempt hair and lifeless eyes, but even though she was a complete stranger to Farrell, he recognized her immediately. The woman had a daughter who strongly resembled her. And when she spoke to the man in the photograph, and Farrell saw that she was missing a tooth, he knew for certain he was looking at Mary's mother.

He caught Archie's eye, then Jeffries's, too. As a unit, the three men moved toward the door. In moments, and with only a short scuffle, the three shoppers were escorted to Jeffries's car.

* * *

"Sally?" Farrell closed the file folder he'd been examining. Jeffries stood against the door, his arms folded. He had agreed to let Farrell talk to Mary's mother, but he was going to observe the process. "May I call you Sally?" Farrell asked politely.

"Like I care what you call me."

He didn't let her ruffle him. "Then Sally it is."

"You don't got nothing on me. You got no reason to arrest me."

"You're just here to answer some questions." Farrell smiled politely.

"I got nothing to say to you. I don't have to talk to you unless I got a lawyer."

"You're right about that. But I thought you might want to find out about your little girl."

Sally didn't blink. "What little girl?"

"Sally, let me remind you that your daughter has a birth certificate. And now that we know your name, we can track it down and tie you to her like that." He snapped his fingers.

Sally, who according to identification in her purse was Sally Margaret Matthews, twenty years old and born and bred in their fair city, shrugged. "So?"

"Aren't you interested in what happened to Mary?"

Sally gave up pretending. "I read the papers."

"So you know she's okay."

She shrugged. "I figured."

"Can you handle this without me?" Jeffries asked Farrell.

"No problem."

Jeffries left, and Farrell took a seat on the other side of the table from Sally. He knew Jeffries—and Archie, too—would be watching through a two-way mirror, but Sally probably didn't.

"I was there the day the house was raided," he said in a conversational tone. "As a matter of fact, I was the one who found Mary in the closet."

"I didn't put her in no closet."

"Didn't you?"

"I wasn't even there that night. Someone else was taking care of her."

Farrell nodded, as if he believed her. When she relaxed a little he added, "Of course, you were *seen* there that night by one of the neighbors, so we know that's not quite true."

Sally slumped. "I didn't put her in no closet. She was asleep on the bed last I knew. I had to leave fast. I didn't have time to get her."

Farrell nodded again, as if in his world, that happened all the time. "She was badly frightened."

"Well, I didn't frighten her, did I? You were the ones that broke in while she was sleeping."

"The courts don't look kindly on mothers who abandon their children. You've never called to ask about her, have you? You haven't tried to find her."

"So?"

"She's a beautiful little girl." He cleared his throat. "I've spent some time with her since I found her."

Sally looked as if she wondered what this had to do with her.

Farrell let his emotions shine through in his voice. "I'd do almost anything to make sure she isn't hurt again."

Sally suddenly seemed interested. "That so?"

"Yeah." He shook his head ruefully. "I don't have kids of my own. Mary's almost like a daughter to me."

"That so?" Sally tossed her dirty hair back over her shoulders.

"Does her father spend time with her?"

"I don't know." She grinned.

Farrell cocked a brow in question.

"I don't know who her father is," she said triumphantly, as if she'd told a wonderful joke.

"Oh." He nodded. Under the table, his hands balled into fists. "She needs a father."

"Maybe she does." Sally was still grinning, but her eyes narrowed. "Maybe I ought to find her one, you know?"

He waited, not quite holding his breath.

"Am I in big trouble?" she asked, in what seemed like a change of subject.

"I'm afraid so."

"Can you help me?"

"How could I do that, Sally?"

"Well, you and me, we could come to an understanding, right?"

He felt sick inside, but this was exactly what he'd been hoping for. "What kind of understanding?"

"Mary needs a daddy, and it sounds like you might want her."

"And?"

"And I got the right to give her away, but I got to get something in return...."

"In other words, you'll give me Mary if I do you a favor?"

Sally looked cagey. "Yeah, something like that."

Farrell sat back and closed his eyes.

Farrell put his arm around Gemma and brought her to rest against his shoulder. He didn't know why he hadn't told her about finding Mary's mother. He had come to Gemma's house late, well after his interview with Sally Matthews. Jeffries had come back into the room, and together they had explained that in addition to everything else, she was now in serious trouble for having offered Farrell her daughter in exchange for his help. Selling a child, no matter what the currency, was against the law.

He hadn't told Gemma, although that had been his conscious purpose in arriving at her doorstep. But once inside, he had taken her in his arms instead, and now they were upstairs in her bedroom after passionately making love. She was snuggled against him, and he knew that soon she would be asleep.

His heart was overflowing with emotion. A long time ago he had given up his childish hopes of ever loving or being loved by anyone. Gemma had come into his life accidentally, and he had very nearly lost her before he found her. But there had been a spark inside him that a childhood of neglect and alienation hadn't been able to extinguish. And Gemma had fanned it into flame.

He loved this woman with a passion that was grander because he hadn't believed it possible. He wanted to tell her, but he had never had any practice. Still, he wanted to tell her....

"Gemma?"

"Hm...?"

"I didn't know I could be this happy."

She made a soft sound of pleasure. "Me either."

"I didn't want any of this."

"You just didn't *know* you wanted it."

"Maybe..." He stroked her hair. "I don't want it to end."

She was silent, but she didn't move away.

He didn't know how to tell her what he was feeling. She could talk openly about her emotions; he had spent a lifetime learning to repress his.

Instead, he started with what had happened that night. "I came to tell you something. I didn't come for this."

"Are you apologizing?"

He laughed. "Are you kidding?"

She touched his face. "I like it when you do that."

"What?"

"Laugh that way."

"I do it a lot more often than I used to."

"That you do."

"I do have something to tell you, Gemma. Are you awake enough to listen?"

He could feel her body tense. "Go ahead."

"Mary is going to be freed for adoption."

She sat up and looked into his eyes. "What?"

"We found her mother tonight. And she's agreed to relinquish her rights."

"Why?"

He had hoped to avoid this, but he had guessed that Gemma would want to know it all.

Gemma listened without saying anything until he had finished. "She tried to exchange Mary for her own freedom?"

"She had nothing else to bargain with."

"What if she changes her mind?"

"She doesn't want Mary, Gemma. That part was crystal clear. And since three cops heard her offer to give me Mary if I helped her out, she can't really change her mind."

"What's going to happen to her now?"

"She has a record, but so far it's mostly minor offenses. She abandoned Mary, but if it looks like she's trying to do the right thing now by giving Mary up for adoption, the judge will probably be lenient. Unless she's linked directly to activities at the drug house, she'll probably be put on probation...until she's arrested for something else.''

''Mary's really safe? You're sure?''

''I talked to Marge Tremaine and told her what happened. She says the paperwork will start immediately. She also said that you can apply to adopt Mary.'' He paused and took a deep breath. ''Or that we can.''

''We?''

Farrell had dodged bullets, chased criminals on foot through rush-hour traffic, handcuffed and hauled in men twice his size, but nothing compared with the difficulty or danger of his next words.

''I know we've only known each other a little while....''

She didn't answer. She wasn't going to help him in this.

''Gemma, I never thought I wanted to marry or have children. I didn't think I could offer a woman or children anything. And it's hard to believe, I know, that being with you and Mary could change how I feel so quickly. But one of the things I learned in all those foster homes was to grab what I needed when it came around, because if I didn't, it might never come my way again.''

''Farrell, I—''

He rested a finger against her lips. ''I want to spend my life with you. I want to spend it with Mary, and the children we have together. I know this is sudden. I know it's too soon to speak, but circumstances,

Mary's adoption, make it necessary. You probably don't trust—''

This time she was the one to put her finger on his lips. ''Farrell, no. Please, you've got to listen to me now.''

She looked as if she wanted to cry. Everything inside him froze. In the weeks they had been lovers, he had misunderstood. He had believed that the passion they had found together was more than it was. He had seen love when there was only attraction. He had moved too quickly....

She sat up and moved away from him. In a moment she got up and pulled her robe off the chair and slipped it on. Then she sat back down on the edge of the bed and turned to face him.

''I've never told you much about my marriage to Jimmy.''

''It's never mattered to me.''

''I have to tell you. You have to know, so you'll understand....''

He didn't want to ask her what he had to understand. She was going to say no to marrying him and adopting Mary together. That was as clear as anything in his life.

His voice was hollow, the voice of the man he had been before falling in love with her. ''You don't have to make excuses. If you don't want to marry me, that's good enough.''

She pulled the robe tighter around her. ''Do you

remember the day you told Marge what it was like to be a foster child?''

''What does that have to do with anything?''

''The only way you could make us understand how you felt about Mary's situation that day was to tell us why it mattered so much to you. I have to do the same thing.''

He didn't want to hear this. Her relationship with her dead husband had nothing to do with him, but he was powerless to tell her so, because he didn't want her to stop talking. When she stopped, where would they be?

''I married Jimmy the summer after my last year of college. He was bright, good-looking, charming in every way. It was a small school. If we had voted for Most Likely To Succeed, Jimmy would have won hands down. I thought I was the luckiest girl in the world. Everyone loved him, and I thought I did, too.''

''So you were living a fairy tale. I don't understand what this has to do with me.''

She continued as if he hadn't spoken. ''A year passed, then two, and I began to see what I'd been too young and immature to realize at first. Everyone loved Jimmy, but Jimmy loved himself most of all. The world revolved around him. He knew how to get anything he wanted, and he did, regularly. If he couldn't get it in the usual ways, he'd manipulate others until he had what he wanted. He wasn't above lying or wearing people down. Just as long as things went his way.''

Farrell watched her. She wasn't quite looking at him. She was looking at her past, and she didn't like what she saw.

Gemma continued. "You know, I was raised to take care of people. My mother was a stay-at-home mom, and I adored her. She took such good care of my sisters and me when we were growing up, and I wanted to be just like her. She and my father were so happy, and when I married Jimmy, I wanted us to be just like them. So even though I began to see things about him that disturbed me, I closed my eyes."

He interrupted. "I don't know what this has to do with me. Do you think I'm like him?"

"No!" She shook her head so hard he couldn't doubt what she said. "You're nothing like him. We were married for five years before I realized that he'd been leading me on about wanting a family. I wanted children, and Jimmy had always promised that we'd have them. Somehow, though, he always came up with an excuse why we had to wait. By then I was beginning to see him for what he really was and to have serious doubts about our future together. My parents had moved to Florida, so I made arrangements to go and visit them to think about what I was going to do. I was twenty-seven, and it was clear to me that I'd married a man who wanted things, not people, in his life. I think Jimmy realized that I might leave him. He was sales manager for a conservative company that strongly promoted their family image, and divorce would have been frowned on. One day while I was away, his boss took him aside and asked him about his plans for the future. Jimmy decided that children would be good for his career.''

''He told you this?''

''I figured it out later. Jimmy was too smart to admit something like that. He realized that if I knew what he was thinking, I'd never agree to stay with him, much less bring children into the marriage. No, he knew me too well. He came down to Florida, cried like a baby and told me that he couldn't live without me. He asked me to go into counseling with him. I was ecstatic. I came home. We went to counseling for a few months, and Jimmy fooled me and the therapist. At the end he told me he was ready to have children, and I believed him because I wanted them so badly.''

''But you didn't have them?''

''I got pregnant quickly, but it was a tubal pregnancy.'' She looked straight at him. ''I didn't want to admit anything was wrong, and I waited too long to see my doctor. I lost the baby and my chance to have another. I can't have children, Farrell. I had an emergency hysterectomy.''

''Gemma...''

She shook her head, warning him not to say anything. ''I wasn't as devastated as you might think. I mourned terribly, but I knew that even if we couldn't have children of our own, Jimmy and I could still adopt. But Jimmy had other ideas. He waited until I got out of the hospital, then he informed me that he wanted a divorce.''

Farrell couldn't remain silent. "That doesn't make any sense. If he didn't really want kids, he had the perfect excuse. And his job…"

"No, it made sense to Jimmy. You see, he had a new job by then, and no one was asking questions about his personal life anymore. But even though he wasn't sure if he'd ever want children, he *was* sure he wanted a wife who could have them. For Jimmy, adoption was out of the question. He felt it was his duty to pass on his own exceptional gene pool. Jimmy wanted everything he owned to be perfect, and in his eyes, I wasn't perfect anymore."

She had tried to finish as if she were telling a story about somebody else. But now she looked at him, and he saw the misery in her eyes. "He moved out. For months I just sat at home, frozen with grief. I had always wanted children, and now I couldn't have them. I had wanted a man like my father, and instead I'd married a man without an ounce of integrity. Jimmy didn't sit at home, of course. He found a young woman who worshiped him, one who could probably bear a dozen babies. Then, the night before his attorney was going to file the divorce papers, Jimmy ran a stop sign, and that was that. On the last day of his life, he couldn't stop long enough to let someone else have the right of way, and it killed him."

She shook her head. "Jimmy wasn't much for details. He hadn't gotten around to changing his will. I was still the beneficiary for his insurance policies, his pension. He bought insurance the way he bought everything else. Only the biggest and the best. It's the ultimate irony, isn't it, that Jimmy left me enough money so that I can spend my life raising other people's children?''

Farrell knew that the words he said now would be the most important of his life. He wished that he knew how to put his feelings into words. But all he could do was try.

''I'm sorry. I know how badly you were hurt.'' He wanted to reach out to her, but he knew better than to touch her yet. ''He was a bastard, Gemma.''

''That he was.''

''But you told me you know I'm nothing like him.''

''You're not, Farrell. Jimmy could talk about everything. What he was feeling, what he was supposed to be feeling, what he wanted me to think he was feeling.'' She shrugged. ''He could charm anyone until they couldn't see which end was up. Even my family was fooled, until the truth was right in front of them. Jimmy would say anything I wanted to hear. You tell the truth whether I want to hear it or not. And believe it or not, that's what I...'' She shook her head, as if she couldn't finish.

''I can see why you might have trouble trusting a man again.'' He was making his way carefully, like a man in a pitch-black room.

''I trust you.''

''Then what does this have to do with us,

Gemma?'' he asked gently. ''After everything that happened, are you afraid? Do you need more time? I can give you all the time you need, even if it makes the adoption trickier. I can—''

''Farrell, I can't marry you, no matter what I feel. Don't you see? I was married to a man for almost seven years. I gave him everything. And in the end, he tossed me right out of his life because I couldn't give him children.''

''Do you think that matters to me?''

''Yes!'' She took a deep breath. ''A while ago you said something about the children we would have together.''

''Give me some credit here. I didn't know you couldn't have children. Do you think I would have said something like that if I did?''

''No. I know you wouldn't have. You're a good man. An honorable man. You'd marry me anyway, and just tuck that away. But sometimes, when you saw other people with their newborns, you'd wish, just a little, that you were holding your own child in your arms.''

''No, that's not—''

''Farrell, you have never had a family of your own! Never! And I can't give you one. If you married me, you would never have biological ties, not to one person on the face of this earth. Don't you think I know how important that is? I have family. I have nephews. Mark's hair is the color of mine. Shawn looks like my baby pictures. I don't have to bear children to see family all around me. I can love my nephews. I can love Mary. I can love the other children who come into my life. But I can't love you, because I know that in the end, you'll resent me for depriving you of your own babies.''

He couldn't find a thing to say. He was struck by two things simultaneously. One, that she believed every word she was saying, believed them so vehemently that her mind would not be changed tonight. The second was that she didn't *want* to believe them. But if he couldn't find a way to change her mind, they had no future together. In the very center of Gemma's heart was a place so bleak, so damaged by her ex-husband, that it would take a very special kind of healing to make her whole again.

She had healed him, or, at least, she had begun the process. Now he had to find a way to do the same for her. And he thought he knew what it might be, although the thought of it made him feel sick inside.

''You're wrong about everything,'' he said quietly. He reached for her hand and clasped it.

''I don't think so.'' She let him hold her hand, but hers was limp inside his, as if she were already schooling herself to let him go.

''We've talked enough tonight.'' He squeezed her hand, then turned away from her to find his clothes. ''Keep tomorrow night clear for me, Gemma. I'm coming over after dinner. We'll finish this then.''

''It's finished now, Farrell.''

"No, you had your say. I get a turn. That's only fair."

"Nothing you can say will change my mind."

"I'm not going to say anything. I just have some things to show you."

She didn't answer.

"But there is one thing I didn't say tonight because I haven't had any practice." He zipped his pants and reached for his shirt; then he faced her again.

"Don't, Farrell, I—"

"I love you, Gemma, and I think you love me. I know this happened quickly, and that you don't trust it yet. But I never expected it to happen at all, so I'm going to fight hard to keep you. Nothing you've told me changes the way I feel. And nothing changes my intention of making a family with you. A real family."

She shook her head mournfully.

He came around the bed and pulled her head to rest against his belly. "Go to sleep. Don't think about this now. Just go to sleep. We'll settle this tomorrow."

Her cheek was wet against his skin. He smoothed her hair and prayed that tomorrow he would have the courage to make her understand the truth.

Chapter 8

Gemma watched Mary running through the back-yard with Shawn right behind her. Katy had a doctor's appointment, and she had asked Gemma to baby-sit Shawn for the afternoon. The two children had played together several times since the picnic at Patty's, and they were well suited. Whenever Shawn visited, Mary seemed to evolve right before Gemma's eyes, as if she had just needed a role model so that she could learn how a child was supposed to act. On the other hand, Shawn was learning how to behave with a younger child, which was good, since Katy had told Gemma over lunch that she was pregnant again.

Right now the little boy was holding himself back, as if he were afraid that if he really caught Mary, the game would be over. Mary stepped into the rope net that webbed the skeletal pirate ship and began to climb, giggling as she crept higher and higher.

Gemma held her breath, but her foster daughter didn't stop or even falter until she had reached the top. It was a new milestone in Mary's development. This was not the child who had clung so pathetically to Gemma and Farrell. This was a child growing confident, a child who was growing in all the important ways.

A child who might one day be Gemma's very own.

Gemma dropped to the picnic bench and watched Mary begin her descent. She suspected a new game would ensue now. Mary would climb up and down until she tired of this new achievement, and Shawn would find some way to work this strange behavior into his own game. In years to come, would Shawn continue to adapt for this girl cousin? In ten years, or fifteen, would they still be friends, or would the rivalries and passions of adolescence separate them until they were adults again?

Whatever happened, it seemed that Gemma would be there to watch Mary grow, to suffer the pangs and joys of growing up with her. Thanks to Farrell Riley.

The grass was warm against her bare feet, and she wiggled her toes, taking her eyes off the children for a moment. Toes were as good for contemplation as belly buttons, and there were more of them. But more didn't change a thing. She could contemplate all day and well into the night, and nothing was going to change. She could not bear children. One man had already left her because of her infertility, and she could not ask another to give up having a family of his own.

Last night she hadn't gotten any sleep after Farrell left. She had tried to convince herself she was wrong, that her inability to bear children wasn't a good enough reason to destroy her future happiness. But as many times as she had gone over it, she hadn't changed her mind. When Jimmy had left her, she had sworn she would never be that vulnerable again. She would rather be lonely than pitied or resented.

Tears stung her eyes, and she took a deep breath. She loved Farrell Riley. She knew that she had never really loved Jimmy. She had loved Jimmy's image, the glow that surrounded him, the man he pretended to be. But the Farrell Riley she loved was the man inside the human shell, the passionate, sensitive, yearning man. The man who deserved the biological ties, the family he'd never had.

"Ma…" Mary ran full tilt in Gemma's direction and threw herself into her lap. She clasped Gemma around the neck and buried her face in Gemma's shoulder. And again she used the word she had heard Shawn use with Katy. "Ma…"

Gemma hugged her until the little girl began to wriggle in protest. There were no breaths deep enough to keep tears from sliding down Gemma's cheeks. "Oh, Mary."

"Ma…" Mary touched her cheek and frowned.

"I'm just happy," Gemma explained. And she

was. Mary was going to be her real daughter now. In the ways that mattered, she already was. Gemma hadn't even dared to dream this might happen so soon. Yet even while she stroked Mary's hair and murmured her name, the tears continued to slide down her cheeks.

The box under Farrell's arm was as heavy as lead. His heart was nearly as heavy. He had taken the afternoon off work, and he had spent it digging memories out of his attic. He hoped he never spent another afternoon exactly the same way. He would rather take his chances on the worst streets of Hazleton than dig through his past. But if this was what it took to convince Gemma that he wanted her forever, then he would do it every day without flinching until she saw the truth.

He hadn't told her when he would be coming, and he hadn't called before he left the house. He imagined he was catching her at dinnertime, which was what he had hoped for. He wanted to see Mary. If he couldn't make his case tonight, he didn't know how often he would see the little girl in the future. The thought of losing Mary, like the thought of losing Gemma, was something he couldn't contemplate.

As a child, he hadn't been able to fight for what he wanted.

But he was not a child anymore.

He knocked and waited, looking around as he did. The pansies in planters flanking the front steps were wilting in the late-afternoon sun, as if Gemma had forgotten to water them. Mary's plastic tricycle lay turned on its side next to the front door, and dried leaves huddled against the morning paper, which had never been taken inside.

Gemma appeared at the front door, a Gemma without a smile or one trace of makeup. Her eyes widened. "I thought you'd be by later."

His other reason for coming at dinnertime was to throw her off guard. He could see he'd succeeded. "I was hoping you'd feed me. I brought dessert." He held up a bakery box containing a fresh apple pie. "If you don't have enough, I could just eat the pie."

She smiled, almost as if she couldn't help herself. Then she sobered. "Don't you think we should do this after Mary goes to bed?"

"Absolutely. I'll wait."

She shook her head, but she let him in. And once inside, he had no intention of leaving until this was settled in his favor.

Mary covered the awkward silence in the hall by dashing into Farrell's arms. Gemma grabbed the pie just in time, and he lifted Mary with one arm, protecting the box under his other arm.

"Can I take that, too?" Gemma asked.

"I'll put it in the living room." He didn't explain. He carried Mary with him, setting the box on a table out of her reach.

In the kitchen, he watched Gemma open the refrigerator and peer inside. She didn't look at him. "I was just going to cook a hamburger patty for Mary. I have some carrots from last night. I hadn't even thought about what I'd make for myself.''

"Why don't I order a pizza?"

The suggestion seemed to startle her. "Pizza?"

"Yeah, you know, crust, sauce, pepperoni. No work for anybody except dialing the telephone."

"I never order pizza."

He suspected there were a number of things she hadn't learned in her first marriage that she would learn in her second. He was not marrying her to be taken care of. He was marrying her to share her life.

"Sit," he ordered. "All you have to do is think about what toppings you want."

"I don't care."

"Then I'll get a supreme, and you can take off whatever you don't like."

She sat, almost as if she were in a trance. He grinned at her, forcing a confidence he didn't feel, and picked up the telephone. He knew the number by heart, since pizza was a cop's best friend. When he hung up the phone, she was still sitting and staring at him as if he'd just been transported to earth from a spaceship.

"Okay, where's the hamburger? Our little girl may like this pizza just fine, but she needs something healthier to start her off."

"Oh." Color rose in Gemma's cheeks, and she started to get to her feet.

"Sit," he ordered again. "And stay there. You look beat. Just tell me where to find everything."

She didn't argue. With her supervision, he found and unwrapped a hamburger patty and started it sizzling in a small frying pan. He found the cooked carrots next and slipped them into the microwave; then he poured Mary a plastic tumbler of milk and set her in her high chair with a slice of bread and jam.

By the time the hamburger and carrots were on a plate in front of Mary, he had found two ice-cold beers and poured them for himself and Gemma. Mary filled the strained silence with comments on the food in front of her, some of them amazingly close to standard English. As soon as she started putting sounds together in a slightly different order, Farrell's little girl was going to be quite a linguist.

The pizza arrived before the silence between the two adults stretched too thin. Farrell retrieved it and paid the deliveryman. Then, back in the kitchen, he dished it up, with a small piece for Mary, too.

He joined Gemma at the table. "You've given me a good taste of your life. You need a taste of mine. That way, when you marry me, you'll know exactly what you're getting."

"Farrell—"

He shook his head. "Eat up before it gets cold."

Mary was an instant pizza convert. She gobbled her slice, then a slice of apple pie, fretting when she couldn't have another. Farrell made the disappointment up to her by giving her a horsey ride around the house while Gemma cleaned the kitchen.

Gemma rescued the little girl after a good long gallop and took her upstairs for a bath, but Farrell was the one who read her a good-night story and tucked her into bed. Mary pointed at pictures in the simple storybook, as if she was memorizing the names of every animal and object. Just as soon as she had the vocabulary she needed, Farrell's little girl was going to be quite a reader.

He left the door open, just in case she needed anything, but one last peek in her direction convinced him she was falling asleep. He stood at the top of the stairs for a moment, girding himself for what was to come; then he went down to find Gemma.

He found her in the living room. "Do you want your pie now? I could make some coffee to go with it."

She shook her head. "I couldn't eat another thing."

"Then we'll save it for later."

She looked as if she wasn't sure there would be a later. In fact, she looked as if she was sure there *wouldn't* be. "She adores you."

"She knows it's mutual."

"You're so good with her. You're a natural with children."

"Who would have guessed it?"

She didn't ask him to sit beside her, but he did, anyway. "I had some news this morning."

"Oh?"

"I'm moving up to detective."

"That's wonderful." For the first time that evening, her eyes lit up. "That's really wonderful.... Is
it a dangerous job?"

He smiled, because she hadn't managed to keep the
concern out of her voice. "No more so than any other
job on the force. And I'll be spending a lot more time
on investigations. The hours won't be as regular, and
I'm sorry about that. But if I work long hours one
week, I can take time off the next."

"I'm proud of you."

He wondered what else he could say about the pro-
motion. He wanted to keep talking about other things.
He would have been happy to talk about almost anything to keep from discussing what he'd come for.
But the time had arrived.

"Farrell, I—"

"Gemma, I—"

They both stopped. Gemma flushed. "I've given
this a lot of thought, Farrell. That's all I've done. And
I still—"

He held up his hand. "I have some things to show
you. Can I do that first? Then you can tell me what
you think, and I promise I'll listen. I promise I'll always listen to you. But this time, I need to go first."

She looked doubtful, but she nodded.

He stood and retrieved the box from the table
where he'd set it; then he brought it over to the sofa.
"Come sit beside me. You can see better."

She scooted closer. "What is it?"

"It's my childhood, Gemma. My life."

He had been very careful about how he had placed things in the box. Now he opened it, spreading the cardboard flaps so that the contents were in view. He lifted out a worn scrapbook with a padded plastic cover. The cover was torn, but it had been neatly taped. One of his foster mothers had discovered the scrapbook in the destructive hands of a foster brother, and she had helped Farrell repair both the cover and some of the inside pages. She had been one of the important people.

He was not a man to make speeches, but now he knew he was about to make the longest speech of his life. "I've told you a little about the way I grew up. But not enough."

"I thought it was something you probably didn't want to talk about."

"You were right. But you need to know me better." He balanced the scrapbook on his knees and opened it to the first page. Dust filtered through the air. The scrapbook had been stored away for years, and although he had carefully wiped off the cover, he hadn't touched the inside pages.

The photo on the first page had been imprinted on his brain from hours of staring at it as a child. He hadn't seen it for a long time, but he hadn't needed to.

"This is my mother. Her name was Noreen, Noreen Wakefield. She grew up on a small farm in Iowa. Wakefields owned that farm for five generations."

"She was lovely." Gemma touched the edge of the photograph. "You look a little like her."

"I've been told that before." He did resemble the woman in the photograph—the same dark hair, the same straight nose. But his mother was smiling with the exuberance of youth, and he had never felt that kind of joyful abandon.

He touched the edge of the photograph. "She was seventeen when this photograph was taken. Just out of high school. She moved to Des Moines right afterward. She moved to bigger and bigger cities after that to escape her roots. She did a good job of it."

He turned the page. "These are her parents." The snapshot, probably taken with an ancient box camera, was faded and unfocused. It showed two people in front of a small frame house. An old pickup was parked beside them. "I never met my grandparents. A great-aunt, my grandfather's stepsister, sent me this photo when I was in high school. She would write me occasionally. She was very old and unwell, but even though we weren't related by blood, she tried to stay in touch with me. Her name was Hattie."

He turned the page again and pointed to the first of two photos. "That's Hattie." The snapshot was slightly more focused then the one of his grandparents. Hattie was a prim-looking woman, with the weathered face of someone who had worked hard and seldom pampered herself.

"This is Hattie's sister, Clara. I never met her. I think she died before I was born." The photo was similar to the one of Hattie, and he moved on to the next page.

There was no photograph here, just a small plastic bag filled with dirt. "This is soil from the family farm. When I got out of high school and the state of Illinois couldn't tell me what to do anymore, I hitch-hiked to Iowa. Hattie was dead by then, but I wanted to see where my family had lived. The farm is still in cultivation, but it's owned by a huge conglomerate now. The house is used for hay storage."

Gemma gazed up at him. "What happened? Didn't anyone in your family want it anymore?"

"It was auctioned to pay off debts back in the seventies." He turned the page to one showing two young men, standing with cocky indifference under a large oak tree. "These are my mother's two brothers, Alfred and Gary. I lived with Gary once for a few months, until the state stepped in and put me into a foster home."

"Why?"

"Let me show you the rest of the album first."

She looked puzzled, but she nodded. "Okay."

He turned the page and revealed a stack of letters. "These are Hattie's letters. I kept every one of them."

He turned the page again. "This is my father, Paul Riley."

The man in the photograph didn't resemble Farrell in any way. He had a wide face and curly blond hair. He was dressed in a cheap polyester suit, and his shirt was unbuttoned to show a substantial portion of bare chest and three gold chains. "And *this* is my father," he said, turning the page.

The second picture was a fading newspaper photo of the same man, but this time he wasn't wearing a sly smile. He looked surly and mean. The headline beside it read Local Man Arrested In Robbery.

Farrell turned the page again without looking at Gemma. "This is the transcript of a hearing dated just after my birth. I filed for and got this when I was twenty-one."

"A hearing?"

"My mother tried to get child support from my father, but he claimed that I wasn't really his son. For all I know, he may have been right. I saw Noreen on and off through the years before she died, just often enough to keep the state from severing her parental rights, but she never would tell me if Paul Riley was my real dad. The court seemed to think he was. They told him he had to pay support for me, but it didn't really matter, because he never had any money—at least, none that he could claim on his income tax."

He turned to the last page. It was a collection of short newspaper articles, all detailing the conclusion of criminal trials or subsequent sentencing. Paul Riley was the subject of them all.

Farrell closed the scrapbook. "I had similar articles about my mother, Gemma. I tore them out and threw them away the last time I looked through this. I'm not sure why. Noreen wasn't any better than Paul, although at least she admitted I was her child. She and her brothers left the farm in Iowa and never looked back. She wanted the good life. She told me once that she didn't want to end up like her mother, bitter and depleted, so she went looking for something else. Only, she didn't take any of the values she'd learned in church as a child. She stole and lied and used her body to get whatever she could from men. She got pregnant with me and tried to use me to get money from Paul. When that didn't work, she gave me to the state to raise.''

"What about your grandparents? Didn't they try to help you?''

"I was born late in my mother's life. My grandparents were old, and they had washed their hands of all their children by the time I was born. Alfred and Gary had turned out like my mother, using whatever they could to get whatever they wanted. My grandparents had mortgaged the farm to help their sons out of one jam or the other. In the end, they were so deeply in debt they couldn't recover.''

"But none of that was your fault, Farrell. How could they take it out on you?''

"In one of her letters Hattie said that my grandparents were rigid people who only saw the world a certain way. They thought that anything that didn't fit into their views was no good. My mother was obviously no good, and so, in their eyes, I couldn't be, either. And a child born out of wedlock didn't fit into their picture. They never even wrote to me.''

"Maybe your mother turned out the way she did because of them."

"Maybe she did. And maybe I was better off not having them in my life. Unfortunately, like I said before, I had one of my uncles for a while. Gary took me in when I was seven. He looked good on paper, I guess. He had a wife, a job. He'd been in trouble with the law, but the court thought that he'd cleaned up his act. They didn't know he wanted me because he needed a child to stand watch for him."

"Stand watch?"

"His talents ran to burglary. He set me up with an ice cream cone and a puppy he got from the pound, and the puppy and I would walk back and forth, up and down the block, while he broke into houses. If I saw a police car, I whistled. Unfortunately, Gary was cockier than he was smart. He got caught on our third trip out. I got sent back to foster care, and the puppy went back to the pound."

"Farrell..." Gemma laid her hand on his arm. "You're breaking my heart. Why are you telling me this?"

"Those are the people I came from, Gemma. They're my blood, the stuff that I'm made from. At the worst they were criminals. At the best they were rigid and bitter, with no joy or love in their souls for their only grandchild. I thought you should know."

"Why? Do you think it matters to me what your family was like? You're *you,* and you're nothing like them!"

He let that sink in a moment. He wanted her to think about what she'd said. "I'm not," he said quietly. "You're right. I'm the man I am because of some people I met along the way. Not because of the people whose bloodlines I carry."

Gemma watched Farrell's face. He had not shared this story of his family often. She knew him well enough to know that. But he wasn't ashamed. She knew that, too. Farrell had grown past the family who had given him life. He knew who he was and what was in his own heart. He knew which side of the law he stood on, and he was a proud, confident man.

Gemma couldn't think of anything to say in response to what she had learned about him. Farrell's family was as different from hers as the county jail was from Shore Haven. She understood what he was trying to say, and she wanted to accept it, to reach out to him and tell him that they could make a different kind of family together. But she was still so tied up in her own misery, her own failures, that the words wouldn't come.

Farrell seemed to understand. He reached inside the box for a second album. This one was stuffed full. He opened it before she could speak. "I had ten foster homes. Six of them didn't make it into this album. Four of them did."

He opened the album to the first page. "These are the Jensens. I was only with them a year, but Sarah taught me to read. She wasn't a warm, welcoming woman, but she took her job seriously. I was a shy

seven-year-old. I'd been moved twice in first grade.
At the beginning of second grade I went to live with
Gary, and he didn't send me to school. By the time
the Jensens got me, I was so far behind that the
schools decided I was slow. Sarah wouldn't have that.
No child in her care could possibly be slow. So she
drilled me every night until I was in tears. But she
taught me to read, and I never had trouble in school
after that, no matter how many schools I attended.
Sarah made me understand I could do anything I
wanted if I just tried hard enough.''

He smiled at the picture of the Jensens. It wasn't a
photograph, but a childish drawing of two blond and
overweight adults. He turned the page to a yellowing
school paper printed neatly on wide lines. ''My first
A. Sarah's doing. She's the one who bought me this
scrapbook.'' He turned the page again. ''My first
good report card. Sarah smiled when she saw it. It
might be the only time she did.''

Gemma put her hand on his arm. ''You don't have
to go on, Farrell.''

''I think I do.'' He continued showing her mementos of the other homes where he'd learned the things
he needed to become an adult. She listened to him
tell about the Watkinses, who had taught him to take
care of himself with older, rougher boys. The Petersons, who had given him music lessons and bought
him exactly the right kind of clothes so that he would
fit in with the other thirteen-year-olds at his school.
The Lamberts, who had attended every school con-

ference and even every football game the year he had warmed the bench for junior varsity.

He ran his finger along the snapshot of a nondescript older woman. "Mrs. Lambert was the one who helped me repair that first scrapbook. When the county tried to move me in my senior year, she and her husband threatened them with a lawsuit. She was there when I graduated from the police academy, too, although she was in the last stages of cancer. Through the years I started to think of those four families as 'the important ones.' They weren't my families by blood, but they gave me the things I needed to become a man."

He closed the second album with its collection of photographs and pictures, its school papers and report cards.

He set it back in the box, then turned so he could see Gemma's face. Her eyes were clouded with tears, and she couldn't speak.

He did. "You were right when you said I needed my own family, Gemma. You were right, because I *do* have things I need to pass on to my children. I need to teach them that they can do anything if they try hard enough, just the way Sarah Jensen taught me. I need to teach them to take care of themselves and not to be afraid, the way Sam Watkins did. I need to show them I understand how important it is to explore new parts of yourself and to fit in, the way the Petersons did. And I need to show them that I care what they do and what they feel, the way the Lamberts did.''

He took her hand. His was warm and strong, a hand that wrapped around hers protectively. ''Those are the things I need to pass on to my children, Gemma, the very best parts of myself. Not my genes. Not my heritage. The man I am *despite* that heritage. You've come to terms with your inability to bear children. Now you have to come to terms with my acceptance of it.''

''Farrell…''

He spoke the next words slowly. ''I don't care where my sons and daughters come from, Gemma, but I do care desperately who their mother is.''

Tears flowed down her cheeks—healing, renewing tears. She hadn't meant to cry. It seemed wrong, when her heart was so filled with hope and with love for him. He lifted her hand to his lips and kissed it. ''Marry me. Share my life. Let's make a real family together.''

She moved into his arms as naturally as if she had never moved out of them.

He kissed her, and she kissed him back. As he held her, in her mind she saw the family they would make, a family filled with love and warmth and laughter.

She pulled away at last, and he wiped the tears off her cheeks with his thumbs.

''I love you,'' she whispered. ''I will forever. When we have grandchildren and great-grandchildren—''

"Ma?"

Gemma turned and saw Mary standing in the doorway. Her thumb was firmly in her mouth and her blanket was trailing behind her. Mary, the first of the children they would raise and love together. Farrell put one arm around Gemma and held out the other. Mary flew across the room and scrambled into his lap.

Farrell Riley enclosed his family in his arms.

*   *   *   *   *

BABY ON THE WAY
Marie Ferrarella

To Pat Teal,
with all good wishes
for a full recovery.
Love,
Marie

Dear Reader,

Everyone deserves a second chance. "Baby on the Way" is about second chances and two people who needed them and each other. When Officer J. T. Walker came to Madeline Reed's rescue late one night and helped the young widow give birth to her son, he had no idea that he was getting a second chance, or that he was giving one. But as different as J.T. and Maddy were, they had one thing in common. They had both lost someone they loved, and both thought that love only came around once. They were wrong.

All you need to love again is an open heart that's willing to take a chance on the greatest gift the world has to offer. Maddy and her baby helped J.T. open his heart again by drawing him, kicking and screaming, out of his lonely world and into theirs: a world filled with warmth, laughter and, most of all, with love.

I hope their story brings you a measure of joy this Mother's Day, and if you don't have someone at this moment, may you find someone to love, and to love you, very, very soon.

All the best,

Marie Ferrarella

Chapter 1

Nights were the hardest.

Nights were when all the memories, both good and bad, would come crowding back into his head, giving no quarter, taking no prisoners as they slashed through his heart. The bad memories all revolved around the loss of Lorna, around having to do without her.

You would think, J. T. Walker thought as he steered his patrol car down a long, lonely stretch of road, that after two years he would finally have come to terms with it. Come to terms with the emptiness, the sorrow.

Well, maybe he had.

After all, he was still here, still alive, still moving through life, fitting one day onto another like some giant mismatched string of pop-beads. And he was no longer sleepwalking through his life, the way he initially had when the news had reached him. That had to mean something, right?

Yeah, he thought cynically, it meant that he was a survivor.

Only question was, what was he surviving for? Nothing that he could see. Lorna was gone, as were his hopes for a family, swept away by the carelessness of a drunk driver early New Year's Eve in one horrific turn of the wheel, one terrible miscalculation.

Gone, just like that.

Leaving him to grieve, to continue as best he could in a world that had the audacity to continue spinning without Lorna.

Without laughter, without joy.

If only he hadn't been working late, an extra shift so that he could have the next day off to spend with his wife. If only he hadn't told her to go on ahead of him to her parents' house, that he would meet her there after he got off.

If only...

Damn it, he was getting maudlin again.

Annoyed with himself, J.T. shook his head to drive the thoughts away, like a soaked dog shaking to rid himself of the water that was stubbornly clinging to his coat.

The thoughts wouldn't leave as easily as droplets of water, but he was a police officer and he had a duty to perform. To patrol the darkened streets and make sure that the citizens of Bedford, California, who slept peacefully in their beds, could continue to do so untroubled. Dwelling on the past, on things that couldn't be changed no matter how much he wished and prayed that they could, was utterly fruitless.

When was he going to accept that?

Damn it, Lorna, why did you leave me? Why?

The silent question echoed back at him in the silent squad car, mocking him. The radio crackled, but no message followed. Only static. It was a peaceful night. Peaceful everywhere but within his mind.

Tired, annoyed with himself, J.T.'s hands tightened on the wheel of the squad car he usually shared with Officer Adam Fenelli.

He was alone tonight.

Fenelli had caught his youngest son's bronchitis and had called in sick earlier this evening. They were shorthanded at the station as it was and there was no one to partner with him, nor anyone offering to switch into his squad car for the shift.

Not that he blamed any of them. He wasn't exactly great company anymore, preferring to ride in silence. On the quiet side to begin with, he'd lost all interest in carrying on purposeless conversations just to pass the time. Time passed anyway, whether he talked or not. Fenelli never seemed to take any notice of his lack of communication, doing enough talking for both of them.

A half smile attempted to curve J.T.'s lips. Fenelli was a good man who never stopped trying to reach him, to get him to open up. The older officer might as well have saved his breath.

J.T. figured he had nothing worth saying anymore.

The streets of Bedford were silent, its store lights dimmed to just the barest of glimmers. Street lamps stood like thin sentries, their lights bright against the inky sky as they marked the coming of the midnight hour.

It was a weekday and, for the most part, everyone was home, asleep, in preparation for the beginning a new day. They could sleep. He couldn't. So he'd volunteered for the night shift and tried to close the day with its brightness away.

To his surprise, Fenelli had made the shift over with him, remarking that he could use the change. J.T. knew it was because the older officer was worried about him, but there wasn't anything Fenelli could do to help him. Nothing did any good.

J.T. was simply marking time.

Another wave of darkness threatened to creep over his soul, and it might have, had he not seen something in the road just then. Up ahead, just beyond the boundary of the shopping center and a couple of miles before the next residential area, he thought he saw two red lights pulsing.

J.T. squinted, trying to make out the shape. The squad car's heating system was out of sync and the windshield was beginning to fog up again, as it did periodically, drastically cutting his field of vision. He slowed his vehicle down to a crawl. Having no handkerchief available, J.T. rubbed the glass with the palm of his hand as he continued to stare straight before him.

After a minute or two he began to barely make out the rear lights of a stalled car. The red spheres were pulsing like twin heartbeats, sending their syncopated rhythm into the darkness, two beacons in the night.

Some motorist was probably out there somewhere on foot, J.T. guessed, although he hadn't passed anyone in the past fifteen minutes. Maybe whoever it was lived in the development up ahead and had gone there.

He sighed. Stalled cars were not uncommon, but he was bound to check it out, just in case. From where he was, he couldn't make out the license plate, but the car was a relatively new model sedan and in good condition. There had been no reports of a stolen vehicle on the scanner, so he doubted it was anything other than what it seemed—a car that had more than likely run out of gas or developed some kind of annoying, disabling problem.

Parking several yards behind the vehicle, J.T. got out of the squad car, his hand resting lightly on the butt of his service revolver. Just in case. Every policeman knew that the seconds between leaving his own vehicle and approaching another on the side of the road were the most crucial, risk-filled seconds of his life. The warning had made its rounds even here. Bedford was as peaceful as they came, but be that as it may, it never hurt to be cautious.

The scream shattered the night, his thoughts and his calm.

Hurrying the rest of the way, straining for any sights or sounds of danger, J.T. had his gun out of its holster by the time he reached the driver's door. There had been no one visible as he'd run the short distance from his car to the stalled one, but the scream had come from somewhere and there was no one around anywhere else. No stores, no homes hiding behind a residential wall, nothing. The scream had to have come from the car.

One hand holding his gun ready, J.T. yanked open the door of the car with the other. Part of him embraced the idea of trouble. Anything to get his adrenaline moving, to occupy the space where loneliness had taken up permanent residence.

That was when he saw her.

There was a blonde slumped over to the side, her body wedged behind the steering wheel, her abdomen distended with the swell of an unborn child.

"Lady—" he began, and got no further. She screamed again, this time all but destroying his eardrums and peeling back his skin. The last time he'd heard a scream like that, Fay Wray had gotten her first terrifying look at King Kong.

He noticed that her right arm was extended out onto the passenger seat, as if she were trying to claw her way out of the vehicle.

In pain from the roots of her hair down to the soles of her feet, Madeline Reed had trouble focusing on the face of the man looking into the car. Seeing the gun he held, her first thought was that he could shoot her and put her out of her misery.

"I'm sorry," she gasped. "I'm not…much on…pain and this—" she stopped to suck in air with the fervent hope that it could somehow arrest the onslaught that was coming "—this is pretty bad." She'd just made the understatement of the century, she thought, biting down hard on her lip.

He didn't need to ask her how far along she was. Unless she was carrying quintuplets, the woman in the car was at term with every indication that she was in the verge of exploding.

She also looked stuck. How the hell had she gotten herself in that position?

"Water break?" he asked.

She tried to nod her head and found she couldn't. "A hundred years ago, when I started…started…out on this…*trIPPPP!*"

This one was the worst, she thought, the very worst. But every pain that had assaulted her since she'd left the shop and begun her trip home had been greater than the last. Which meant that the worst was yet to be. It wasn't a comforting thought.

"How did you—never mind." He could see she was in no condition to have an extended conversation or even offer any explanations. Maybe she had just fallen over trying to reach for her purse, which he could see was on the floor. How she got here didn't matter. That she was here did.

Kneeling, J.T. found the mechanism that controlled the seat's various positions. He tried to push the seat back farther, only to discover that it was already as far back as it could go. He sat back on his heels, studying the problem. He heard her vainly attempt to muffle the next scream.

"I've got to get you out of the front seat."

Madeline turned her head toward him, surprised that she could. "No...kidding..." she gasped.

Damn it, why did this have to happen now? Why not an hour from now? She'd be ready for this an hour from now. She would have gotten home and if the contractions had begun then instead of when she'd been on the road for less than five minutes, she would have been able to make a few calls, place her suitcase in the car and go to the hospital in style instead of feeling as if she was about to be torn apart from the inside out.

She wasn't even due for another week and a half. This wasn't supposed to be happening.

"You wouldn't...happen...to have...the...jaws of...life...with you...would you?" When he shook his head, she pressed her lips together to keep from screaming again. "Then...you'd better...be... Superman."

J.T. said nothing in response. Instead he pressed another button that allowed the back of her seat to go down until it was almost in a reclining position. Very carefully, he drew her back into a sitting position, then turned her so that her legs were out of the car.

The woman was small, but her center of gravity was low. J.T. braced himself. This wasn't going to be easy for either one of them.

"Put your arms around my neck," he instructed.

"Are...you...asking me...to dance...?" Maddy quipped, trying hard to keep her wits and humor about her. Otherwise, she was going to dissolve in a flood of frightened tears. The policeman was only trying to help her, she told herself. It wouldn't be fair to him if she became hysterical.

Fair.

None of it was fair.

She swallowed the lump that made a sudden appearance in her throat.

The pregnant woman's flippant question took him by surprise. She was probably hallucinating, he decided. He needed backup. Fast.

"Maybe later."

As gently as possible, he drew her up to her feet. When she swayed, his arms tightened around her, drawing her to him. Damn it, he could remember holding Lorna against him just like this. A bittersweet feeling swept over him.

He fought off the wave of sorrow.

"Right now," he said to her, "it looks like you've got a baby to deliver."

A line from *Gone with the Wind* suddenly materialized within her fevered brain. "I don't...know nothin' about…birthin'…no babies,'' Maddy managed to exhale as she struggled against the darkness that threatened to engulf her.

She was vaguely aware of a sinking sensation. The policeman had eased her onto the back seat. His arms were strong. Protective.

Maddy sank down, struggling not to cry out against his ear.

Chapter 2

"Birthin' babies." The words echoed in J.T.'s head. What the hell was she babbling about?

The woman was out of her head, J.T. judged. Pain did that to a person. He should know.

At least he hadn't dropped her when he'd placed her in the rear of her car. Grateful for small favors, he straightened. As he began to leave, he felt his wrist being seized in a steel grip.

He looked at her in surprise. She didn't look capable of exerting such strength. Her fingers tightened around his wrist, cutting off circulation.

"Where…are you…going?" she gasped. He couldn't just leave her here, could he? Maddy thought frantically. She couldn't do this alone.

"Just to my car." He pointed with his free hand,

even though he knew she couldn't see. "I've got to call for an ambulance."

"Too late."

This baby wasn't about to wait for any ambulance to make its appearance. It was trying to make an entrance. Now.

Scared, still holding on to his wrist with one hand, Maddy dug the nails of the other into the upholstery in an effort to somehow ground herself. She arched her back, trying to ease the pain.

He felt sorry for her. Even with her face contorted with pain, she was a beautiful woman. What the hell was she doing out here alone at this time of night? Where was this woman's husband?

"Look, you need professional help." Help he didn't feel qualified to give. "I've got to call for an ambulance. They'll be right here."

She was afraid. Afraid of being alone. Until he had found her, she'd been struggling to fight off encroaching terror. Her car had died just as she'd felt herself going into hard labor.

Maddy looked at him, her eyes beseeching him. "No...don't go... Please." Gritting her teeth, she tried to raise herself on her elbows, and only marginally succeeded. "You're...part of...911, aren't... you?"

J.T. didn't see what that had to do with it. "Yes, but—"

Oh damn, here came another one. Maddy began

breathing more rapidly. "Then...do...what you were...trained to do... *Help me.*"

That was what he was trying to do, but he couldn't accomplish that by just talking to her. He felt her loosening her grip for a moment and took the opportunity to peel her fingers away from his wrist. He could feel the flesh throbbing, could see the imprint of her fingers on his skin. He thought labor was supposed to make you weak. Labor had apparently turned this woman into some kind of superwoman.

"Maybe we can get you to the hospital." Harris Memorial was less than fifteen minutes way. Eight if he broke a few speed rules. He glanced toward her ignition and saw that there was no key in it. "Let me have your car keys—"

Maddy moved her head from side to side frantically. "Car's...dead." And so would she be in a few minutes if this pain didn't stop, she thought. How did women *do* this?

He could carry her to his car, J.T. thought, as long as she didn't fight him. The distance wasn't that far, and except for her belly she was a petite woman. "Then I'll get you into mine—"

But even as he reached for her, Maddy scrambled back against the upholstery. She couldn't stand the thought of being moved, wasn't up to it.

"This...baby's...coming...*now.*" Her words were framed in short, melodious sounds as she practiced the breathing exercises she'd learned. She was desperate and completely out of options. To her surprise, the exercises helped.

But not enough. She felt like a lobster being cracked open.

J.T. knew he had no choice. He was going to have to deliver the baby. He'd been in this position once before. There'd been a huge storm the November before Lorna had died. They'd been coming back from a concert when the woman's husband had flagged them down. He'd tried to drive her to the hospital, only to find the roads impassable. The man was practically babbling, saying something about there being no time to circumvent the eucalyptus tree that had fallen directly in the path of his car.

In what turned out to be almost the most incredible twenty minutes of his life, he and Lorna had delivered the couple's baby. He'd never felt closer to Lorna. Or more convinced that he wanted to begin a family himself.

He remembered how he'd felt, delivering the tiny baby girl born that night. Being the first to hold her in his hands. She'd been such a tiny bit of a thing, her eyes bright, alert. He remembered looking at Lorna over the baby's head.

The bittersweet memory overwhelmed him for a moment, cutting through the past and the present until he wasn't sure just what was real.

Why was he just standing there like that? Maddy wondered frantically. Why wasn't he doing something?

Another contraction seized her in its tight jaws, sucking her breath away so that continuing the exercises became impossible. She was vaguely aware of grabbing his hand, nearly breaking his fingers as she bent them in hers.

"Help…me," she pleaded.

He saw the terror in her eyes. All thought of racing to his car to make the call for assistance vanished. He couldn't leave her alone.

"All right." J.T. climbed into the car with her.

"What's…your…name?" A woman should know the name of the man picking up her dress and tucking it up around her hips, she thought.

Intense concentration as he tried to remember procedure momentarily blocked her words. J.T. looked up at her. "What?"

"What's…your…name?" she repeated with effort. "I…need…to know…the name of…the man… delivering…my baby." She tried to smile, but the look dissolvéd into a grimace as she fought another contraction.

He raised his voice, knowing she wouldn't hear him otherwise. "J.T."

Her lashes were damp from tears or sweat, she wasn't sure which. "That's…not a name…that's… part of…the…alphabet."

He'd always been J.T., to Lorna and to everyone else. The only person who'd ever called him by his full name had been his mother. He'd been named after both of his grandfathers.

"John Thomas." When she looked at him with a silent question, he went a step further. "John Thomas Walker."

Maddy nodded. It was a good name, an unpretentious name. Her husband's name had been John. Johnny. *Oh Johnny, I wish you could be here.*

"John Thomas," she repeated, her lips dry, her body damp. "I...hope you're...not...the type...to panic...because...I am." It was all she could do to keep the panic at bay now.

He tried to assure her as best he could. The woman looked to be fully dilated. It shouldn't be much longer now. "Piece of cake."

"Right...with...a big file...stuck...in it." A sharp, pointy file with inch-long teeth that were slicing across her flesh with every breath she took. "Here...comes...another one!"

J.T. grasped her hand, letting her hold on as tightly as she could.

"It doesn't last," he promised, her, leaning over so that he could wipe her forehead.

She barely felt his touch. It was too gentle to register. "Easy...for you...to...say."

There was nothing easy about this for him. He felt as if he was reliving one of the most important nights of his life. And none of it was actually real.

They made eye contact for a split second and his eyes held hers.

"No," he told her firmly, "it's not." He sought for a way to distract her. He vaguely remembered it was supposed to help at a time like this. Lorna had sung to the woman, some ancient Irish lullaby that had helped soothe her. J.T. hadn't even attempted to join in. He had a voice that could crack eggs. "What's your name?"

"Mad—" Maddy began giving him her nickname. But Maddy wasn't the name of a woman who was about to give birth. The name belonged to the madcap person she'd always been, but she couldn't be that way anymore. She was going to be someone's mother. Mothers were supposed to be regal, not childish. "Madeline Reed."

He could see the baby's crown. The ordeal was almost over for her. "Well, Mad Madeline Reed, looks like you're about to be a mother."

She wished she had posts to cling to, something to give her leverage. "Tell…me…something I… don't…know."

"Boy or girl?"

She blinked, trying to make sense of the question. "I…get…to…pick?"

"No, do you want a boy or a girl?"

"What I…want…is…for it…to…be…*over!*" She wasn't going to be able to make it. Exhaustion was beginning to claim her.

"Almost," he promised. "All you have to do is push when I tell you."

"Tell…me…now," she begged. Maddy didn't know how much longer she was going to be able to stand this. She hadn't been prepared for anything this intense. But then, she hadn't planned this pregnancy, it had just happened. But she was glad that it had, because now at least she was able to have a part of Johnny. "I've…got to…push."

It had to be structured, regulated. Otherwise, he was afraid she would rupture something.

"Not yet," J.T. warned.

His mind scrambled as he tried to remember everything he'd ever learned about deliveries under adverse conditions.

"Now?" she pleaded. Whether he said yes or not, she was going to start pushing. She had to.

"Now. One—two—three, push!"

He got to three, but there was no point to it. Maddy had begun pushing at one. Pushing with all her might, pushing so hard that she felt everything inside her body was on the verge of coming out.

Exhausted, Maddy fell back against the seat like a rag doll. Any second now, another contraction was going to come rolling in, determined to flatten her. She struggled to draw together what tiny scraps of energy she still had left.

"Good."

Why was he patronizing her? Wavering, Maddy pulled herself up again. "No…it's…not. If it…was…good, there'd…be a…baby…here."

"Almost," he promised.

How could he say that to her? She felt as if she was doomed to push forever, with no results. "Want…to…take…the…next…shift?"

The baby was practically here. Just a little more, he thought, excitement pulsing through him. Just a little more.

"Not possible."

"Spoilsport."

Here it came again, pain. Leaping at her like a panther about to take down a fleeing gazelle. "Oh, God—"

He heard the panic in her voice and moved her face until her eyes were forced to take in only him. "Push," he ordered. "Harder."

She didn't think that was physically possible. Scrunching her eyes shut, envisioning the baby sliding out of her, Maddy pushed with every fiber of her being. And when she was finished, she collapsed, gasping, unable to suck in enough air to keep herself from suffocating.

It wasn't over.

"Almost there."

His voice came to her from a distant haze. Why wasn't the baby here yet? She'd pushed and pushed— it was supposed to be here.

"Something's...wrong."

"Nothing's wrong," he told her firmly, his voice deliberately harsh to keep the panic he heard in hers at bay. "This is a baby, not a can of soda in a vending machine that drops down as soon as you insert the right amount of change. Now you're going to have to push again. Ready?"

"No."

He looked up at her. It was hard to tell, but she looked pale. Damn, but he wished he had called for backup the moment he had seen the stalled car. "Come on, you can do this. Close your eyes and push, Madeline."

"Maddy," she corrected. She needed to hear someone call her that. Needed to cling to something that was stable in her life. She'd been Maddy when she'd met her husband. And Maddy at his funeral.

"Maddy," J.T. repeated. It fit her. "Let's get this baby born."

Closing her eyes, praying, Maddy pushed until she was completely inside out.

A minute later she heard the cry of a baby.

Chapter 3

He didn't want it to happen.

He had no choice in the matter.

Just holding the newborn in his arms forced the feeling upon him. It was a deep sensation that began in the center of his chest—it was almost a pain, really, but not quite—and then spread out to his extremities until all of him was encompassed in the spiraling warmth that was being generated.

The widest pair of blue eyes looked up at him with wonder, placing him at the center of a universe that would only continue to grow. But for now, he was it. The beginning, the end and the middle.

This was the look he'd envisioned in his own child's eyes. His and Lorna's.

The heart that had been frozen over and immobilized within him began to stir. And defrost.

He didn't want it to happen.

But it was happening anyway.

J.T.'s mouth curved as he smiled down at the child.

It was too quiet, too still. Madeline wasn't hearing anything. Was there something wrong with her baby? A newer, sharper panic began to overtake her.

"Is…it…all right?"

Her breath was beginning to return to her in small snatches, but there still wasn't enough for her to be able to form a complete sentence, even a small one, without gasping. Her chest burned and every other part of her felt as if it was throbbing with pain, but the pain in her heart was the worst. Her baby had to be all right, it had to be.

J.T. was only vaguely aware of the sound of the woman's voice or the question that she was asking him. His eyes stung and he was barely holding his own against the onslaught of feelings that were threatening to overwhelm him completely. He'd forgotten what this had felt like, to hold a new life in his arms. To feel the wonder.

"More than all right," he told her softly. "He's beautiful."

He wouldn't lie to her. She had no idea how she knew that, but she did. "He?"

J.T. looked up at Maddy, upbraiding himself for getting so distracted that he'd forgotten about the woman who still needed his help. He nodded even as he looked around for something to wrap the baby in. "You have a son."

Maddy pressed her lips together, suddenly struggling with tears that sprang up out of nowhere. Johnny would have been so proud, if he'd known. But he hadn't. He'd died before she had a chance to tell him that she was pregnant.

We have a son, Johnny. Congratulations.

It was dark within the back seat, with only moderate illumination coming in, thanks to the street lamp, but he still managed to see the tears standing still in Maddy's eyes. Maybe it was because he could hear them in her voice.

Moving forward awkwardly, being careful not to jostle the baby pressed against his chest, he leaned over and presented the newborn to her. J.T. tucked her arm around the small body. Their eyes met for a moment and held just the way his and Lorna's had, over the newborn they'd delivered.

J.T. dropped his.

"Careful, he's slippery."

She merely nodded, accepting the tiny weight into the crook of her arm, for the moment not trusting her voice to keep from breaking.

It was enough that her heart felt as if it was bursting at the seams.

"There's a blanket in the trunk," she finally managed to say.

Looking around the driver's side of the car, he found the latch to the trunk and popped it. When he rounded the rear of the vehicle, he found the blanket in the trunk on top of a laundry basket, which appeared to be crammed full of sheets and towels. Laundry wouldn't help him. He needed something with which to cut the umbilical cord, but at least he could clean the baby up a little before wrapping him in the blanket.

Tucking the blanket under his arm and taking a couple of towels out of the basket, J.T. returned to the back seat.

He set the blanket at her feet and draped one of the towels over the back of the passenger seat. "You always travel with clean laundry?"

"My washing machine broke Saturday." Maddy said, smiling at her son. Everything always happened for a reason, wasn't that what her mother was constantly insisting? "I did my laundry at my mother's." And if she hadn't, or had taken the basket out when she was supposed to, she wouldn't have had the blanket and towels available for the baby.

Very gently, he began cleaning off the baby. "Was that where you were coming from? Your mother's house?"

Despite the pain she was in, Maddy watched, fascinated by how this powerful-looking man could be so gentle as he handled her son. She wondered how many children he had of his own.

She shook her head in response to his question. "No, it was a party. We just landed a huge redecorating account and felt like celebrating," she explained, but even as she did, she realized that he probably didn't know what she was talking about. She and her family ran Rossini Decor, a one-hundred-and-ten-year-old firm that still believed in doing things the old-fashioned way, with dignity, honor and honesty. Not to mention taste.

We. He interpreted the pronoun in his own way. "You and your husband?"

The word brought a fresh volley of tears to her, tears she refused to set free. This was supposed to be a happy time—why did she feel so terribly melancholy?

Struggling for control, Maddy raised her eyes to his. "No."

She said the word with such finality, J.T. knew that he'd trespassed somewhere he wasn't supposed to go.

Divorced? he wondered.

He looked down at her hand as he returned the freshly cleansed infant to her. She still had on a wedding ring. If she was divorced, it had happened recently. And not by choice, he guessed. Otherwise, the ring would have come off.

"I'd better get you to the hospital." J.T. glanced back at his car, gauging the distance. He could always bring it closer, until the two cars were almost parallel, but he didn't want to risk a transfer. But he couldn't leave his car unattended at this time of night. Fenelli picked a fine time to come down with the flu, he thought. He turned back to her. "All right if I call that ambulance now?"

Maddy bit her lower lip. He was referring to how

she'd almost snapped his head off earlier. "I'm sorry. I didn't mean to sound ungrateful."

He didn't want her apologies, and he didn't want her to be getting any wrong ideas. "No call for you to sound anything at all. We're supposed to serve and protect. Just doing my job."

For one moment there, he sounded just like Johnny. Her arms tightened around the baby he would never see. "Yes, I know. My husband was a policeman."

About to get out of the vehicle, J.T. stopped dead. "Was?"

Such a small word, such a huge meaning. Her heart felt heavy enough to sink down to her toes. "He died in the line of duty eight months ago."

The number leaped out at him. That means she'd only been a month or less along when her husband had died. J.T. looked at the baby in her arms.

"Did he know?"

"No."

And that would forever be one of her greatest sorrows, that she'd held the news back from her husband, planning to surprise him with the news on the long romantic weekend they had planned. Johnny had been so eager to have children.

Her voice was filled with sorrow, though she hardly said anything. The heart he was so convinced was incapable of feeling anything went out to her. "I'm sorry."

Maddy exhaled slowly, trying to steady her breathing. "Yes, so am I." As J.T. began to get out of the car, she suddenly called after him. "Don't call the ambulance. Take me in yourself."

He stood outside the passenger door, unconvinced. "I don't think I should try to move you—"

"Why not? You're strong, John Thomas," she told him, then added, "and I'm stronger than I look," hoping to convince him.

John Thomas. It felt odd having someone other than his mother call him that. As far back as he could remember, he'd always been J.T., even to Lorna.

He stood for a moment, thinking, then made up his mind. "Okay, I'll bring the car closer."

Maddy smiled to herself as she held her son close and waited.

The transfer from her car to his turned out to be easier than he'd anticipated. Maddy held her son against her and J.T. carried them both from her back seat to his. His fear of dropping her faded. Even with the double load, Maddy felt as if she weighed close to nothing. He'd carried commission reports that weighed more than she did.

The wind had picked up just before he placed her down on the back seat and he caught a whiff of a soft, tantalizing scent that swirled around him like perfumed magic.

J.T. told himself that he was hallucinating and blocked it out.

"I'll have you there in a few minutes," he promised, getting in behind the steering wheel.

Safe in the back seat, Maddy felt comfortably isolated from everything that was hurtful. "No hurry. I have everything I want right here," she murmured, looking down at her baby.

J.T. looked into the rearview mirror, but she was busy with her son. She looked radiant. He felt something stirring within him, emotions that creaked and flexed stiffly like unused muscles.

J.T. turned the car toward the hospital and forced himself to ignore it. This wasn't about him, this was about a private citizen he was taking to the hospital, nothing more.

"Anyone you want me to call for you?" he asked as he passed through an amber light just before it turned red. The freeway entrance was directly ahead. From where he was, he could see that the traffic was minimal.

"Just my mother." The baby began to fuss and she started rocking him against her. "She'll take care of everyone else. I think I should warn you that she'll want to thank you in person." If she knew her mother, Lorraine Rossini would insist on it. "They all will."

He raised his eyes to the rearview mirror, but Maddy's eyes were lowered as she sat looking adoringly at her son. "All?"

She laughed. He almost sounded wary. "I have a large family. A large, close-knit family."

He wondered what that was like. He'd been an only child and both his parents were gone before he'd blown out the candles on his twenty-fifth birthday cake. His whole world had been Lorna.

"Must be nice," he murmured, out of a lack of anything else to say.

"It is," she assured him. And now she had one more to add to the family. Overcome, she pressed a kiss to the small, not quite downy head. "It is."

He wouldn't know about that, J.T. thought, and he supposed he never would. His hopes of having a family of his own had died that New Year's Eve night with Lorna.

Chapter 4

J.T. had intended that to be the end of it.

He'd done what was expected of him. More, really. He'd brought her in to the hospital, then placed a call to Maddy's mother as she'd requested. He'd patiently listened to Mrs. Rossini shriek with joy as he'd informed her of the details of her grandson's birth. He'd done all that before leaving the hospital.

Beyond that, his responsibility was supposed to be over.

He certainly didn't have to have Ambroise, another policeman from the local precinct, drop him off the following morning where he had left Maddy's car. There was no need to jump-start the dead vehicle. And there had been no need to drive the car to the residential development where she lived and leave it parked safely in her driveway. None of that was necessary or by the book. He couldn't begin to explain why he did it, other than it just seemed like the right thing to do.

Ambroise had followed him and then waited to take him back to his place. A tall, strapping man with skin like ebony, Evan Ambroise made no effort to hide his approval of the deed. He flashed a broad grin as J.T. got back into his car.

"Glad to see you're finally getting out, even if it is just to park cars." He laughed at his own joke as he guided the car out of the development.

J.T. shrugged, staring straight ahead. "Just cleaning up a few details."

Ambroise gave a knowing grunt. "This detail have a name?"

J.T. didn't bother acknowledging the question. He knew where Ambroise, a married man with six children and another on the way, was going with this. Both Ambroise and his wife, Claire, had invited him over countless times since he'd lost his wife. They, along with his partner, kept insisting he had to get out, to socialize, to reclaim his life. Nobody seemed to understand that he didn't want to reclaim it. That it was too empty for him to take back now.

"I helped a woman deliver her baby last night, then took her to the hospital," J.T. said, his voice hardly fluctuating above a monotone.

"Married?" There was a note of concern in Ambroise's voice.

"Widowed." J.T. paused, then added. "That was her car." He slanted a look at the other man. Ambroise was grinning again. "Don't make a big thing out of it," J.T. warned.

"Okay, I won't." He glanced at J.T. as they approached the apartment complex where he'd picked him up earlier. "But maybe she will when she finds out her car isn't where she left it." He pursed his lips together to keep from grinning again. "Don't you think you should tell her it's safe at her place? Seems to me a new mama has enough to worry about without thinking someone stole her car right out from under her."

J.T. rubbed his hand over his face. Why hadn't he thought of that? Because he hadn't been thinking clearly since last night, that's why. Not since he'd held that baby in his arms.

Hell, not since he'd first seen Maddy. She'd reminded him a little of Lorna, petite and blond—and pregnant, the way he'd always wanted her to be.

But he wasn't about to admit that to Ambroise. Even a hint of the truth and the word would be all over the precinct. The last time Ambroise had kept anything to himself, it had been a toothache and even that was shared after the first initial ten minutes of silence.

"I was getting to that."

Ambroise nodded, pleased that J.T. had found an excuse to see the woman again. Wait until he told

Claire. "Good. Wouldn't want one of Bedford's finest to be mistakenly accused of carjacking."

J.T. ignored the grin on the other man's face. The deep chuckle that followed it was harder to block out. It followed him after he'd left Ambroise's car all the way to his own door.

But Ambroise was right. He'd made a mistake. Maddy was going to have no way of knowing where the car was unless he told her.

Which meant he was going to have to see her again.

"No good deed goes unpunished," he muttered under his breath, remembering something his mother had once told him.

With a sigh, he got into his car and drove to the hospital.

J.T. walked slowly to the bank of elevators in the rear of the hospital. For a place that housed the sick, it was incredibly cheerful looking, its colors bright and uplifting without being annoyingly sunny. And the smell was absent. That daunting medicinal smell that made a man's stomach turn to jelly.

He didn't particularly want to be here. Especially not twice in two days.

"This is not a big deal," J.T. told himself. "I'm only dropping by to tell the woman about her car." And while he was at it, he supposed it wouldn't hurt to see how she and the baby were doing. After all, every case had to be followed up. This was just a routine follow-up, nothing more.

J.T. refused to entertain the notion that maybe he wanted to see her just to see her. The fact that they had experienced something special last night, something that tended to bond people for years to come, was not allowed to enter into it. He'd brought her son into the world and had been a critical part of nature's miracle, but he was putting that behind him. There was no point in letting it get to him, no point in dwelling on it at all.

If he did, if he let himself get even moderately involved, it would prove to be much too painful down the line, and he had had a bellyful of pain, enough to last a lifetime.

His.

When he got out of the elevator on the fifth floor, J.T. went straight to the nurses' station and asked for directions. There was no sense in wandering around the corridor, wasting time while trying to find her room. He just wanted to go in, deliver his message and leave. The faster he found her, the sooner he would be on his way.

The older nurse he'd asked paused to look at him over her rimless glasses. "Another one, eh?"

"Excuse me?"

The woman shook her head. "Never mind. I just had no idea we were getting ourselves a celebrity here." She laughed at the private joke she shared with herself. "Keeps the place lively, I guess."

He had no idea what she was talking about. "Is Madeline Reed on this floor or not?"

"Oh, she's here all right. Room 512. Just take the corridor down that way." She pointed toward the left. "Follow the voices, you can't go wrong."

He didn't bother asking what that was supposed to mean.

As he drew closer to the end of the corridor, J.T. heard the murmur of voices. As promised. When he reached Maddy's room and opened the door, he came face-to-back with almost a human wall of people, some milling around the single bed, others lounging by the window. Everyone looked to be in great spirits. At first glance, it looked as if some firm had decided to hold their annual company picnic in her small room.

J.T. stood in the doorway, hesitating for a brief moment. He could always come back. Or better yet, just call the hospital later and ask for her room. He should have done that in the first place, he thought. Although she probably wouldn't have heard the phone ring with all this noise.

Just as he turned to leave, someone grabbed his arm in both of hers.

When he looked, there was a short, beaming older woman in a bright red dress attached to his arm.

"Are you J.T.?" she asked. By her expression, she already seemed to know the answer.

His eyes narrowed. "Yes."

His surprise melted away almost immediately as he

took in the woman's dancing blue eyes, fair complexion and dark blond hair. Aside from the fact that she was somewhat heavy-set, she could have passed as an older version of Maddy.

"I thought so. You looked just the way she described you. I just wanted to hug the man who saved my baby." Before he could say anything in protest, the woman threw her arms around him and squeezed, He saw the family resemblance immediately.

Her mother's squeal of pleasure alerting her, Maddy shifted her attention toward the doorway.

Poor John Thomas, she thought. Her mother tended to be a bit overwhelming as well as dramatic. But that had ceased to embarrass her a long time ago.

"Mother, I was giving birth, not dangling from a broken redwood branch forty feet off the ground."

"Same difference," Lorraine Rossini sniffed. "I could tell you horror stories."

Still holding onto J.T., Lorraine forged her way to her daughter's bed. The sea of people readily parted down the middle to allow them to pass.

He felt like Moses, except no one was allowing him to go free.

"I know you could," Maddy answered, suppressing a wide smile. But it had no trouble reaching her eyes as she looked up at her latest visitor. "You came back."

She made it sound as if he'd promised that he would. Why would she have thought that? "I wanted to tell you that I moved your car."

An older man, barely five-six, with black hair streaked with silver, moved directly into his path. "You impounded her car?" It was a gruff challenge.

"Calm down, Dad," a woman in the crowd counseled. "Let the man talk."

J.T. frowned, directing his response to Maddy rather than to the man who might or might not have been her father. "No, I parked it in your driveway."

An older woman, not her mother, gave him a long, interested look. He'd seen potential Sunday dinners at a soup kitchen get less scrutiny. "How did you know where she lived?"

"He's a policeman," he heard Maddy's mother explain. "They know everything."

Again, he kept his eyes trained on only Maddy. It was easier that way. "I looked in your purse," he told her. He'd taken the purse out of her car just before they left for the hospital. "I didn't think you wanted someone ticketing your car," he added, then upbraided himself for thinking that he needed to explain.

He realized that her mother was still holding on to his arm.

"That was very thoughtful of you," Lorraine said, beaming.

J.T. became uncomfortably aware of the fact that the woman was looking at him as if he were the latest model sports car just off the conveyor belt and she wanted to purchase a sports car—as a gift.

He extricated himself from her grip and took a step backward.

"Well, I told you," he said to Maddy, "so I'd better be going." He gestured around the room. "You look like you've got more than enough company to keep you busy."

As if on cue, the murmur of voices suddenly rose again, all protesting that they hadn't realized how late it was and that they had to be leaving, going to school, to the store, or somewhere else. Anywhere but here. En masse they began to file by Maddy's bed, kissing her cheek and then making their way out the door. All of them looked J.T. over before they retreated.

And then only her parents were left in the room.

"We have to be going, too, darling," her mother declared. "So nice to have met you, John Thomas." She paused beside him, placing her hand lightly on his. "I said a prayer for you last night."

He stared at her incredulously. "Why?"

"Why, to say thank-you for being there for Maddy." She looked back at her daughter. "She always takes too many chances. We wanted to drive her home from the party, but she insisted on going by herself. Told us we worried too much and that she was still a week and a half away from her due date." She glanced back at her daughter. "Obviously the baby didn't have a calendar." Lorraine smiled up at him. "I'm glad she's got herself a guardian angel to look out for her."

Her husband mumbled a goodbye as he hustled her out the door, leaving J.T. standing there, stunned, with his mouth hanging open.

As the door closed behind him, J.T. slowly turned around and looked at Maddy.

Maddy grinned. "Overwhelming, isn't she?"

He inclined his head. "That would be one word for it."

"She means well. Why don't you come closer?" Maddy urged. "I'd like you to meet someone, now that he's really all cleaned up."

For the first time, J.T. saw the glass bassinet beside her bed.

Chapter 5

As a rule, J.T. had few unguarded moments, but he'd let one slip by him now as he glanced at the baby he'd helped bring into the world.

Maddy saw the way he was looking at the infant, like someone in the presence of magic. It reflected her own feelings about her less-than-day-old son. She felt her mouth curving in a smile. The man wasn't nearly as tough as he was trying to make the world believe he was.

"Would you like to hold him?"

J.T. took an automatic step forward, then his instinct for self-preservation kicked in and he halted where he was. It would be a lot better for him if he kept his distance. He'd already felt too much for a child that wasn't meant to be in his life. It made no sense to perpetuate something that had no future to it.

He shoved his hands into his pockets, as if to keep them from betraying him and doing something stupid. "No, that's all right. I just stopped by to let you know about your car."

She wasn't listening to what he was saying—she was looking at his eyes.

"Are you sure? He's much less slippery now than he was the first time you held him." The nurses had bathed and powdered the newborn before they'd brought him to her. With any luck, his diaper was still dry. "Smells better, too."

Despite his best efforts, J.T.'s mind drifted back to last evening. To what it had felt like, holding this brand-new life in his hands. Without meaning to, he dissolved the distance and came to stand over the bassinet.

"Oh, I don't know. He smelled like a miracle to me," J.T. said softly, looking down at the sleepy little being bundled up in white and blue, only one tiny, clenched fist peering out beside his small cheek.

He had no recollection of crossing to the bassinet. He had even less of an explanation for why he was doing exactly what he told himself not to do.

He picked the baby up anyway. His eyes closed for a moment as he drew the tiny, warm infant to him. The baby's warmth penetrated all the layers around him, straight through his chest.

He'd expected pain. He'd gotten incredible, dev-

astating sweetness instead. Very carefully, he stroked
the shock of black hair.

"I don't remember ever seeing one with quite so
much hair," he commented, glancing toward Maddy.

"That's from my father's side of the family," she
told him, mesmerized as she watched J.T. And attempted to imagine Johnny in his place. "Do you
have children of your own?"

The question sliced through him like the point of
a rapier. "No." He looked up at her, his face stony.
"No, I don't."

It was then she saw the pain, though he immediately masked it. She found herself wondering about
him. "But you wanted some," she pressed. He looked
at her sharply and she backed up. She'd overstepped
her ground. "I'm sorry, my mother always says I
can't leave anything alone. It's just that you looked
so sad just now—" she tried to explain. "And so
natural holding Johnny."

His brows drew together and he looked down at
the infant, who continued sleeping. "Johnny?"

Maddy shifted in the bed, reaching up to adjust her
son's blanket. Her fingers brushed against J.T.'s fore-
arm and she could feel his muscles instantly tighten.
"I decided to name him after my husband—" She
raised her eyes to his. "And you. That way he can
grow up having two heroes."

What could he say to that? How was he supposed
to respond? Was she expecting him to remain in her
life in some capacity because fate had had him at the

right place at the right time and he'd delivered her baby? He wasn't about to get his life embroiled with anyone else's. It was bad enough that his partner and some of the men at the precinct insisted on drawing him into their circle no matter how often he fended them off. He was a loner and the position suited him.

Besides, he didn't care for empty praise. "I don't know about your late husband, but there's nothing much of a hero about me. Your son would do a lot better finding someone else to admire."

She liked modesty and thought it a highly under-rated attribute.

"You came to my rescue, that makes you a hero in my book." She hurried on before he could protest. "Besides, there's a bond between you two now, whether you like it or not."

The baby stirred against him, sending out fresh waves of warmth that were impossible for him to block out. "What makes you think I don't like it?"

That was easy. He had a way about him that convinced her he declared "day" whenever someone said "night" just for the sake of not going along with the crowd.

"Oh, I don't know. Something in your eyes tells me that on your report card your teachers used to write: Does not play well with others."

He'd been on the receiving end of that comment more than once. It wasn't that he wanted his own way, he just didn't believe in joining a team for the sake of joining. He liked keeping to himself, something few of his early teachers understood.

J.T. shrugged off her insight. "I tend to be a loner, if that's what you mean."

She took note of the fact that he wasn't putting the baby back down, and it pleased her. "That's what I mean. Ever notice that the word 'loner' shares some of the same letters as 'alone'?"

He didn't care to be analyzed, no matter how well meaning she might be. Or how easy on the eyes. "Never gave it much thought."

Yes, he did, she thought. He'd given it a great deal of thought and chosen his way. And now he was trapped in it, she judged, because he knew nothing else. "Being alone is not always a good thing."

"It is for me." His tone told her to back off.

Rather than back off, she merely regrouped and sought another way into the barricaded citadel. "Then there's no Mrs. John Thomas?"

His tone grew sharper. "Are you asking for my life history?"

J.T. expected her to back down. Tougher people than she had when confronted by his stern countenance. But he quickly discovered that he was in for an education when it came to dealing with the likes of Madeline Rossini Reed.

"Yes," she told him brightly. "If you're willing to part with it."

He laughed shortly. He'd half thought she was going to demand it as her right since they'd shared something so intimate as the birth of a child. Since she gave him a way out, he took it.

"Well, I'm not."

Maddy cocked her head. She wondered if he realized that he was rocking the baby, who had begun to fuss just the tiniest bit. She was willing to bet that he'd make a great father, no matter how blustery he sounded.

"Why?"

The unselfconsciously voiced question caught him off guard. "I thought you were giving me a choice."

He watched as a smile curved along her lips. The same sensation he'd felt when the baby moved against him returned. He fought it off.

"I was being polite."

Still holding the baby, he moved toward the window and looked out on the harbor with its scattered, bobbing boats. Sailing had never held a fascination for him, but he liked looking at the various sailing vessels. There was something peaceful about it.

"And now you're being nosy."

If he meant to embarrass her into backing away, he failed. "I've been accused of being that, too."

He glanced at her over his shoulder. "But it hasn't cured you."

"Nope."

The question had been rhetorical. He turned back toward the harbor. If he concentrated, he could see her reflection in the pane of glass before him. J.T. took a deep breath.

"My wife died in a car accident on New Year's Eve. We were going to try to start a family. It was our mutual New Year's Resolution." He turned around to look at her. "Anything else you want to know?"

Her heart went out to him. "Yes. How are you coping with it?"

He lifted a shoulder in a half shrug. Mostly he tried not to think. "I manage."

That wasn't quite her take on the situation. "Are you sure?"

He'd stood for enough. "Lady, the only thing I'm sure of is that the sun rises the next day whether you've got a family or not, even if you think it shouldn't." Crossing back to her, he placed the infant in her arms. What had he been thinking, coming here?

Unfazed by the annoyance in his face, she took the baby. "I felt the same way when Johnny was killed."

"And now you don't." Sarcasm dripped from every syllable, challenging her.

A part of her, she knew, would always go on hurting, would always miss the man who had been such an important part of her world. The man who had created a child with her and left a part of himself behind.

"No," she replied quietly, her expression serious for the first time that day, "now I realize that he would have wanted me to go on with my life. That he loved me too much to see me immobilized by grief and unable to move ahead. I would have wanted that for him—after he cried a little bit of course,'' she added with a smile. And then the mischief faded slightly. ''But I would have wanted him to be happy.''

Lorna was selfless like that, too. But it didn't matter if she was or not, or what she would have wanted for him. He was what he was, felt what he felt. Like a man walking through hell every day of his life, just marking time.

''Yeah, well, it doesn't always work that way.''

She reached for his hand, surprising him. ''It can if you want it to.''

''Maybe that's the trouble.'' He drew his hand from hers. ''Maybe I don't want it to.''

How the hell had he gotten onto this topic? She was a stranger, someone he'd stopped to help in the line of duty, nothing more. What was he doing, spilling his guts out to her, telling her how he felt? Telling him about Lorna and their plans?

Annoyed with himself, he began to back away toward the door. ''Look, I'd better be going.''

She didn't want him to leave, not like this, not when he was so obviously in pain, but there was nothing she could do.

Maddy nodded toward the infant in her arms. ''Will you come back to see us?''

He had a way out now. ''Aren't they discharging you tomorrow?'' As far as he remembered, hospitals generally liked sending their patients home after two days, especially if there were no complications.

"Yes." She looked at him complacently. "You can bring us home."

Again, she caught him completely unprepared. "Now, why would I want to do that?"

Undaunted, she answered, "Because you're Johnny's hero."

Impatience flared through him. He didn't want her thanks, her glorification, or anything that went with it. "He's less than a day old. He doesn't have any heroes."

"It's never too early to start," she countered cheerfully, determined to bring this man into the sunlight, "and yours was the first face he saw."

J.T. waved his hand around the room. "I just saw more people in here when I came in than at the county fair. Why can't one of them bring you home?"

She lifted her chin and said calmly, "Because I'm asking you."

Shaking his head, he surrendered. Anything to put an end to the onslaught of words. "You always been this pushy?"

Victory had her eyes crinkling at the corners. "Always. I was the youngest. If I didn't push, I got lost in the shuffle."

Something told him that Maddy never got lost in the shuffle. Any shuffle.

He sighed. What harm could it do? He'd have her home in under twenty minutes and that would be the end of it. "I brought you here, I guess I can bring you home, too."

The funny thing was, even as he said it, he wasn't nearly as annoyed about being cornered into doing this as he would have thought he'd be.

Chapter 6

Lorraine Rossini exchanged glances with the two
sons who had accompanied her to her only daughter's
hospital room as she took in the news. With a sigh,
she placed the infant seat she'd brought in preparation
for her grandson's homecoming on the brightly up-
holstered blue chair in the corner.

When she spoke, she didn't bother masking her disappointment. Her voice rose a little more with each
word she uttered.

"But any one of us can bring you and the baby
home, Maddy. What possessed you to ask a perfect
stranger to do it?"

She'd tried to call her mother last night with the
news, but hadn't been able to get through. What few
relatives hadn't piled into her room yesterday, her

mother was busy notifying. Her parents were one of
the few people left on the face of the earth who didn't
have Call Waiting. The message she'd left on her
brother Tony's answering machine had obviously not
been picked up.

Maddy indicated her sleeping baby, silently asking
her mother to lower her voice. "He's far from perfect,
Mom. And maybe that's why I'm doing it."

Her oldest brother ceased prowling around the
room and looked at her. "Oh God," Bill groaned.
"The stray puppy syndrome strikes again."

Unlike their childhood years, which had been spent
in one-upmanship, bruised egos and skinned knuckles, today she and her brothers worked fairly harmo-
niously together in the family business, which was
fortunate. But she knew her brothers still had a tendency to look upon her as the baby, and as such,
given to foibles.

Frowning, Maddy reflexively began to protest the
simplistic label her older brother had applied, then
stopped. Maybe it was as simple as that. In a way. At
any rate, dueling over semantics was a waste of time.

"John Thomas lost his wife a little more than two
years ago," she told her mother and saw sympathy
spring instantly into her hazel eyes. Her mother had
the ability to feel empathy for absolutely anyone.
"And he's gone through some of the same things I
have, except that he hasn't moved on yet."

Standing over the baby, her youngest brother, Joe,
glanced in her direction and gave her a knowing look.

Only thirteen months older than she was, he, better than anyone, knew how her mind worked. "And you're planning on moving him?"

Maddy sniffed, in no mood to put up with a lecture. The rest of her family was far too cautious. They played it safe when it came to decorating, too. She was the one who pushed for the outlandish, for the bright and cheerful infusion of colors.

"Nothing wrong with one person reaching out to another."

Always the pragmatic one, it was Bill's turn to frown. "As long as you don't fall over while you're reaching."

She knew they all meant well and that what they said was motivated by concern. When Johnny had died they had all closed ranks around her like a huge protective coat of armor. She would have been lost without them.

"How could I do that?" Maddy asked, pointedly looking at her mother. "You're all just a single phone call away."

"Closer than that if you want," Joe volunteered, clearly enamored with his new nephew. Single, he had no desire for a wife and kids in the immediate future, but doting on Maddy's suited him just fine.

They had been wonderful, but they did have a tendency to overwhelm and she did need a little space. "I don't need a support system right now."

Lorraine laughed knowingly. "Say that again around the 2:00 a.m. feeding."

"I probably won't—" Maddy acknowledged. Her mother had volunteered to stay with her the first two weeks. Maddy had wanted to go it alone. They had compromised with her mother coming over to spend the nights. It was either agreeing to that, or having her mother camp out at her door. "And you'll be right there to hear me not say it if I know you."

Her mother nodded. "You know me." She turned toward her sons, both of whom towered over her. "All right, let's clear out before your policeman gets here and gets scared off again." She shooed Joe away from the bassinet and both of them toward the door. "He looked like a rabbit about to bolt yesterday."

"Wouldn't you if you'd come up against that crowd? Besides, he just didn't want to intrude," Maddy explained. She saw the look on Bill's face. "And you can save the raised eyebrows for later." She kissed each brother in turn as they filed by her bed and smiled at her mother. "I'll see you later tonight."

"Count on it," Lorraine told her just before she slipped out the door.

J.T. arrived twenty minutes later, a skeptical expression on his face as he entered the room after knocking on the door. From the looks of it, she'd been ready for a while, a suitcase by her feet and the baby dozing in a blue-and-white infant seat.

He'd come because he said he would, but he still hesitated.

"Are you sure you wouldn't rather have someone from your family bring you home?"

"I'm sure," she told him brightly. Now that he was here, she rang for the nurse who'd promised to show up with the mandatory wheelchair. "They'd only fuss unbearably and make me feel like an invalid." Her eyes teased his. "Something tells me you don't fuss."

"Don't see the need."

J.T. looked around. There was a profusion of flowers on every available flat surface in the room. The thought occurred to him that maybe he should have brought her flowers yesterday, but they probably would have gotten lost in this floral sea. Besides, it wasn't as if he'd initially come to visit a friend. She was, after all, just a woman he'd helped all in the line of duty, nothing more.

If she wasn't a friend, how did he pigeonhole her? he wondered.

Rather than tax his brain and have it go places he didn't want it to go, J.T. decided to drop the whole matter and just concentrate on getting through it.

Like everything else in his day.

"You want to take any of these with you?" He indicated the flowers just as the nurse entered with the wheelchair.

Maddy smiled a greeting at her as she sank down into the chair, Johnny safely tucked into her arms. It was left to J.T. to pick up her suitcase.

"No, I've already told the nurses to distribute them

around the hospital to people who don't have any. Flowers cheer things up, don't you think?''

There were flowers on Lorna's grave. There was never any cheer there.

''No,'' he replied grimly.

The look in his eyes warned her not to continue on that route.

''Don't forget the infant seat,'' she cautioned as he fell in behind the nurse who was pushing her out the door. He retraced his steps and picked up the seat.

''Did your captain mind?'' she asked as he came out into the hall. They headed to the elevator. The nurse, he noticed, had mercifully chosen to be quiet.

J.T. pressed the Down button. ''Mind about what?''

''You taking time off to bring me home.''

The doors opened and he moved his hand in the way of the beam, allowing the nurse to push Maddy and the baby into the car safely.

''This is my own time.'' J.T. got in beside them, pressing the button for the first floor. ''I work the night shift, remember?''

''So those were your regular hours?'' She smiled. ''Lucky for me.'' Twisting around, she looked at the nurse. ''He delivered my baby. I was in labor and my car stalled out in the middle of the road.''

The nurse looked at him with genuine appreciation. ''Lucky for you he came along,'' she echoed Maddy's sentiment.

He'd never taken well to attention, either good or

bad. J.T. shrugged at the observation. "If I hadn't happened along then, the cop patrolling in my place would have."

The elevator stopped on the second floor and two people got in, shifting to the left of the wheelchair. Maddy looked up at J.T. "You see the glass half empty, don't you?"

He didn't see how it was any of her business how he saw anything, and he didn't particularly like the fact that she was asking him in front of an audience. Because he knew that ignoring the question would only make her ask it again, he played along with her assessment. It wasn't really far off anyway.

"Half empty, dirty and cracked."

Instead of saying anything, Maddy nodded to herself. It looked as if she had a lot of work cut out for her. But then, she'd already surmised as much and, at any rate, she felt equal to it.

He'd been in her driveway the day before, but hadn't really taken account of the place until now. She lived in a large two story building, the kind that housed a family with multiple children, all of whom had their own rooms. Pulling up the hand brake, he scrutinized the place she'd resided in for over five years. Ever since she'd gotten married.

"You live here?"

She thought it a strange question, seeing as he'd parked her car for her yesterday. "Yes."

He looked at her. "Alone?"

She had, she thought, until now. "Why? Don't you like it?"

She loved the house, loved every corner of it. There were special memories tucked away in every room and it bore her mark from top to bottom. Knowing that all his taste was in his mouth, Johnny had given her free rein to decorate as she chose.

He shrugged, knowing he'd get lost in a place like that. Having sold the house he and Lorna had bought together, he lived his days out in a bare apartment. It held a refrigerator, a table, a bed and a bureau, more than enough for him.

"Just seems like a huge house for one person, that's all."

"One and a half now," she corrected, glancing toward the back seat where her son dozed.

It was time to get him inside. Maddy couldn't wait to see him sleeping in the frilly bassinet her mother had insisted on buying for her. She began to open the passenger door, but J.T. reached over and placed his hand over hers to stop her.

"Wait a second," he ordered. She looked at him quizzically. "Don't just go jumping out of the car. You're still weak."

He didn't strike her as the type to play Sir Galahad. "You don't know me very well, do you?"

The smile she gave him told him that she intended on correcting that.

She could intend whatever she wanted, he thought, that didn't change anything. After he brought her inside her home, his responsibility, even by the wildest stretch of interpretation, was at an end. He'd go his way and she'd go hers. End of story.

"No, but I don't believe in taking chances. Sit." It was a sternly worded command, not a request. Getting out of the vehicle, he rounded the hood and came up to her side. "Okay, now you can get out."

Her grin grew wider. "Yes, sir."

But the grin faded just a little as she gained her feet and the brisk, cool world around her shifted just a little out of kilter. Stunned, Maddy automatically grabbed his shoulder. She felt his arm close around her, pulling her to him as he steadied her.

A warmth spread through her that had less to do with her near faint than with the man who had prevented it. Taking a breath, she looked up into his face. "I guess you were right."

His expression was stoic. "I tend to be."

She smiled, making no move to regain her footing without him. "I'll try to remember that."

He shouldn't be holding her like this, no matter what the reason. It was too familiar. And felt too good. "Can you stand up?"

If she hadn't felt so nice against him, she would have felt foolish. But she didn't. Testing them, she found that her knees felt far less rubbery than they had a minute ago. "Yes."

He had every intention of releasing her then. He didn't mean to go on holding her. And he knew he didn't mean what he did next. He had no idea what came over him. Maybe it was her nearness, or maybe it had to do with the fact that she looked so much like Lorna.

Or maybe it was because he'd been alone for so long. He absolutely refused to believe it was because of the woman herself.

But whatever the reason, whatever the explanation, what happened still happened.

Bending his head, he brushed his lips against hers.

Chapter 7

His instinct for self-preservation warred with desire. The former told him to back away, the latter wouldn't allow it. Before he could stop himself, the kiss flowered, then deepened. Something leaped up and seized his gut, wrenching it so that he could hardly breathe.

There was an unbearable sweetness about the kiss, about her. If he let himself go, he would have gotten lost in both. The temptation to do just that was enormous. It had been so long since he had felt anything, so long since his life had done anything but cast empty shadows on the wall.

He touched her face with his hand, her skin heating beneath his. He remembered another lifetime, when things were different.

What the hell was he doing?

Like an explosion of cold air, reality hit. He was kissing a woman he was just doing the most casual of favors for. He never behaved rashly, never led with his feelings, didn't even *have* feelings, for crying out loud. And he never, *ever,* acted on impulse.

But he'd done all three just now in the space of a heartbeat.

Shaken, trying to get his bearings, and angry at himself beyond words, J.T. dropped his hand from her face and backed away.

"Hey, I'm sorry—" He had no idea what to say. Any apology seemed utterly insignificant.

He'd stirred something within her, reminding her that she hadn't always been a widow, that it wasn't all that long ago that she'd been a desirable woman. He looked flustered, she thought. Like someone caught with his hand in the cookie jar, knowing that he wasn't supposed to be there.

Her eyes smiled a beat before her mouth curved. "Why? Do I taste like onions?"

J.T. stared at her for a second before he realized that she was using humor to get them through what had to be an awkward moment for her as well as for him.

"No, I mean—I didn't mean for that to happen."

Unless she missed her guess, John Thomas Walker never did what he didn't want to do. And, right now, he didn't like the fact that he wanted to kiss her. It was a guilt thing. She could understand that. She'd gone through it herself. It was the first step to making peace with the cold, hard fact that you were alive and the person you loved wasn't.

"Sometimes acting on impulse can be a good thing." He was still uncomfortable, she thought. She didn't want him to be. "And you have nothing to be sorry for. You didn't exactly pin me against the car." Her eyes held his for a moment. "And if I hadn't wanted you to kiss me, you wouldn't have."

He laughed shortly. Was she kidding? "You don't have enough strength to wrestle a flea, you just proved that."

She realized that he didn't understand what she was telling him. What she sensed about him. "I didn't need strength. You're not the type to force yourself on a woman."

He frowned. The woman was too damn trusting for her own good. No wonder her family hovered around her. She needed to be protected.

"You haven't even known me for more than a couple of days, how do you know what kind of a man I am? Just because I wear a uniform—"

But she shook her head. He was on the wrong trail again. "It has nothing to do with your uniform, John Thomas. I can see it in your eyes."

He tried not to let the warm familiar feeling overtake him. He reminded himself that she was a stranger, barely an acquaintance.

Yeah, an *acquaintance* you just *kissed,* an inner voice mocked him.

J.T. snorted, dismissing her naive assessment. "Is that anything like reading palms or tea leaves?"

She knew what he was doing and she wouldn't let him. "It's a great deal more accurate. Eyes are the windows of the soul."

And he had beautiful eyes, she thought. Maddy smiled up into them to make her point.

A soul. He didn't believe in all that anymore. Didn't believe in anything, except that pain was endless. "I don't have one. I lost it over two years ago."

She looked at him for a long moment, at the sadness she saw just beneath the anger. "Then it's about time you found it again."

In the back seat, the baby began to whimper. "What it's time for is to get you and the baby inside."

Because it was at least true in part, Maddy offered no resistance.

Leaving her house less than half an hour later, J.T. made himself a silent promise that he wasn't going to see her again. After all, there was no reason to.

And, except for driving by her house once on the pretext of patrolling the area, one that wasn't in his route, he'd kept his word to himself.

The temptation to drop in on her the afternoon he'd driven by had been great. But what could he do? Just show up on her doorstep and mumble something inane about seeing how she and the boy were doing? She would have seen right through that and he would have opened the door to further involvement. He'd already told himself he didn't want that. Didn't want to be involved with anyone.

So when a call was patched through to his squad car near midnight a week and a half later, no one was more surprised that he was to hear her voice.

He'd forgotten how melodious it sounded. Snapping out of it, he demanded, "How did you get through?"

She'd waited as long as she could for him to come around. When he didn't, she'd decided to take matters into her own hands. The man couldn't be allowed to regress into his cocoon again.

"I told the woman at the dispatch desk that it was an emergency, that I was your sister." Maddy didn't have to see his face to know that J.T. was far from pleased. But it was all for a good cause. "I'm sorry if I violated protocol, but I wanted to reach you and you haven't come by."

J.T. sighed, deliberately ignoring the look that he knew Fenelli was giving him, the one that was sported by proud fathers when their late-bloomer sons finally took their advice and plunged into life.

"All right, you reached me. So what's the big emergency?"

"I want you to be Johnny's godfather." Grateful that he didn't cut her off, Maddy took advantage of the silence to hurry through the rest of what she had to tell him. "The ceremony's taking place this Sun-

day at St. Mark's on Alton at two o'clock. I guess
I'd better get off now. Call me.''

J.T. stared at the two way receiver in his hand as
static took the place of her voice. The woman was
unbelievable. Swallowing an oath, he replaced the receiver as little more forcefully than was really necessary.

Fenelli shifted in his seat, a grin wide enough to
do the Cheshire Cat proud on his florid face. J.T.
could sense it before he even saw it. ''So, what
haven't you been telling me?''

J.T. stared straight ahead into the inky darkness.
''Nothing.''

Fenelli chuckled. ''Nothing's got a really sexy
voice.''

He'd been partnered with Fenelli for four years.
When he'd opted to take the night shift, Fenelli had
made the switch with him even though he'd told the
older man it wasn't necessary. Now that he thought
of it, that gave Fenelli a great deal in common with
Maddy, J.T. thought. ''It's a long story.''

The streets were long and dark, slumbering like the
residents in the houses they passed. ''Hey, we got
time and I like long stories.''

J.T. snorted. ''Yeah, I know. You tell them all the
time.''

Fenelli had grown up the next to youngest in a
family of seven. He had a hide like a rhino and never
got insulted. ''Turnabout is fair play.''

J.T. knew his partner wasn't going to let up until

he told him. After deliberating, he gave him the story in a nutshell.

"I helped her deliver her baby. It was the night you were out with the stomach flu." He looked at his partner accusingly. "If you had been on patrol, you would have been the one to deliver it."

Fenelli refused to rise to the bait. He was as optimistic in his views as his partner was pessimistic. He insisted that was why they got along. He was also a great believer in fate. "Hey, there's a reason for everything. Maybe I wasn't supposed to be on duty that night, ever think of that?"

"No," J.T. snapped. But he did. He'd thought about it a lot this last week and a half. Thought about it every time his thoughts turned to Maddy which was a lot more often than he was happy about. The bottom line was that he knew his life would have been less complicated if Fenelli hadn't called in sick.

The next morning, J.T. went to Maddy's house to tell her that she was simply going to have to find someone else to be the baby's godfather. The words were right there, on the tip of his tongue. He'd rehearsed them on the way over, just in case he forgot.

But when she opened the door and he looked at her, the words somehow became lost.

She was standing there, wearing a blue cotton dress that would have seemed shapeless on anyone else. On her, it accented curves that hadn't been there just a week and a half ago. Other than the baby she had tucked into the crook in her arm, there seemed to be no evidence at all that she had given birth recently.

He realized that one of the little white buttons on her dress was open, allowing him a view of full, firm breasts he shouldn't be been privy to. He also realized he was staring and quickly lifted his eyes.

She'd just finished feeding the baby and congratulated herself on her timing. She opened the door wider in silent invitation.

"I was hoping you'd come by."

Finally finding his tongue, J.T. got right to the point as he walked in. "Why me?"

She closed the door behind him, flipping the lock. "Because you were there to help me through a difficult time. Because yours was the first face that Johnny saw and I'd like to find a reason for him to see it again every once in a while."

No way, sorry. Uh-uh. Nope. He shoved his hands into his pockets, feeling oddly powerless in the presence of this petite woman. "So exactly what's a godfather supposed to do?"

This was actually easier than she'd anticipated, Maddy thought. She shifted Johnny to her shoulder and began to pat his back, waiting for the tiny telltale burp. "Technically or really?"

He looked at her darkly, struggling not to react to the woman in any way but impersonally. He would have had an easier time winning a cheerleading contest.

"I'm not interested in technicalities."

She enumerated what she was hoping for. "Show up once in a while and play catch with him. Maybe occasionally take him to a ball game. Remember his birthday and Christmas." She smiled at him, her features softening as she remembered. "Show him what his father would have been like if he'd lived. I want Johnny to be proud of the fact that his dad was a policeman."

J.T. struggled to resist. He knew he didn't want to say yes, saw further complications if he did. But the word "no" just wouldn't come out as easily as it had for most of his life. Not to her. He wasn't about to analyze why.

"It doesn't bother you that I might not be the same religion as you and your son?"

It was a requirement, but there were ways around that. Tiny white lies could be forgiven. In the grander scheme of things, she was saving a soul. Or at least bringing a man back among the living. She'd had her family to help her through her difficult time. She'd already figured out that J.T. had no one.

Maddy shook her head to his question. "He's got uncles for that."

J.T. spread his hands. He was off the hook. "Then he's got uncles to play catch with."

She laughed. "You obviously haven't seen my brothers play ball. They're great interior decorators and each one has a fantastic eye for color and proportions. But doing anything remotely productive with a round little object flying through the air at them

is another story.'' Turning the baby around, she held
him up in front of J.T. so that the infant's cherubic
face was close to his. ''How can you say no to this
face?''

J.T. took the excuse she offered him as a graceful
way to surrender. But in his heart he knew that it
wasn't Johnny's face he couldn't say no to.

''I can't.''

Chapter 8

Like a passive observer in a dream, J.T. watched himself get into his car the following Sunday afternoon and drive to the Church. He still wasn't quite certain how he had managed to get himself roped into agreeing to be the baby's godfather. He certainly didn't think of himself as the godfather type.

Godfathers were mostly inactive roles, anyway, he consoled himself. He hardly remembered who his had been; he certainly hadn't made a significant difference in his life. This was just something that required his going through the motions, nothing more. Once he did, that would be the end of it. Really.

It struck him that he'd said words to that effect concerning Maddy before. He was actually trying to convince himself that, this time, they would stick—and not having altogether that much luck at it.

With a sigh, he took a right turn just past the intersection and slipped into the church's parking lot. The familiar-looking edifice brought a sudden lump to his throat. It surprised him that Maddy should have chosen St. Mark's for the baptism. St. Mark's was where he and Lorna had gotten married.

And where he had felt bound, because Lorna would have wanted it that way, to hold the funeral service for her over two years ago.

He hadn't been back since then. He'd buried his belief and his soul in the same grave where he'd buried his wife.

Bracing himself, J.T. got out of the car and took the five steps up to the front of the church. A man he recognized from the hospital was standing at the doors, obviously waiting for him. The man, older by a few years and, by his estimate, a couple of inches taller, took hold of his arm the moment he came into range.

"Hi, I'm Bill. They're waiting for you," was all he said by way of a greeting.

He didn't like being touched. J.T. removed his arm from the other man's grasp. "How do you know you have the right man?"

"Maddy described you."

J.T. resisted the temptation to ask him to elaborate. But he couldn't help wondering just what it was that she had said.

There was a baptismal font to the left of the entrance. Usually it was separated from the rest of the foyer by an ornate wrought-iron gate, but that was drawn back today and a small group of people were gathered in a semicircle around the font. A priest stood in the center. Maddy was holding her son, who was dressed completely in white from the miniature suit down to the slightly oversize socks that ran up his legs and over his knees.

She smiled a greeting at him as he approached. Everyone was obviously waiting for him.

"I was beginning to think you had a change of heart," she told him, transferring the baby into his arms.

"I did," he told her. "I came."

There was a glint of vague recognition in the eyes of the priest who officiated at the baptism, but J.T. didn't acknowledge him, didn't let on that he knew the man—that the priest had been the one who had presided over his wife's funeral mass. There was no point in it.

He had no reason to rekindle any sort of relationship with the man or what he represented. That part of him, J.T. thought, was dead.

So what was he doing, he wondered, standing here, professing to be this tiny human being's godfather, the guardian of his immortal soul? Reciting words that were being fed to him by a man of the cloth? He wasn't any more suited for the job than a snow leopard was suited for the tropics.

It was her fault, all her fault. J.T. slanted a glance at Maddy. He couldn't seem to say no to her. But he would. He'd just get through this ceremony and then whatever else she was planning, she could just count him out.

The christening wasn't the end of it.

Somehow, in his heart, he'd known it wouldn't be. The moment the ceremony was over, he overheard two of the men he'd been told were her brothers, Bill and Tony, talking. There was to be a party to celebrating her son's big day right after they all left the church.

Well, it could just go on without him, J.T. thought. He hadn't signed on for anything extra, and he wasn't about to mingle with people he didn't know.

His escape was foiled.

The second the priest withdrew, gratefully accepting the envelope Bill had slipped him for the ceremony, J.T. found Maddy hooking her arm through his and drawing him outside toward where her own car was parked. The baby was tucked against her other shoulder, apparently content to remain there indefinitely.

Maybe the baby was, but he wasn't, J.T. thought. No, he wasn't…so why wasn't he drawing away, for god's sake? Why was he allowing her to remain at his side like this, directing his every move?

He refused to entertain the thought that a small part of him liked it.

"Thanks for standing up for Johnny."

J.T. looked down at the small face. He knew that,

at this age, a smile was not within an infant's repertoire, but something very close to a smile was on the small, rosebud mouth and he found himself being almost as captivated by the child as by the mother. Again.

Still, he tried to sound distant. "I doubt if he knew the difference."

She firmly believed that babies were far more aware of things than anyone gave them credit for "He might not, yet, but I do and I appreciate it."

She kissed the small head before placing the baby into his infant seat. Johnny began voicing his protest at being separated from his mother. His lungs had done a lot of developing in the short time since she'd brought him home from the hospital.

Maddy looked up sweetly at J.T. "Do you know how to get to DiAngelo's?"

Having lived in the city all of his life, J.T. sincerely doubted there was a place in Bedford he didn't know how to find. However, he looked at her suspiciously. "Yes, why?"

She returned the suspicion with innocence. "That's where the party's being held." She indicated the baby. "I thought the guest of honor should be there and I'd really rather that you drive us. Bill drove my car over and he can't seem to understand that he's not racing go-carts anymore."

He glanced over to where his vehicle was parked. "What about my car?"

"We can bring you back after the party."

"And Bill?"

"He's getting a ride from someone else."

The woman had an answer for everything. He played dumb, even though he'd overheard her brothers talking to her mother about the reception. "And what party are you talking about?"

She explained as if she were talking to someone who had come from another world. In a way, she was beginning to think that he had. A very somber, joyless world. But it was up to her to change that. It was her way of paying him back for coming to her aid. It was, in her estimation, the least she could do. Besides, because of the mutual loss they'd each suffered, she felt a kinship toward him.

"It's customary to have a celebration after a christening. My mother thought there'd be less cleanup involved if we hired a hall instead of having it my place. Or hers," Maddy added with a smile, remembering the look on her mother's face when she had contemplated the kind of mess forty or so people could leave behind in their wake.

It seemed to him that ever since he'd met Maddy, he was constantly attempting to find ways to beg off from things. "Um—"

She recognized that sound. He was going to say no. Maddy hurried to head him off. "It'll just be a small thing, for the people who came to the church."

Out of the corner of his eye, he saw people who had filled a number of the last pews filing out. He'd thought they were there for someone else. He should have known better.

"They didn't bite you then," she was saying. "They won't bite you at the restaurant. I promise."

He found himself coming up with reasons why it would do no harm to go along with things, just this one more time. What was this overpowering effect she kept having on him?

And why couldn't she just take a hint?

And why couldn't he just say no to begin with?

Shaking his head, J.T. fixed her with a look that was not altogether disgruntled. "You were spoiled as a child, weren't you?"

"Me? Spoiled? Nope." Her grin was wide with victory. "I earned everything I got. In case you haven't noticed, I have the tenacity of a bull terrier."

There was certainly no need to tell him that. "I noticed."

Trouble was, he was noticing a lot of things about her. Like the habit she had of letting her smile begin in her eyes before it reached her lips, or the way she had of looking up at him just before she was about to put him on the spot.

It had to come to an end, and soon. There was no place in his life for the feelings that were beginning to push their way forward.

He had no business wanting to see her, to be in her company. He knew it was just asking for trouble and he'd sworn to himself that he'd never be in that kind of a position again. A position where fate could sud-

denly spring up out of nowhere, grab him by the
throat and choke him because it had senselessly
robbed him of what was his. He'd been through it
once, and once had been hell.

If he ventured into the land mine laden field again,
he would have no one to blame but himself.

He drove Maddy and Johnny to the reception,
blaming himself.

"You're not dancing."

Her softly worded observation came floating to him
from behind his chair. He'd mistakenly taken a seat
at a table he discovered to be occupied by her mother,
a woman who did not have to stop for a breath the
entire time she spoke. It obviously ran in the family
on the female side only. Mercifully Mr. Rossini had
seen fit to take his wife onto the dance floor at every
opportunity, allowing him to regroup for the next assault.

He'd just been planning his escape when Maddy
came up behind him. J.T. didn't have to turn around.
The next moment, she was in front of him.

"There's a reason for that," he told her.

But she was already taking his hand, drawing him
out of his chair. "Good, you can tell me all about it
while we're on the floor."

A man had to take a stand somewhere. "Maddy, I
don't dance."

The statement seemed to have no effect on her as

she continued to lead him to the dance floor. "You can stand, can't you?"

He stopped and she turned to face him. The woman was incorrigible. "You want me to stand still on the dance floor?"

"To begin with." As if posing a mannequin, she placed one of his hands behind her back and wiggled her hand into the other one. "The rhythm'll take you."

It wasn't the rhythm that was taking him anywhere. It was her. The song that was playing was a slow one and she was so close against him that he could feel each breath she took as she swayed in tempo to the music.

"Just let yourself go," she coaxed softly. "Nobody's going to rate your performance, I promise."

He looked down into her face and caught himself struggling with the urge to kiss her. The woman was a witch. "Even you?"

Her smile curled all through his body. "Most of all me."

What did he have to lose? "You asked for this."

J.T. closed his hand over hers and drew her closer as he moved his hand to the small of her back. He'd never actually danced, only observed other people doing it. For a few minutes, he supposed he could fake it. It was easier than trying to argue with her.

At least with dancing he had a fifty-fifty chance of getting it right.

She raised her face up to his and smiled at him in

that way of hers that was beginning to nibble away at his inner lining. "Yes, I know."

He forced himself to look over her head. It was simpler that way. "What does your family think?"

"About?"

He could feel her warm breath against his chest, could feel something tightening in his gut in response. "You asking me to be the baby's godfather."

"They think I made an excellent choice." Well, eventually they will, she added silently.

He sincerely doubted that had been the response she'd gotten, but he didn't feel like engaging in what he knew would be a long, drawn-out process to try to draw the truth out of her. "Got an answer for everything, don't you?"

She laughed lightly. "No, but you've been asking the right questions, and so far, I'm safe."

Yes, but was he? he wondered. Two weeks ago, he would have said that nothing could get him to feel anything but anger again, and now there were a host of emotions shifting around inside of him, emotions he wasn't about to examine.

So for now, he decided that that safest thing was to say nothing. Instead he did what she'd told him to do. He let the music take him away.

Chapter 9

It had to stop, it really did.

He'd been telling himself that for the last three months. Three months during which he found himself slipping deeper and deeper into the trap. The one that sprang when you least expected it, breaking your spirit, breaking your back.

Breaking your heart.

Granted, Maddy had a way of brightening his life, of actually making him look forward to the next day. He'd finally come to grudgingly admit that to himself. His partner swore he'd changed, become easier to get along with. He'd told Fenelli he was hallucinating, but in his heart, he knew his partner was right.

But that was just the trouble.

He didn't want to change, didn't want to look forward to the next day. Didn't want to get into that kind of relaxed mode because that was exactly when it happened, when fate came to kick you in the teeth as it took away everything it had given you. And more. If you never let yourself be vulnerable, if you never had anything, then you couldn't lose everything. It was as simple as that. He'd come to learn that it really wasn't better to have loved and lost, it was better not to have loved at all because if you don't love, you have no clue what it is you're missing.

Lorna had taught him what it felt like to be in love, to center a world around someone else. If she hadn't done that, he wouldn't have felt as if he were walking around with a gunshot wound to his vital organs the last twenty-eight months.

He should have learned something from that.

Self-preservation was supposed to be an inherent human instinct.

So just what the hell was he doing, looking forward to seeing Maddy each day? How had all that happened, anyway? he wondered in self-disgust. For a loner, he was certainly out of his element.

It had to stop.

Now.

Before he lived to regret it.

Having made up his mind, he worked out his plan and waited for the elation of freedom, of release, to come. It didn't.

No matter, it would, he promised himself. He reached for the phone.

* * *

Maddy had gone back to work three weeks after Johnny was born. Rather than take her mother up on her offer to baby-sit every day, Maddy set up a play-pen in the back office and brought the baby in with her, whimsically dubbing him a consultant. She worked with her three brothers, each of whom brought something a little different to the business her grandfather and then her father had built up.

For her part, Maddy ran the financial end and did some of the decorating. Bill did the buying, Steve had a background in architecture and Tony, with his gift for gab, did the canvassing and brought the customers in. Until recently, they had worked beside her parents. The elder Rossinis were retired now, though that didn't prevent them from showing up at the trendy shop several times a week, especially now that their grandson could be found on the premises.

Everyone doted on the boy, although Maddy swore that his eyes lit up whenever J.T. entered a room.

When she told him that, J.T. felt it was just her way of trying to snow him, though for the life of him, he couldn't figure out why she would want to. In any event, he told himself he didn't take the words to heart.

He'd gotten extremely good at lying to himself.

Determined to put an end to his growing relation-ship with both Maddy and her son once and for all, he called her at her office. He got Bill instead. The fact that Bill immediately recognized his voice just reaffirmed J.T.'s belief that he had spent far too much time with a family he had no desire to merge with.

Only an insane man steps off the ledge of a cliff twice in one lifetime.

He cut through the small talk that Bill attempted, asking to speak to Maddy. "She's out of the shop with a client. Do you want her cell number?"

He'd refused to take down the number all the times she had offered to give it to him, feeling that it was just one more way to entangle his life with hers. He didn't want the temptation of having such easy access to her. But this was different.

"Yeah, why don't you give it to me?"

J.T. jotted down the number as Bill rattled it off. Hanging up with a terse, "Thanks," he pressed the numbers her brother had given him. It took five rings to finally reached her.

"Hello?" Her voice, always cheerful, sounded like sunshine against his ear.

"Maddy, it's J.T."

"John Thomas?" she said warmly, pleasure vibrating in every syllable.

It made him feel guilty because he had to tell her what he knew she didn't want to hear. There was the murmur of another, deeper voice in the background. Annoyance took him by surprise. It was sprinkled with a touch of jealousy. That in itself convinced him he was doing the right thing.

"Who's that?"

"My client." He heard her making an excuse to

the other man before asking him, "To what do I owe this unexpected honor? The last I recall, you didn't want my cell number."

"Your brother gave it to me when I called the shop."

He heard concern seep into her voice. "Is something wrong?"

J.T. could almost see her in his mind's eye, holding the tiny black phone he'd seen her with to her ear, her lips almost touching the base of the receiver. The warmth and yearning that came over him seemed almost automatic. Silently cursing his juvenile behavior, he told himself to grow up.

"Are you free for lunch?"

There was a pause on the other end. He knew the backhanded invitation had taken her by surprise. But he didn't want to do this on the telephone. It was the coward's way out and he had never been a coward. Except maybe about this.

"I can be. In say, half an hour?"

There was a smile in her voice. It reached out and touched him, compounding his discomfort.

"Half an hour's fine," he told her.

They made arrangements to meet at a restaurant not too far away from where she was with her client. She'd have to drop the man off at the shop first, but she assured J.T. that she could make it in plenty of time.

Hanging up the phone, he began to plan what he was going to tell her. He'd never been good at voicing his feelings. No matter how he phrased it, none of the words sounded right to him. He figured they never would.

But it had to be done.

Before it was too late.

Maybe it already was.

Traffic had been worse than she'd anticipated. Lunchtime was a mad scramble of people trying to find time for their private lives within the space of forty-five minutes to an hour. She made the best time she could, considering.

He was waiting for her when she arrived at the restaurant, a trendy little place where people went to get a little solitude. She didn't exactly know why, but she could feel nerves dancing throughout her body. Maybe it was because he'd never invited her out before. He'd shown up at her shop and on her doorstep, and agreed to meet her in places she suggested, but he'd never initiated anything himself.

Maybe he'd finally passed a major hurtle.

And maybe he hadn't, she thought. Walking toward him, Maddy braced herself the second she saw the look on his face.

This wasn't going to be good.

She'd fooled herself these last few months, she realized, telling herself that crawling into his life the way she had was something she was doing for his sake, to draw him out among the living. But that wasn't quite the case.

Not entirely.

Oh, she'd started out with those intentions, wanting to help get this man out of his shell. But somewhere along the way, she'd found herself getting tangled up in a whole different set of feelings. Feelings that had more to do with the man he was than with the man she was trying to get him to be.

More to the point, she found herself falling for him.

Big mistake, Maddy thought.

He probably realized it and thought so, too. Maybe that was what this was about. Maybe he was about to gently ease her out of his life.

Something within her froze.

As he half rose in his seat when she approached, she saw that there was a determined look in J.T.'s eyes that even the romantic lighting in the restaurant couldn't hide.

Funny, if she hadn't been acutely aware of the shift in her own feelings, she would have taken the look to be no different than the one he'd given her all the other times he'd resisted her gentle and not-so gentle nudges to get him involved in something outside of his own pain.

Uneasiness made her see things more clearly.

"This is a pleasant surprise." She slipped into the seat opposite him. He'd chosen a secluded table, she noted. Was that to give them privacy, or because he didn't want anyone seeing her in case she caused a scene? Maddy tried to stay upbeat. "Usually I have to do the suggesting." She took the menu in her hand without glancing at it. Instead she looked at him. "Turning over a new leaf?"

Damn it, how could a woman in a business suit look so damn alluring? Why did she have to look this good? But then, when had she ever really looked bad? Even that first night, when he'd found her swollen with child, her hair all but plastered to her head, she'd still looked radiant. In the throes of agony and obviously scared, she'd still managed to look better than any woman had a right to, outside of a movie screen.

He wanted her. Badly. And that was just the trouble. He didn't want to want her. Not on any level. Not for sex and definitely not for something more.

He realized that she'd asked him a question. Something about turning over a new leaf. "No."

"It's not about the apartment, is it?" She was grasping at straws and she knew it, but she was trying to divert his attention.

Nearly a month ago, she'd managed to wheedle a grudging invitation out of him to see his apartment. Appalled by the Spartan way he lived, with little more than the basic necessities as far as furniture went, she'd started out by making subtle suggestions about how he could change things. Suggestions led to her bringing him photographs, which led to her dragging him to the actual store where the pieces of furniture or accessories were.

In what she knew was a moment of weakness, he'd surrendered, allowing her to do what she wanted to his apartment. In the space of a few hours, she'd pulled strings and gotten things delivered, turning the cold residence into a home.

She'd known she had surprised him with her abilities, although he'd tried hard not to show it. Surveying the final results, he'd gruffly asked her if she hadn't already had enough to do, with the new baby and the business. She'd answered that she believed in squeezing every last drop out of life. That performing miracles, as she termed her work on his apartment, gave her life additional depth.

That was when he'd finally allowed that the changes suited him and that he liked what she had done to the place. Coming from him, she'd considered it the highest praise possible.

But praise was the furthest thing from her mind now. He wasn't here to talk about the apartment. She knew that. But like an ant in the path of a rushing tidal wave, she was bound to try to put up barricades in hope of surviving the inevitable.

If she survived, she could rebuild.

He'd been here over half an hour, waiting, he thought, having his stomach tie itself up in small knots because he both wanted and didn't want to do what he was about to do.

"No," he said curtly, "it's not the apartment. I already told you I liked it."

She tried not to let his tone get to her. "So you did." She took a bread stick from the basket and began to shred it slowly. It was time to stop waltzing. "What is it you wanted to see me about?"

The only way to get through this was to say it and be done with it. "I want my life back."

Chapter 10

Maddy sat before him, silence hanging between them. Damn it, he was supposed to feel relieved, not guilty.

"I want my life back," J.T. repeated.

She folded her hands before her like a school girl sitting at attention in a classroom, listening carefully lest she miss something.

Maddy leaned forward, her eyes intently on his. "And it's being held hostage by who?"

She knew the answer to that better than he did, J.T. thought. "You."

Maddy cocked her head. "Excuse me?"

He didn't want to go into it, didn't know how to make her understand. Hell, he wasn't sure if he even understood the whole thing himself.

All his previously rehearsed words deserted him. None of them made any sense anyway.

He took a breath, as if that could somehow help. "I don't want my life getting tangled up with anyone's."

"I wasn't aware I was trying to entangle you."

They could have been talking about the weather for all the modulation he heard in her voice—a sure sign, he realized, that he'd hurt her. Maddy sounded enthusiastic about almost everything.

"Well, try or not, you were. He was." She looked at him, not comprehending. "Johnny," he explained. Both she and the boy had begun burrowing into his life, taking up more and more space. Hell, he woke up every day looking forward to seeing them. That was a bad. Very bad. "And I can't go through all that again."

"Through all what again?" Stunned, feeling numb, Maddy desperately tried to make some kind of sense out of what he was telling her. "Feeling something?" she hazarded. The flicker in his eyes told her she was right. "J.T., if you don't feel, you're not alive, you're only going through the motions."

He raised his chin defensively. "Well, that's enough for me. That's all I need to do, to go through the motions." J.T. rose. Sorrow was beginning to shade her eyes and he couldn't bear to look at them, knowing he was responsible. But if he gave in, it would be even worse in the long run. "I just wanted to tell you that, so that you'd know.'' He paused one moment. ''It's not you, it's me.''

''I know that,'' she said quietly. ''But I don't want it to be you.'' She raised her voice as he began to walk away. ''I don't want you to be alone like that, John Thomas. If it can't be me, make it someone else.''

The words had followed him all the way to his car. All the way through his day and all the days and nights that followed. She cared that much about him, worried that much about him, that she was willing to let him be with someone else as long as it meant he was happy.

What the hell was wrong with her? he demanded silently, slamming his locker door, taking his anger out on anything in his path. Nobody was that selfless.

She was.

She was better off with someone else, he told himself, striding to his squad car. Someone who could care for her the way she deserved. And he was better off getting back to square one, where he'd been all this time. Before he'd met her.

During the day, J.T. existed within the walls of the apartment she had redecorated for him and tried not to think of her. For two weeks, he tried. He volunteered for second shifts, covering for anyone who didn't come in. Trying to outrace his thoughts. And the feeling of loneliness that had crept out again.

Loneliness.

He hadn't realized the specter was gone from his life until it returned again with all its hopelessness, all its darkness.

It was as black as it had been before, except that this time, he had been the one who brought it into his life.

He had the shell that he'd demanded back and it was cutting off his very breath. It didn't fit anymore. With each day that passed, it grew tighter around him and more confining. Making him claustrophobic.

He was a walking time bomb, ready to go off and he knew it.

And still he didn't pick up the phone, didn't drive the short distance to her house. He felt that if he could only hold his ground long enough, things would be all right. He'd get over her, like the flu.

Fenelli stood it as long as he could. And then, the second hour into one of their shifts, he turned and looked at his partner as they drove by the silent industrial park on the west end of Bedford. "Look, maybe you don't want my advice—"

J.T.'s profile remained stony as he looked straight ahead into the night. "I don't."

Fenelli ignored his dismissal. "But you're going to get it anyway because if you don't do something, and soon, a bunch of us guys are going to take you behind the precinct and shoot you," he informed him. "It'll be a mercy killing—" He slanted a look at J.T. "For you and for us."

Irritated beyond patience, J.T.'s head snapped around and he looked at his partner. "What the hell are you talking about?"

He was talking about the hurt he knew J.T. was trying to avoid. The hurt, unless he missed his guess, J.T. was going through right now.

"I'm talking about the fact that we take chances in life no matter what we do." Fenelli turned around the block. "That being a cop is taking a chance. That stepping off a curb is taking a chance." Fenelli pushed on though he knew that the analogy hit far too close to home. "Some lousy drunk might come careening around the corner and knock you straight into Kingdom Come."

"The point?" J.T. growled.

Fenelli pulled over to the curb and looked at the young policeman he'd taken under his wing when he'd first been assigned to him, wet behind the ears.

"The point is we don't know what's coming today, tomorrow, or even an hour from now. None of us do. All we can do is take the little bit of happiness we might be lucky enough to find along the way, and the way I see it, you got lucky twice. Don't blow this second chance you got, J.T. you'll regret it for the rest of your life—short though that may be because we are going to shoot you if you don't get back with her, make no mistake about that." Finished, he moved away from the curb again and started down another long stretch of street.

J.T. blew out a breath. ''Maybe you have something there.''

Fenelli grinned, though he didn't turn to look at J.T. He'd gotten through, at least a little. ''Yeah, maybe I do.''

Maddy didn't know she could care for someone so quickly, or hurt so much so fast when they left. But she could and she did.

Each day that passed since J.T. had walked away from her and out of the restaurant was busy.

Each day was empty.

Empty despite the baby she adored and the work she loved. Empty despite her family who, as always, had rallied around her with a minimum of questions and a maximum of support.

She'd get over it, she told herself, struggling with her feelings. She'd survived John's death; she would get over this.

But not anytime soon.

Because it was Mother's Day and her family had come out en force to gather at her house in order to celebrate the day, Maddy pinned a smile to her lips and tried to act as if she wasn't weeping inside. Who knew, if she pretended hard enough, maybe she'd begin to believe it herself.

After all, that was what had happened with John

Thomas in the first place. She'd tried so hard to draw him out, she'd gotten drawn in.

So she mingled, and hosted, and made small talk. All the while thinking of him and wishing he were here.

Well, he wasn't going to be here. He'd made it perfectly clear that he didn't want to see her anymore and he hadn't been around for almost three weeks. Why should today be any different?

She paused to scoop Johnny up from his playpen and hug him to her. "You're the only man I need in my life," she murmured against his cheek.

Johnny squirmed in response.

A faint melodious chime echoed somewhere in the background. "Doorbell, Maddy," Bill called to her. He was standing closer to the front door than she was. "Want me to get it?"

She shook her head. "No, that's okay." Walking by Bill's latest girlfriend, a forensic expert attached to the coroner's office, Maddy placed Johnny in her brother's arms. "Entertain Johnny, I'll get it."

Maybe it was a friend dropping by, she thought, making her way to the front door. Everyone in her family was already here, and then some. Her brothers had each brought their current flames and her dad was busy surveying the lot under her mother's watchful eye.

A smile curved Maddy's lips as she turned the doorknob. Her father wasn't twenty anymore, but he acted it at times. It was one of the things she found endearing about him.

Her smile froze in stunned disbelief the instant she opened the door.

Was this just wishful thinking?

She blinked, but he continued to stand there.

"It's you."

J.T. almost shifted in his discomfort before he stopped himself. He was holding a large bouquet of flowers in his hands and felt absolutely devoid of the courage that saw him through every day.

"Yeah, it's me." Because she was looking at them, he became aware of the flowers he was clutching. He'd told the florist to throw every flower she could think of into the bouquet. One of them had to be Maddy's favorite. "These are for you." He thrust them toward her. "Happy Mother's Day."

Taking them, she still looked a little uncertain. She hadn't thought that something like Mother's Day registered with J.T.

"Thank you." She took a deep breath. The fragrance was wonderful. Maddy raised her eyes to his. "I thought it might be a peace offering."

"Actually it's that, too." Out of steam, he paused, searching for more words and coming up woefully empty. "Can we have it? Peace?"

"I never went to war, John Thomas," she told him quietly. "You did."

He lifted a shoulder in a half shrug before letting it drop. "Yeah, I guess I did."

"Who is it, Maddy?" her mother called out to her from within a room.

"Just a friend, Mother," Maddy replied.

He laughed shortly, indicating the full house behind her. "Seems every time I come to see you, there's a crowd around." In response to that, she pulled the door to behind her, leaving it slightly ajar as she remained on the doorstep. He put his own interpretation on the action. "Does that mean I can't come in?"

He would see it that way. "No, that means I thought you'd want privacy. Your own space seems to be very important to you."

He looked down into her eyes. God, but he had missed just looking at them. Just looking at her. Missed the graceful, tempting curve of her throat, missed kissing her mouth. Missed her.

"It isn't as important as I thought." Unable to help himself, he reached out and caressed her hair. He saw wonder and confusion spring up in her eyes. "Maddy, I want my life back."

The familiar line stung. "I thought that's what you got by leaving."

"No, not that life. The one you gave me." His voice grew a shade deeper. "The one that opened up every time I heard you laugh. Every time I saw you with Johnny."

"I never took that away," she pointed out, afraid to allow herself to become hopeful. "You turned your back on it."

"I know." It was his fault, all of it. "Can I turn around again?"

"That depends." She held the flowers to her breast like a shield. As if that could protect her heart from what was coming. "Do you want to?"

"More than anything," he swore.

Her smile was pure sunshine. "Then turn around. No one's stopping you."

He wanted to press his mouth to hers, to have the sweetness wash away the taste of the last lonely weeks. But he wasn't finished yet. "There's one more thing."

She raised her brow, waiting for a shoe to drop somewhere. "And that is?"

He started and then stopped, hesitating. "Maddy, I'm not good with words."

She thought of the way he made her feel when he was around her, of the way she felt when he kissed her.

"Not everyone is. You have other attributes. Besides, that's why we complement each other so well." The smile turned into a grin. "I can talk, you can listen."

But he shook his head at the analysis. "This time, I want to talk, and you can listen."

"All right. Talk."

Silence followed, wrapping dried leaves around him. J.T. pressed his lips together as he looked off to his left at the greenbelt that lay just beyond. He was a better cop than a civilian.

Frustrated, he shoved his hands into his pockets. It was then that he felt it, a small velvet box that rubbed against his fingertips.

He looked at her. The words came, short, simple. "Marry me."

She couldn't have been more surprised if she'd literally been blown out of the water. "Shouldn't you start out by saying you love me?"

"I do. I love you." He liked the sound of that. What had kept him from saying it before? "That's why I left."

The flowers slipped from her fingers to the cheery welcome mat beneath her feet. With loving fingers, she touched his face.

"Love me and stay," Maddy urged softly.

His arms closed around her, drawing her to him. "Only if you want me to."

She laughed. "I guess you'll never make detective if you haven't figured that out yet."

He took out the box from his pocket and flipped it open to show her the contents. The old-fashioned square-cut diamond gleamed bright, catching the afternoon sun within its borders. He heard and felt her catch her breath. "Maybe you'd better help me study for the exams."

"Every day of my life," she promised, threading her arms around his neck. "And yes, I'll marry you."

"That friend still there, Maddy?" Her mother's voice reached her, coming from within the house.

"No," Maddy called out over her shoulder. "He left." Turning her head, she looked up at J.T. and smiled. "Someone better showed up."

"And he intends to stay," J.T. told her before he brought his mouth down to hers and kissed her. And officially began the first leg of his second chance.

* * * * *

A DADDY FOR HER DAUGHTERS
Elizabeth Bevarly

For Mom,
Happy Mother's Day!
(Don't worry—you're getting a present, too.)

Dear Reader,

I was so flattered and pleased when Silhouette invited me to write a novella for their Mother's Day collection this year. Not just because I'm a mother myself, experiencing all the joys and surprises (and terrors!) that go along with such a job, but because I've always had such a good relationship with my own mom.

Like Naomi in my story, "A Daddy for Her Daughters," my mother always allowed me to be whomever I wanted and needed to be, and encouraged me to do whatever it took to achieve my dreams. It's thanks to her that I became a writer, because unlike a lot of other people in my life, she never told me—not once—that I couldn't do it.

So here's to all the moms out there: to those who are struggling to raise the best possible kids they can—the ones who are second-guessing their every move and lying awake at night, wondering if they're doing enough—and to those who are resting happily on their laurels, knowing they did a fabulous job. Happy Mother's Day to you all.

And, speaking now as a daughter, thanks. (I love you, Mom.)

Warmly,

Elizabeth Bevarly

Chapter 1

Sloan Sullivan knew it was going to be a bad day the minute his boss told him he was going to have to lend a hand. And not just for today. But for a whole month.

It wasn't that Sloan already felt as if he lent a hand—several hands, in fact—at the Atlanta, Georgia law firm where he had been a partner for years. But, too, this month simply wasn't looking to be a good month to schedule in something like lending a hand. He had back-to-back appointments and professional functions out the proverbial wazoo throughout February. And March was pretty booked, too.

In fact, as he sat at the big table bisecting the boardroom of Parmentier, Barnaby, Shepperton and Ganz, flipping frantically through his organizer, Sloan couldn't find a single opening for lending a hand until spring. And even then, he was going to have to pencil in lending a hand, because that was coming up on the Masters Tournament, and he always went over to Augusta for a few days, because there were always parties to attend, so he might very realistically have to make an erasure and postpone lending a hand until sometime during the summer instead.

To be perfectly honest, Sloan just didn't have *time* to lend a hand, regardless of the season. He was much too busy with other things—mostly work. An estate attorney's work just never seemed to be done.

He ran restless fingers through his dark hair and glanced up from his organizer, only to find his silver-haired boss gazing expectantly back at him from the other end of the massive, smoked glass table. "I'm sorry, Edgar," he said to Edgar Parmentier, the senior partner of Parmentier, Barnaby, Shepperton and Ganz. "But this really isn't a good time for me. Normally, I'd jump at the chance to lend a hand. You know that. But I just can't find the time right now. Surely, you understand."

But Edgar only glared at him with that gimlet-eyed stare that always made Sloan want to run for the nearest, well gimlet—shaken, not stirred. "What I know and understand, Sloan," he said, "is that you'd just as soon pretend that everyone in the world lives the same way you do—pampered, privileged and prosperous. You don't want to lend a hand, because then you'll have to admit that not everyone's life is as cushy as yours is.''

"That isn't it at all," Sloan objected. Even if, maybe, he couldn't quite disagree with his boss. He really didn't like to think about things like poverty and indigence and disadvantage and people who needed a hand. Hey, who did?

"That's exactly it," Edgar insisted. "You Sullivans have lived in your ivory tower—or, at the very least, in your stately manor—for too long. It's time at least one of you saw how the real world lives. Come on, man," he further jeered. "Show some backbone. This will be good for you."

Sloan told himself to object to his employer's assessment of his family—of himself—then realized that, in all honesty, he couldn't. He *was* pampered, privileged and prosperous. He'd grown up being pampered, privileged and prosperous. And he *liked* being pampered, privileged and prosperous, too. The Sullivans were one of Atlanta's most illustrious families and had been for generations. And Sloan had no intention of giving up his pampered, privileged and prosperous lifestyle anytime soon.

So, in fact, there was no reason for him to object to Edgar's words. Somehow, though, he wasn't comfortable with his boss's evaluation of him. It made him sound so shallow. And hey, there must be *some* depth to his character. Right? He'd come this far, after all.

Sloan shook the thought off. "But, Edgar—" he began again.

"It's *always* a good time for doing good deeds, Sloan," his boss cut him off. "And the Lend a Hand Month council has scores of excellent causes lined up this year. Pick one."

The older man dipped his head toward a brown felt fedora turned upside down at the center of the table. Inside were more than two dozen folded slips of paper, each recorded with some kind of month-long good deed that needed doing, and for which Edgar Parmentier had volunteered one of his employees— with or without that employee's go-ahead. So far, four of the eight partners at PBS and G had chosen from the hat. Whatever good deeds were left after the partners' meeting would be divvied up among the associates and office workers of the law firm. Come February, five days hence, PBS and G would be well represented among the do-gooders. Whether its employees liked it or not.

Of course, the vast majority of employees didn't mind lending a hand at all. And Sloan wouldn't, either, if it just came at a better time. But he had things to *do* next month. Lots of things. Lots of really important things. Tennis dates with Bambi Winston. The Farringdons' annual open house. Babs and Leonard Bayard's cocktail party. It was a never-ending series of social obligations. And work, too, he reminded himself. Why, setting up the Maury and Antoinette MacCorkindale estate alone was going to take weeks.

"But, Edgar—" he tried again.

"Choose," Edgar commanded, jabbing a stubby finger at the fedora.

With a frustrated sigh, Sloan reached into the hat and drew out a slip of paper. So far, the good deeds chosen had been anything but appealing. Dennis Robertson was going to be spending each of his February weekends painting the interior of a nursing home. Fred Schwartz would be serving baloney and beans at a local food shelter during half of his lunch hours. Lauren Riordan would be reading books to preschoolers at a nearby women's shelter during her lunch hours. And Anita Spinelli was going to spend her next four weekends putting together food baskets for the underprivileged.

Sloan held his breath as he unfolded his piece of paper to see what inconvenient blow fate had dealt him. Would he be singing rondos to a group of Cub Scouts? Baking cookies for a church bazaar? Walking dogs for the elderly? What? He unfolded the scrap of paper…and was surprised to see that he was actually halfway suited to the job he would be required to do—and only two evenings a week, at that.

Halfway being the operative word here. Because although the *basketball coach* part was familiar enough, the *rural Georgia high school* part was not.

Still, it appeared that the Fighting Razorbacks of Stonewall Jackson High School in Wisteria, Georgia—roughly forty-five minutes from Atlanta—needed an assistant coach for the next month, because their regular one had been laid up by a hunting accident. Sloan, of course, had never actually coached basketball before, but he'd had the honor of warming the bench for Vanderbilt. And, of course, he'd played basketball in high school—very well, too. In fact, as starting center, he'd taken the Fighting Ptarmigans of Penrose Academy right to the state championship twenty years ago. Well, the state championship for tony private schools, at any rate. Still, if he'd won one for the Ptarmigans, he could certainly do the same for the Razorbacks.

Then, for some reason, the image of a razorback having a ptarmigan for lunch erupted in his brain. How strange…

Immediately, Sloan shook off that thought, too. They were high school students he'd be coaching, he reminded himself. It would only be two nights a week. And only for a month. How tough could this assignment be?

It wasn't until Sloan parked his Jaguar roadster outside the gymnasium at Jackson High School that he began to regret his final words after drawing this assignment from a hat. He'd never visited rural Wisteria before, and hadn't realized just how *rural* Wisteria was. Jackson High School, for instance, was one of only two in the entire town. And this one, he couldn't help but notice as he'd driven over them, was definitely on the wrong side of the tracks.

He knew it was the wrong side of the tracks, because on the *other* side, Wisteria had been very picturesque, filled with white frame houses and tidy yards and old-fashioned mom-and-pop type shops. There had even been an ice-cream parlor on one corner of the downtown—and how quaint to think of the business district as "downtown," Sloan thought again—not to mention a town square which was really a square, and which, during the warmer months, was no doubt green and lush and landscaped to perfection. This side of Wisteria, on the other hand, was…

Not.

Not picturesque. Not filled with white frame houses and tidy yards and old-fashioned mom-and-pop type shops. Not quaint. There were no ice-cream parlors, and nothing that had the potential to be green or lush or landscaped in any way. What he *had* seen lots of on this side of Wisteria were auto parts stores—which were more part than auto, truth be told—junkyards, trailer parks and what appeared to be illegal dumping grounds. Oh, and of course, Stonewall Jackson High School, whose gym was a massive, looming, bleak structure that couldn't possibly keep out the rain, or last beyond the next big gust of wind.

It stood apart from the school, which seemed to be in no better shape than the gym, truth be told, all of it squatting amidst the biggest gravel parking lot Sloan had ever seen in his life. Then again, much of the gravel didn't appear to be parking lot. It just appeared to be…gravel.

The small gray stones crunched beneath his two-hundred-dollar sneakers when he stepped out of the car, and the damp February breeze brought with it the oily stink of a paper mill that must lie on the outskirts of town. Strangely, he hadn't noticed the smell on the *other* side of the tracks. But here...

Sloan did his best to breathe shallowly.

A sign above the main entrance to the gym hung a bit listlessly on one side, and many of its plastic letters were missing. Still, Sloan was able to get the gist of *ad Razo ba ks Eat Their Y ung! Go Te m!* Not that he necessarily wanted to get the gist of it. But he did anyway.

Evidently, the Razorbacks meant business, he thought as he zipped his hooded sweatshirt over his sweatpants and Vanderbilt T-shirt to ward off the chill. Then again, Sloan had been brought up to date on the team by the Jackson High principal before coming to Wisteria. The kids were indeed poised for the regional championship, and they were definitely kicking butt. Even this late in the season, they were still undefeated, and had royally trounced a couple of schools everyone had considered shoo-ins for the regional, perhaps even the state, title.

Then again, according to the sign, they did eat their young, Sloan reflected wryly. That showed a real flair for offense. He began to suspect that he had grossly underestimated just how demanding this volunteer position was going to be.

His suspicions were only reinforced when he

pushed open the gymnasium doors and strode through the decrepit lobby to the cavernous—and likewise decrepit—gym itself. The bleachers were empty, which surprised him, even if the team was only practicing right now. Generally, when a team was doing as well as the Razorbacks were, there were always fans in the stands to encourage them and cheer them on, even at practice. Parents, too, often showed up to watch. Yet the Razorbacks didn't seem to have any visible means of support.

Oh, wait, yes they did, Sloan realized belatedly. Because a large group of girls stood on the other side of the gym, chatting. Cheerleaders, probably, he thought, seeing as how most of them were wearing shorts, and a few were in sweats. Or they may be girlfriends of the team members. It was nice that so many of them to be here, showing support for their menfolk.

And just where were the menfolk? Sloan wondered, scanning the gym again. There wasn't a single team member in sight.

Then the shrill cry of a whistle alerted him to the fact that the team was indeed, as kids said nowadays, "In da house." At least, Sloan thought that was what kids said nowadays. He did have VH-1, after all. Even if he didn't watch anything except "House of Style." At any rate, even after that long, piercing shriek came to an end, no team appeared. Only the girls on the other side of the gym ran to the center of the room, presumably, he thought, to create some kind of pyramid for the boys to run through.

But no boys appeared. No, the only thing Sloan saw with the scattering of the girls that he hadn't noticed before was what turned out to be the source of the whistle—a woman who was striding toward the middle of the group of girls. Who, incidentally, he also noted, had yet to climb atop each other and form a pyramid for the boys. The woman caught sight of Sloan just as he caught sight of her, and after saying something to a couple of the girls he couldn't hear, she smiled, lifted a hand in greeting, and began to jog toward him.

She was tall, he noticed, easily five-ten or -eleven, slim, but curvy, with small, round breasts and short, dark hair. She had a basketball tucked under one arm and was dressed almost identically to Sloan, though where his sweats were navy blue, hers were gray. And the T-shirt she wore indicated she'd attended Clemson.

As she drew nearer to him, Sloan noticed that she was about his age—late thirties—with clear gray eyes, touches of silver and auburn in her hair, and a spray of freckles over her nose and cheekbones. Her mouth was good, full and smiling, and her smile was good, too, broad and uninhibited. She wore not a bit of makeup, but somehow, she didn't really need it. She was wholesome and healthy-looking, and Sloan was surprised to discover that he found her attractive. Usually, he didn't go for wholesome and healthy-looking. Usually, he went for flashy and luscious-looking.

"You must be Mr. Sullivan," she said as she halted before him, extending her hand.

He nodded and accepted her hand automatically, and he noticed right away that it wasn't like most women's hands. No, this one was large and raw-boned and callused, with fingernails clipped short, and completely devoid of jewelry.

"Yes, I'm here for the Lend a Hand thing," he said as he let her hand drop. "I'm looking for Coach Carmichael. Do you know where he is?"

Her smile fell some, and she eyed him curiously for a moment. Then she fisted the hand that wasn't holding the basketball on her—surprisingly curvy—hip and smiled again, her gaze never once veering from his. "I'm Naomi Carmichael," she told him. "*Coach* Carmichael. And I can't thank you enough for taking time out of your busy schedule to help us out this month."

Sloan narrowed his eyes at her. "*You're* Coach Carmichael?" he asked, confused. "*Us?*" he asked further, even more confused.

"Yeah, us," she said. Then she gestured over one shoulder with her thumb, toward the group of girls who were eyeing him with open curiosity. "The Lady Razorbacks," she said further. "Thanks for volunteering to be our assistant coach for the next month. We really do appreciate it."

Chapter 2

"The *Lady* Razorbacks?" Sloan Sullivan cried as he gazed passed Naomi, over her shoulder, and out at the gym floor.

Naomi narrowed her eyes at him and wondered at his flabbergasted reaction. Surely he'd known he would be coaching girls, she thought. And even if he hadn't, what was the big deal? Why would the gender of the team be significant? Their regular assistant coach was a man.

"Ye-es," she replied slowly, "the Lady Razorbacks. Will that be a problem, Mr. Sullivan?"

He glanced back at Naomi's face, then at the girls on the floor again, then back at Naomi once more. "But—but—but—I mean... It's just... How could... This isn't..."

Honestly, Naomi thought. For an educated man, he sure didn't have much of a vocabulary. Then again, a man who looked like he did probably didn't have to talk very much to get ahead, even if he was an attorney in his real life.

He was tall—several inches taller than Naomi, and that was saying something. At five-eleven, she didn't have to look up to very many men, a fact of her physique that she enjoyed *a lot*. Still, Sloan Sullivan was easily five or six inches taller than she. And he probably outweighed her by a good sixty or seventy pounds, too—but not because he was overweight by any means. No, she could see, even through layers of clothing, that every ounce of this man was pure muscle. She'd been told by Phil Leatherman, Jackson High's principal, that Mr. Sullivan had played basketball in high school and college. Obviously, the athlete in him was still alive and kicking. He may be a workaholic attorney these days—which she'd also learned from Phil—but he clearly took time out of his busy schedule to keep himself in shape.

She guessed his age to be close to her own thirty-eight, thanks to the faint lines fanning out from his eyes and bracketing his full lips, and the few threads of silver winding through his black hair. The razor-straight tresses were conservatively and expertly cut, and somehow Naomi knew—she just *knew*—he paid more for one haircut than she spent in a week feeding herself and her four kids. Of course, she did buy store brands and use coupons—lots and lots of coupons—

but still. His hands were big and masculine, but she'd noticed when she shook with him that they weren't calloused or overworked. And his eyes were…oh… So blue. A dark, rich, velvety blue, like the morning glories that climbed up the back trellis in the summertime. Oh, yes. The epitome of tall, dark and handsome. Quite the dreamboat was Mr. Sloan Sullivan.

Now, now, Naomi, she cautioned herself. She knew better than to have thoughts like that. Just because it had been more than four years since she'd been intimate with any—

But she didn't allow herself to think about things like that. It was tough enough getting through life as a single woman—a single woman who'd been dumped by her husband, no less—and raising four daughters on a teacher's salary, and trying to keep them, and herself, out of trouble. Naomi didn't need to go looking for more. And this Sloan Sullivan, with his hundred-and-fifty-dollar haircut and his Vandy sweats, was Trouble with a capital *T*. Because only a few minutes after meeting him, Naomi was already yearning for things she hadn't had for a very long time, things she wasn't likely to have again for even longer.

She hadn't met too many men who were inclined to ask out a woman who had four kids. Especially not in a town like Wisteria, where the only single men were widowers in their eighties. And, judging by the looks of him, Sloan Sullivan was a man whose taste ran more toward young, petite, dainty little blondes in slinky dresses, and not towering, butch brunettes who didn't know the meaning of the word *foundation*—either for face or body support.

Still, Wisteria was Naomi's home, and had been for the bulk of her adult life. And Wisteria was, for the most part, a good place to raise kids. It was quiet, the pace was slow and crime was pretty much nonexistent, save the occasional adolescent prank. But, hey. Naomi had been an adolescent, too, once upon a time. Even if she couldn't find a single thing about herself these days that reminded her of that carefree kid.

She pushed the thought away and focused her attention on Mr. Sloan Sullivan again, realizing he hadn't yet answered her question.

"*Will* it be a problem, Mr. Sullivan?" she asked again. "*Do* you have some objection to coaching girls?" And if he did, Naomi thought further, would he mind if she smacked him around a bit, until she'd knocked a little sense into his thick head?

He returned his attention to her face, and she marveled again at how handsome he was. Damn. This was going to make the next month even more difficult to get through than it had already promised to be. It would be hard enough for the team to maintain their fevered momentum with a new—and temporary— coach whom none of them knew. But with their new—and temporary—coach looking like…like… like…*that,* the Lady Razorbacks were going to be totally distracted.

And worse, so would their coach.

"But…but…they're girls," Sloan Sullivan said, his voice tinted with petulance and something akin to distaste.

Naomi nodded and tried very hard—really, she did—not to be too sarcastic when she replied, "Whoa, good call, Mr. Sullivan. You're absolutely right. They are, in fact, girls."

"But girls can't play basketball," he said, still sounding like he'd ingested something that didn't agree with them.

"Oh?" Naomi asked crisply. "Why not, pray tell?"

"Well, because they're *girls*," he said. "They don't have the—"

"Your next word may be your last, Mr. Sullivan," Naomi interjected as diplomatically as she could. "If I were you, I'd think good and hard before I chose it."

Immediately, he snapped his mouth shut. But she could tell he wasn't quite ready to concede the battle. Maybe what he needed was a little push in the right direction, she thought.

"Let me tell you something about girls who play sports, Mr. Sullivan," she said coolly. "Statistically speaking, girls who are involved in sports during their school years grow up to be stronger, healthier women. They have a lower incidence of breast cancer and depression and heart disease, and they have higher self-esteem and self-confidence. They're less likely to become pregnant before they're ready, and they're more likely to leave an abusive relationship. Not to mention, they just have a helluva lot of fun.

"Now then," she continued, her tone a *tad* less brittle than before, "you were saying, Mr. Sullivan? About girls playing basketball? They can't because they don't have the *what?*"

And with that, Sloan Sullivan finally did back down. Sort of. As much as a man of his accelerated height could back down, anyway, Naomi supposed.

"Well, they just play like girls, that's all," he finished a bit more tactfully.

Naomi smiled. "Damn straight they do," she retorted. "Watch this."

Without warning him any further, she spun around and hurled the basketball toward her center—her daughter Evelyn—who caught it effortlessly and began to dribble, rocketing down the length of the court with staggering velocity and equilibrium, weaving in and out of the girls who tried to interfere, until she vaulted toward the opposite hoop and, with a sweet-sounding *swish,* stuffed it for two points.

"In your face, Mom!" she shouted with a smile as she landed gracefully on the floor beneath the goal.

"Mom?" Sloan Sullivan echoed.

Naomi nodded and smiled. "That's my girl!" she yelled. Though whether she was congratulating her daughter or overstating to her new assistant coach, volume-wise, her relationship to the team's center, Naomi wasn't entirely sure. "Katie's mine, too," she added indicating the shorter version of Evelyn, who was, at that moment, high-fiving her sister.

"You have two daughters on the team?" Sloan asked.

"Yep," Naomi told him. "Evy's my center, a junior, and Katie's a guard, a freshman."

"They resemble you," he said, nodding. "And you teach English, as well, I understand?" he asked further, something he'd obviously gleaned from his own chat with the Jackson High principal.

"Yep," she said again.

"You must be a busy woman, Mrs. Carmichael," he observed as he watched the team reconvening at the center of the floor.

"Yeah, I am," Naomi agreed with a smile. "Especially when you include the two other daughters I have at home."

He said nothing in response to that, but turned briskly to look at her, his expression both startled and inquisitive. And there was something about the way he looked at her in that moment that made Naomi feel…funny. Not funny ha-ha, but funny strange, because what she felt seemed kind of familiar somehow, even if she hadn't felt it for a very long time. He seemed to be appraising her, she realized. And she realized that, somewhere deep down inside herself, a little part of her wanted him to like what he saw. Unfortunately, another not-so-little part of her was worrying that she didn't measure up.

But measure up to what? she wondered. She hadn't

cared what any man thought of her for a long time. She didn't care now, she assured herself. She was a thirty-eight-year-old woman with four children, a woman whose husband had hit the road the minute he found out about the impending arrival of number four. She didn't have time to worry about what other people—what men—thought of her. And she didn't have the inclination, either.

But that didn't stop her from caring just then what Sloan Sullivan thought of her. And Naomi didn't like it that she cared as much as she did.

Somehow, she stopped herself from running a hand through her short, dark hair, to smooth out the unruly tresses that she hadn't brushed since that morning. And somehow, she kept herself from biting her lips, hard, in an effort to put a little color in them. Instead, she spun around and shouted out a few instructions to her team, and then watched her girls go to work.

The moment she blew her whistle, they broke off into two camps and began to practice. Where normally, Naomi would have joined them, shouting out more instructions and pointers, this time, she didn't say a word. But she did turn to gauge Sloan Sullivan's reaction as he watched the Lady Razorbacks work out. At first, he had a little trouble keeping up with them, so swiftly and deftly did the girls move. Eventually, though, he got into the spirit of things. His gaze ricocheted from one player to another, darting up and down the length of the court as the girls did.

And with every passing moment, Naomi could see the admiration in his eyes grow.

"Wow," he finally said with much understatement. "They're, uh… They're pretty good."

Naomi smiled proudly. "Yes, they are. They're extremely good. They're going to the state championship, Mr. Sullivan. And they're going to win it. The question now is, are you going to help us get there? Or are you just going to be dead weight?"

He glanced at the rapidly moving girls again, then back at Naomi. "I'm in," he said with a smile. "Let's go all the way."

Naomi reminded herself that he was talking about team sports, and not sexual escapades. Still, she couldn't quite squelch the itinerant heat that wound through her at hearing his words. She would *not* be going all the way with Sloan Sullivan, she hastened to remind herself. She had just met the man, and she would only have contact with him two nights a week for one month.

She wouldn't be going all the way with anyone, she told herself further, forcing herself to be brutally honest, because she figured she needed the reminder just then. Not until she'd finished raising four daughters and sent them all off to live their own lives, at any rate. Of course, seeing as how her youngest, Sophie, was only four, by the time all the girls were out of the house, Naomi would be so old and dried up, no man would want her. And even if, by some wild miracle, she found a man who did want her, by then, she would have forgotten what it was that a man and a woman were supposed to do together.

So, for now, she'd have to settle for "going all the way" with her team. And she told herself, as she always did, that that would be enough. Funny, though, where before, Naomi had always believed herself when she told herself that, suddenly, as she looked at Sloan Sullivan, she wasn't so sure she did anymore.

"Practice ends at seven," she told him, shoving her troubling thoughts away for now. "You busy afterward?"

He seemed surprised by the question, but slowly shook his head. "No, not really."

"I don't live far from here. Of course, nothing is far from anything in Wisteria," she added with a half-hearted smile. "But if you want to follow me home after practice, I'll fix us some supper. And then, after the girls clean up and head to their rooms, you and I can talk strategy for the team."

When she'd first started voicing her offer, Naomi had noted that Sloan Sullivan suddenly began to look terrified. But by the time she finished talking, he seemed much relieved, as if, initially, he'd been afraid she had something else in mind. She smiled sadly at the realization. Poor guy. He'd been scared that she was making plans for just the two of them. Plans that didn't revolve around basketball, even if they'd maybe focused on a little fun and games.

And as much fun as games might be with him, Naomi thought further, there would be little point.

Men like him, although they were certainly good at games and running around, never stayed long enough for the main event. It was just as well he'd only be coaching the girls for a month, until Lou Melton, their usual assistant coach, would be back at work. Because by the time March Madness rolled around, Naomi would need a guy in her court who would be there for the girls and for her. And Sloan Sullivan simply was not that kind of man. He was far more suited to big business boardrooms and high-society cocktail parties, draped with ornamental women who wouldn't know a rebound from a double dribble.

"Planning a strategy for the team sounds like a good idea," he said. And then, for a second time, he assured her, "I'm in."

Oh, that he was, Naomi thought. That he definitely was. Even after knowing him for a matter of moments, Sloan Sullivan was already, definitely, *in*. And all she could do now was hope it wouldn't be hard to get him *out* again, once their month of working together was over.

Chapter 3

Surprisingly, Naomi and her daughters didn't live on the same side of town where they worked and attended school, Sloan noted as he pulled his roadster to a stop in the Carmichael driveway behind the aged, tired-looking Carmichael minivan. In fact, Naomi's was very much like one of the charming white frame houses he had passed on his way through Wisteria earlier that evening, situated only a couple of blocks from the town square. The yard was tidy, if small, a good bit of it arranged in such a way as to suggest that, in the greener months, it was a fairly extravagant garden. And although the place really didn't seem large enough to accommodate a family of six—presuming there was a Mr. Carmichael to go with the rest of the Carmichaels, something Sloan found himimself feeling apprehensive about for some reason—he supposed the homestead would qualify as "cozy."

Not that coziness was anything he wanted to invite into his *own* life, mind you, but, looking at Naomi Carmichael's house, he could certainly see why something like coziness might appeal to other people.

The inside was as charming as the outside, he noted further as he followed the three Carmichael women of his acquaintance inside. The furnishings were old but comfortable, not quite antiques, but sturdy and full of personality nonetheless—overstuffed chairs covered in chintz florals, curio cabinets filled with mementos, large, well-worn, wool-hooked rugs spanning most of the hardwood floors. The living room was painted a dark, rich green, which flowed surprisingly well into the terra-cotta-colored dining room beyond. Built-in shelves in both rooms were crammed full of books and family photographs and an assortment of mismatched knickknacks. More photographs and watercolor paintings of flowers and gardens filled the walls, and plants tumbled from every other available surface. All in all, the Carmichael home looked like a place where a lot of living—and a lot of color—went on.

Briefly, Sloan compared the house to his own downtown Atlanta condo, which was sparsely furnished in what he liked to think of as "clean contemporary." White walls, minimalist white furnishings, white carpeting, and splashes of primary colors in abstract, geometric artwork and accent pieces. It was by no means child-friendly. And it was, to put it mildly, not much like the home into which he had just wandered.

And strangely, for the first time since moving into his place, Sloan wondered if maybe the condo could stand a little improvement in the interior decoration department. This in spite of the fact that he'd paid a small fortune to one of Atlanta's premier interior design firms to do the place for him, exactly the way he had asked for it to be done. Somehow, he suspected Naomi Carmichael had achieved her look without any outside input, and without paying thousands of dollars to someone named Serge.

"Ginny! Sophie! We're home!" she called as she closed the front door behind Sloan, and strode past him toward the dining room, into which her other daughters had strolled and then disappeared.

Assuming he was supposed to follow the women, Sloan did so, and eventually he found himself in the kitchen—which was as old-fashioned, colorful and lived-in looking as the rest of the house, right down to the floral wallpaper, the glass-doored, natural pinewood cabinets, the braided rag rug and the ladderback chairs surrounding a heavy, pinewood table. Once again, Sloan found himself responding to his surroundings in a way that was totally uncharacteristic, feeling oddly contented in an atmosphere that should have been alien and uncomfortable.

In response to their mother's summons, two more girls scurried into the room to join the rest of the family. The oldest of the newcomers, Sloan saw immediately, was the identical twin of the ninth-grade point guard, Katie. The fourth Carmichael girl, though, was considerably younger than her sisters. Even to his untrained eye, Sloan could see that she wasn't yet school age.

"Hi," the smallest one said when she saw their guest. She smiled, her mouth full of perfect little teeth. Sloan had no choice but to smile back. "Who're you?" she asked further.

Naomi intervened before Sloan had a chance to, telling her daughter, "This is Mr. Sullivan, Sophie. Mr. Sullivan, this is my youngest daughter, Sophie."

"How do you do, Sophie?" Sloan asked, his smile growing broader. Automatically, he extended his hand toward the little girl, the way he would have done had he just been introduced to a new law partner or associate.

Much to his surprise, Sophie took his hand and shook it soundly, three times, before releasing it. "It's nice to meet you," she said with practiced courtesy.

Sloan stifled a chuckle at her formality. Like the other Carmichael women, Sophie had dark hair and a smattering of freckles, but where her sisters all had dark-brown eyes, this one had her mother's clear gray. In fact, she was a miniature of her mother, right down to the short haircut. The other girls, though they did resemble Naomi, probably favored their father more. Which reminded Sloan that there must be a father of the girls, somewhere, and he wondered just how he might find out where the man was without seeming forward or, worse, interested.

Because he *wasn't* interested, he assured himself. Not in Naomi Carmichael. No way. Even if he did find her attractive—very attractive, actually—he was in no way interested in her. Not in any kind of a— he shuddered to even think the word—*romantic* sense, at any rate. For one thing, Naomi Carmichael was probably married. Though, he had noticed during practice that she wasn't wearing a wedding ring. Not that that was an indication of anything—the absence of the wedding ring *or* the noticing, he assured himself—because sometimes married people didn't wear rings, especially if they were physically active. For another thing, Naomi Carmichael had children. And for another thing, Naomi Carmichael wasn't his type—not by any stretch of the imagination.

Sloan was just...curious. Yeah, that was it. Curious. He was curious about her because she was so much different from the women he usually met. Over the course of the evening, he'd watched her with the Lady Razorbacks, noting her skillful coaching, her graceful motion, how she nurtured the girls without being motherly, and drilled them without being harassing. And he had quickly come to the conclusion that she was one of those women he normally avoided—strong, self-confident, self-sufficient, no-nonsense. Not that he liked weak-willed, small-minded clinging vines, he hastened to amend. Au contraire. But a man liked to think he was needed. And

Naomi Carmichael gave him the impression that she lived her life very nicely, thanks, without needing any intervention from anyone.

So that was another reason he wasn't interested. Just curious.

"And this is another of my daughters," she said, bringing him out of his troubling thoughts, "Ginny. Katie's twin, obviously."

"Only in looks," Ginny was quick to point out.

"Yeah," Katie readily agreed. "Ginny's a total girlie-girl."

Which, of course, Sloan could have discerned all by himself, seeing as how the girl was dressed like Sorority Barbie, her perfectly coifed hair swept back with a glittery headband, and wearing a pink T-shirt and lavender miniskirt and pink tights, and having apparently just knocked over a department store cosmetic counter in a clean sweep of goods. Compared to her sister's bedraggled—sweaty—ponytail, ragged—sweaty—practice clothes, and cosmetic-free—sweaty—face, she was clearly a twin in looks only.

"Beats being a jock," Ginny easily countered her sister. "At least I get dates."

"Oh, no you don't," Naomi was quick to cut in. "You don't date until you're sixteen."

"But, Mo-om," Ginny began to object. "I went out with Stuart Benson just last weekend."

"Yeah, and six other kids," Katie said. "That's not dating. It's mobbing."

"Is not."

"Is, too."

"Is not."

"Is, too."

"Is not, jockstrap."

"Is too, girlie-girl."

"Enough!" Naomi interrupted.

Immediately, the girls quit their bickering, but they shot each other enough ugly looks that Sloan figured the argument was by no means over. No, it would probably be a while—say the year 2020—before those two settled anything.

"We have a guest," Naomi reminded her daughters. "I know it's hard, but try to act like human beings. You can start by washing up," she told the two who were athletically inclined. Then, taking her own advice, tugging at the damp fabric of her T-shirt, she turned to Sloan. "I'll just be a second. Dinner will be ready in less than twenty minutes."

"That's fast," he said, surprised.

"Listen, if it has to be boiled for more than fifteen minutes or microwaved for more than ten, you won't find it in my kitchen," Naomi told him.

And, oh, how palate-pleasing that sounded, Sloan thought wryly. He made a mental note to stop by his favorite deli for carryout before driving to Wisteria next time.

And then Naomi was gone, abandoning him to her other two daughters. Which, at first, didn't seem like it was going to be a problem, because Ginny immediately cited an intense need to make a phone call and left the room. Sloan waited to see if Sophie would likewise have some kind of pressing social obligation—what did nonschoolage children do with their time, anyway? he wondered—but she remained in the kitchen, eyeing him quizzically.

This was a first for Sloan. He had absolutely no idea what to say that might start a conversation. Normally, he was totally at home with strangers, could make chitchat effortlessly and for hours on end. It was a necessary talent for someone who attended as many social functions as he did. Unfortunately, none of those social functions he had attended before now had prepared him for how to make small talk with someone so, well, small.

So, going for broke, he said, "Hey, what about that Barney, huh? Is he cool or what?"

"I don't like Barney," Sophie told him matter-of-factly. "He's for babies."

"Ah," Sloan replied eloquently. "I see. Yes. Well."

"I'm too big for Barney. I like Thomas."

"Jefferson?" Sloan asked before he realized how ridiculous the question would be.

"Tank Engine," Sophie told him, smiling. "He's a train. And he has lots of train friends."

"Ah. I see. Yes. Well."

"Wanna see my track?" she asked.

And there was something so earnest in the way she posed the question, something so genuinely pleading in her little face, that Sloan found he couldn't say no.

He supposed it wasn't easy being so much younger than everyone else in the house. Not that he understood why she was responding to him, when he was just as old or older than the others. Still, he could see that she craved the attention of someone new, so how could he turn her down? Besides, he'd had a train set when he was a boy, and it might be kind of fun to revisit that sort of thing.

"Sure," he said, smiling at the little girl. "I'd love to see your track. And Thomas. And all of his train friends."

Chapter 4

Naomi left the upstairs bathroom five minutes later, after cleaning up as best she could, and changing into a pair of clean blue jeans and a nondescript, wash-faded, once-red sweatshirt. And also after trying to forget about how horrific her mirror reflection had looked after two hours of practice, and how Sloan Sullivan had seen her that way.

She hesitated in the hallway when she heard voices—Ginny's husky, I'm-on-the-phone-with-a-boy voice coming from the room she shared with Katie, where she had evidently taken the extension, and So-phie's British-tinted, Ringo-the-Thomas-narrator voice coming from her room next door. Silently, Na-omi crept in that direction, peering through the open door to find her youngest introducing Sloan Sullivan to all the friendly, cheerful inhabitants of the Island of Sodor.

She couldn't help but smile at the scene. Sophie lay in the middle of the floor on her stomach, knees bent, feet tracing random semicircles in the air above her, one of them missing a sock. She dragged a long line of colorful engines along one of her more sophisticated track designs, one that wound in and out on itself, under her bed and back again. Sloan sat pretzel-fashion on the floor on the other side of the track, one elbow braced on his thigh, his chin cupped in his hand, looking genuinely rapt with attention. If Naomi hadn't known better, she would have sworn he was actually enjoying himself.

"The troublesome brake van," Sophie was saying, "came around the curve much too quickly. 'Stop! Stop!' cried Edward, who barely had time to move out of the way."

"Uh-oh, looks like that troublesome brake van is being a problem again," Sloan said.

"He's always a problem," Sophie told him, using her regular voice now. "That's why he's the *troublesome* brake van."

"That makes sense." Sloan bent forward, reaching for one of the red engines, pushing it along the length of wooden track before him. "Who did you say this was?" he asked. "James?"

Sophie nodded. "James the red engine. He's very useful."

"Well, he's about to make himself even more useful,'' Sloan told her. "Because just between you and me, I think James could take the troublesome break van any day.''

Naomi bit back her laughter but was helpless to stop the smile that curled her lips. Poor Mr. Sullivan. Once Sophie corralled a willing subject—or even an unwilling one—she didn't let go easily. She could potentially keep the guy up here for hours. Then again, from the looks of things, it didn't seem as if Mr. Sullivan would much mind being kept up here.

And it would keep him *out* of Naomi's hair while she prepared their dinner, she thought further, as would, no doubt, the presence of her other daughters. So with Sloan Sullivan's happily offered, "You're in trouble now, Mr. Brake Van!'' echoing in her ears, she tiptoed past Sophie's room toward the stairs and made her way back down to the kitchen. True to her word, within twenty minutes, she had the table set for six—the first time she could remember it being set for that number since her husband Sam had taken a powder more than four years ago—with stir-fry chicken and oriental salad ready for immediate consumption.

She called her brood to order and, with a series of heavy *thump-thump-thumps* down the stairs, they rapidly arrived, all four girls plunking down in their usual spots and reaching haphazardly for food as they chattered amiably—and nonstop. Only when each of them had filled a plate did Naomi look up to find Sloan Sullivan standing in the kitchen doorway, looking very much like the proverbial deer in the head-lights.

She smiled. "We don't stand on ceremony here, Mr. Sullivan," she told him. "If you want to eat, you have to jump right in. But I apologize if we ran over you."

He shook his head and smiled, but there was something decidedly flummoxed in the gesture. "No, it's not that. It's just... It's just been a long time since I've dined in, that's all," he told her. Then he smiled. "I guess I'm waiting for a hostess to show up and seat me."

Naomi nodded. He did seem more of the dining-out type, she thought. "We had to let our hostess go," she told him, smiling back. "So have a seat," she added, gesturing toward the only chair left vacant.

Belatedly, she realized she had assigned to Sloan Sullivan the place her ex-husband used to occupy when he lived with them, and something about the realization bothered her. A lot. So, not sure why she did it, Naomi jumped up and moved herself to that spot instead, indicating that their guest should take the seat she'd just vacated. He did so without question, and she passed him the food—or what was left of it, once her daughters had finished filling their plates.

As was the Carmichael tradition around the dinner table—and, unlike many families, Naomi made sure they all sat down to a meal together at least five nights a week, even if it sometimes meant eating late—the

girls launched into rapid-fire discussions of their respective days. Naomi asked the usual questions about
school and homework and extracurricular activities,
the girls gave the usual answers, and all in all, everything was exactly as it should be, exactly as it always
was.

Well, except for the drop-dead gorgeous man sitting in their midsts. But other than that...

Not once did Mr. Sullivan interject a word into the
dinner conversation, but Naomi wasn't sure if that
was because he didn't find the subject matter interesting, or he simply felt too intimidated by the tight-
knit Carmichael crew to wade in among them. Somehow, she suspected it was the latter, though, because
he did smile several times during the course of the
conversation at something one of them said. And once
or twice, she caught him looking as if he wanted to
say something, but stopping himself before he did, as
if he were unsure of his reception.

After dinner, Naomi assigned the girls their usual
cleanup tasks, asked Evelyn to put Sophie down for
the night, then, with coffee cups in hand, she and Mr.
Sullivan retreated to the living room to discuss roundball strategy. Funnily enough, though, what they
ended up talking about was something else entirely.
After a moment or two of idle chitchat—thanks again
for your help this month, Mr. Sullivan, and how do
you take your coffee?—the conversation turned
abruptly to the personal, though that was thanks to
Mr. Sullivan himself.

"I couldn't help noticing as we drove here," he said, "that you and your family live much closer to a different high school from the one where you teach and they attend class. How come the three of you don't take advantage of the closer one?"

Thinking the question a legitimate one, Naomi shrugged and offered her standard answer. "Jackson High is where I happened to find a job four years ago, when I returned to teaching. And I like teaching at Jackson," she hastened to add, because people tended not to believe her on that score, even though she was being perfectly honest when she made the assertion. "When the girls were old enough to go to junior high and high school, it just made sense to enroll them at Jackson with me. Sophie attends preschool near the house, and after we drop her off in the morning, the rest of the girls and I all ride to school together. And, of course, we can ride home together, too. It works very well, especially since I have such a hectic schedule."

"And Mr. Carmichael?" her guest asked. "Is his work not convenient to the school nearer your home?"

The question sounded perfectly innocent—and was perfectly understandable—coming on the heels of her response to his first question. For some reason, though, Naomi got the feeling that there was something more Mr. Sullivan wanted to know about than her ex-husband's contribution, if any, to their family life.

Nevertheless, she replied, likewise honestly, "I have no idea where Mr. Carmichael works these days, or if he works at all. I haven't heard from him in years."

Naomi must not have been as good at keeping the bitterness out of her voice as she'd hoped to be, because her guest had been lifting his cup to his mouth as she spoke, but halted the movement abruptly enough when she concluded that some of the coffee sloshed over and into his lap. His blue eyes widened in response to the coffee's temperature—because surely that wasn't incredulity she saw there—and, with his free hand, he hastily began to brush at the small stain that dampened his sweats.

"I, uh, I see," he said, clearly uncomfortable with this new turn of conversation. "So, then, I, uh… I mean, I guess he's not, um… He isn't, ah… He's not, uh…"

"Here," Naomi finished eloquently, taking pity on Mr. Sullivan for the second time in one night. How strange, taking pity on someone whose lifestyle was, she was certain, infinitely easier than her own. "No. He's not," she added. "Here, I mean."

Her guest nodded, but said nothing.

Naomi expelled a soft sound of resignation. "I'm divorced, Mr. Sullivan. I haven't seen or spoken to my ex-husband for over four years now. He even pays his child support through his attorney."

"But Sophie—" he said, cutting himself off immediately when he must have realized he was prying.

"I'm sorry," he immediately apologized. "It's none of my business."

Naomi sighed again. "Look, it's not a big deal. Evelyn, Katie and Ginny, obviously, were old enough to know what was going on. Or, at the very least, to know something was wrong between me and Sam. I don't like to talk about it in front of Sophie, though. Her father left right after I discovered I was pregnant with her. She never knew him."

Naomi inhaled a deep breath and released it slowly, wondering how much she should say about her past to this man she had just met, this man she would only know temporarily, even if they would be working closely together over the next four weeks. Finally, though, she heard herself telling him, "Our marriage had been rocky for a while. Then, one night, Sam decided not to come home. He served me with divorce papers shortly thereafter. I signed them without hesitation, because I knew it was pointless to try to get him back. Frankly, at that point, I didn't want him back. Evelyn, Katie and Ginny helped me a lot with Sophie after she was born, and the five of us have been a very tight-knit group ever since. The last I heard, Sam was living in Atlanta, where he had been doing most of his work, anyway. I don't hear from him. Ever. End of story."

Sloan Sullivan seemed not to know what to say in response to so matter-of-fact a tale about the decline of an American family. Finally, though, he smiled halfheartedly and told her, "You don't have to call me Mr. Sullivan, you know. Call me Sloan. We are going to be working together, after all.''

Naomi smiled sadly, but with heartfelt gratitude. ''Thanks,'' she said, hoping he knew her appreciation was for a lot more than just the first-name basis thing. Then her smile grew happier. ''And you,'' she added, ''can call me Coach.''

He laughed at that. ''Will do. Coach.''

The tension seemed to ebb after that, but they still didn't talk all that much about basketball. Instead, Naomi found herself answering questions. About how long she had been coaching—four years. About what had brought her to coaching in the first place—she had loved playing center for her high school and college teams. And about how she managed to juggle coaching, teaching and raising four daughters—not especially well, quite frankly, seeing as how she was organizationally challenged.

What was even stranger, though, was that Naomi didn't mind answering all of Sloan's questions. Normally, she was wary around men. Not just because of the difficult years with her ex-husband, but because, growing up, she'd always been taller than the rest of the boys, lanky and not particularly feminine. As a result, she'd intimidated most of the boys she'd known, and none had ever been interested in her. She hadn't dated much, hadn't had a real boyfriend until college. She had been a virgin on her wedding night, and she hadn't been with anyone since her ex-husband.

She just wasn't comfortable around men, unless they were talking about sports with her. Which, of course, she and Sloan were. But they were also touching on the personal, and that was something Naomi always strove to avoid with the opposite sex.

With Sloan, though... For some reason, she just didn't mind speaking frankly about such things. She didn't mind talking about herself or her past. Maybe because she knew that, with him being the kind of man he was, there was no way he'd ever be interested in her. So, in a sense, she was simply making friends with him. And hey, who couldn't use a friend now and then, right?

"What about you?" she finally said, when she began to grow tired of talking about herself.

He seemed surprised by the change of subject. "What about me?" he echoed.

"Are you married?" she asked bluntly. "Have any kids?"

He shook his head vehemently. "No. I've never been married. Never had the time," he added with an embarrassed smile. "And I can't honestly see myself with children. I'm not good with kids. Especially young ones."

Naomi found his response strange. Not only had Sloan interacted surprisingly well with all the girls at practice that evening, but she'd also seen how good he'd been with Sophie earlier. He'd seemed very comfortable in his association with her, had been in no way condescending or anxious or reserved, the way people without children so frequently were around kids—preschoolers especially. Still, she didn't call him on it. He must have his reasons for feeling the way he did. However erroneous those feelings might be.

"My work takes up a good part of my life," he told her. "I really don't have time for a family."

"You might be surprised how much time you could take from your work and still get things done," she said pointedly. "You just have to choose your priorities and put those first."

He nodded. "I agree completely. And I've made my work my first priority."

"Fair enough," she said. "At least you're honest with yourself. And others. A lot of men…" She stopped herself before saying anything more. She really didn't want to sound bitter. She wasn't bitter, she assured herself. Just…wary. That was all.

"A lot of men what?" Sloan asked.

She shrugged, but there was nothing casual in the gesture. "A lot of men make their work their first priority, but swear that it's really their family that comes first," she finally said. "Then they delude themselves into thinking that, because they're good providers in the financial arena, then they must be good fathers, and that's all that's important, and everything is fine, and it doesn't matter that they're never home, and never have anything to do with their families at all, and that they've actually assigned their family to last place instead of first."

Sloan said nothing for a moment, then, very softly, he asked, "Is that what happened in your marriage?"

Naomi told herself to change the subject again, that this was something that was not only none of his business, but also something she had no desire to discuss—with Sloan or anyone. Then she realized she was the one who'd started it, the one who'd brought it up in the first place, and that, too, seemed very unlike her.

In spite of all of her misgivings, though, and for some strange reason she didn't want to ponder at the moment, she heard herself telling him, "Maybe. My husband was a general contractor, and that meant he worked long hours, late hours, weekend hours. Even when he was home, he always seemed to be holed up in the office on the phone. We hardly ever saw him. He was never here—physically or emotionally. There were times when I found myself thinking he took on more work specifically because he didn't *want* to come home."

Sloan seemed to be genuinely puzzled by the comment. "Why wouldn't he want to come home to such a beautiful family?"

Naomi smiled indulgently at his remark. She and the girls weren't unattractive, she knew. But neither were any of them, save perhaps Katie, anything remotely resembling "beautiful." Her daughters were handsome. Striking. Had classic good looks. But even Naomi knew better than to consider them "beautiful." Beautiful suggested flowing blond locks, lush, womanly curves, and dainty, fragile dispositions. Her daughters, to a girl, were tall, dark, slender and strong. And as for Naomi, well… There were days when she didn't even feel strong anymore.

Still, she felt obligated to respond to Sloan's question. "If you must know," she began, "I don't think Sam was ever comfortable in the company of so many females."

"What?" Sloan asked, sounding honestly incredulous. "How can a man feel uncomfortable around women? That makes no sense."

Oh, he would feel that way, she thought. A man like Sloan could no doubt charm the socks—and more—off of any woman he chose. He seemed the epitome of the term *ladies' man.*

"Sam was a real man's man," Naomi said. "Very athletic, very car-oriented, fascinated with heavy machinery, that kind of thing. If the girls and I ever needed to go shopping, we'd drop him in the Sears tool department and know we could come back three hours later, and he'd still be happily browsing, or buying, or just talking metal shop with the guys."

Although Naomi didn't tell Sloan, she also knew that Sam's manly manliness was what had caused him to marry her in the first place. She was, in essence, one of the guys—therefore, he could always be comfortable with her, when he considered the majority of women to be alien creatures. But as the years went by, and he gradually found himself saddled with three daughters in addition to a wife, he'd begun to feel as if he were drowning in estrogen. He'd simply stopped feeling comfortable in his own home. And then, when Naomi had gotten pregnant that fourth time—unexpectedly—Sam had begun to fear that another pair of X chromosomes would be invading his turf. So he had left. All of them.

"He just wasn't comfortable around so many women," Naomi abbreviated. "And he spent as little time at home as possible as a result."

"But Sophie," Sloan objected again. "Surely, if he'd known you were pregnant with her, he wouldn't have—"

"Sam knew about Sophie," Naomi said quietly. "When I told him I was expecting again—it came as something of a surprise to both of us—he asked me to terminate the pregnancy. I refused. But the possibility of having another daughter, to him, was—" Naomi inhaled deeply and released it slowly, hoping the bitterness would leave with it "—unacceptable," she finally finished. "So he took off."

Sloan studied her in silence for a moment, then, "Oh," he said, very softly.

Naomi nodded. "Yeah. Oh," she agreed. "Now you know why I really don't like to talk about Sam in front of Sophie."

An awkward moment of silence ensued, until the clock on the mantelpiece began to chime. *One, two, three,* Naomi counted mentally. *Four, five six...* On and on it went, until twelve chimes had sounded.

"Good God, is that the time?" Sloan asked, glancing first at the clock, then down at his watch. "Midnight? But how can it already be midnight? I feel like I just got here."

Chapter 5

Naomi was no less surprised by the hour than he, though she didn't feel as if Sloan had just gotten there. No, in many ways, it seemed as if eons had passed since she'd said hello to him earlier that evening, because it had felt so comfortable having him here in her home. She felt as if she'd had him here on a number of occasions already, and that the two of them were simply indulging in a regular, weekly ritual.

Funny, that, she couldn't help thinking. Normally, she didn't warm up to people so quickly. And she couldn't remember the last time she'd entertained anyone in her home with whom she had felt such an immediate sense of kinship. Certainly she'd never discussed the details of her marriage with someone she'd known such a short time. With Sloan, however, talking about her past—talking about so many things—hadn't felt awkward at all.

"Gosh, I am really sorry," she said, rising from the chair where she had parked herself for what she now realized had been hours. They'd finished their coffee long ago, and neither had expressed a desire for more. Their conversation, however, had obviously flowed quite freely. "I didn't mean to keep you so late."

"It isn't your fault," he replied, mimicking her gesture, pushing himself to standing. "I had no idea it was nearing midnight. When did that happen?"

Although it was true that the girls had all come in to say their good-nights a while ago, Naomi hadn't noted the time then, nor had she marked its passage since. And neither, evidently, had Sloan. Honestly, she couldn't remember the last time she'd lost track of the hour this way, but they'd been talking so companionably—and it had been so nice to talk to someone her own age for a change, she couldn't help thinking further—that she just hadn't been paying attention.

"You have a long drive back to Atlanta," she observed. Not that she was willing to offer him an alternative, mind you. She was just making an observation, that was all.

"It's not a problem," he assured her mildly. "I've had late drives home before."

Oh, she'd just bet he had—much later than this

one, no doubt. She'd wager Sloan had women all over the metro Atlanta area, and that most of his women kept him in their homes well past midnight. Not that she considered herself one of Sloan's women, of course. But she'd bet good money that most of the women he spent the evening with turned out to be women he spent the night with. And probably not a single one of them was sharing her roof with four other females besides. Not unless there was some pret-ty kinky stuff going on. Stuff that Naomi would just as soon not ponder, thank you very much.

"Can I help you clean up?" he asked, surprising her. First of all, men didn't usually offer to do something like that, and second, he had a long drive home. Why would he want to make his departure later than it already was?

She shook her head. "There's not much left. The girls took care of most of it. You go on."

For one scant, strange moment, neither of them moved or spoke, as if they weren't quite sure what they were supposed to say or do. Sloan just stood in front of the couch, where he'd been sitting, and Naomi just stood in front of the chair she'd occupied herself. And in that scant, strange moment, she was overcome by the oddest sensation that something was supposed to happen, that one of them was supposed to do something very specific—she had no idea what. And then the moment was gone, and she was extending her hand toward the front door, in a silent indication that he should use it.

"Well, I guess I'll see you again on Thursday," she said, suddenly feeling awkward and nervous for no reason she could name. "Maybe next time we can get to that strategizing we somehow never got to tonight."

"We didn't, did we?" he said, seeming as perplexed by the realization as she. "Thursday then, for sure."

"You can stay for dinner again, if you'd like," Naomi heard herself offer, even though she'd never formed the invitation consciously in her head.

"I would like that," he said, surprising her yet again. "I'd like it a lot."

Naomi nodded once. "Fine. I promise not to keep you as late next time."

He started to say something else, went so far as to open his mouth to form the words. But he must have had second thoughts, because he closed it again before uttering a sound. He took a few steps toward the front door, then stopped and turned around to look at her. Naomi had started to follow him, but had been looking down at her feet instead of at him, and therefore wasn't paying attention when he came to a halt. Not until she ran right into him, anyway. Not until she felt his hands on her upper arms, steadying her to keep her from stumbling backward.

Hastily, she glanced up, only to find him gazing down at her, and she was overcome by the realization that never in her life had any man ever looked down at her this way. Never had she had to actually tip her head backward to meet a man's eye. But Sloan Sullivan was a large enough specimen that he made Naomi feel almost pint-size in relation. It was an unsettling feeling, acknowledging that a man was so much bigger than she was. But, strangely, it wasn't an altogether unpleasant one.

No, not unpleasant at all.

"I—I—I…I'm sorry," she stammered, confused by the keen heat that spilled through her midsection at the way he towered over her. "I, ah, I guess I wasn't looking where I was going."

She thought he would release her then, but he didn't right away. Instead, he only hesitated a little, loosening his grip on her some, but not quite letting go. "Are you okay?" he asked.

Naomi nodded, not sure she trusted herself to say anything more. By now, the heat that had spread through her abdomen was moving outward, seeping into every extremity, pooling deep in her belly, warming parts of her that hadn't felt warm for a very long time. Too long a time. Way too long a time.

"I'm fine," she finally managed to reply. And she hoped he didn't notice how weak and quiet her voice suddenly sounded.

For another brief moment, he continued to hold her, and then—almost reluctantly, it seemed—he released her. He took another few steps toward the front door—moving backward this time, so that he could continue to look at her—and said, "Let's definitely talk basketball Thursday night. You could fill me in on the year thus far, the girls' strengths and weaknesses, that kind of thing. I feel like I'm coming in to this thing so cold."

That's funny, Naomi thought. *I'm feeling kind of warm myself.*

Aloud, though, she only said, "Um, fine. That would be, ah, fine. You're right. There's a lot we need to go over."

He nodded, but said nothing more, only kept walking backward until his backside hit the front door. Still looking at Naomi, he reached behind himself for the doorknob, turned it, and opened the door. But he seemed reluctant to step through it, seemed as if there were still something very important he wanted to tell her.

But all he did was lift a hand in farewell and then tell her, "Good night. See you Thursday."

"Good night," Naomi replied automatically. And before she could stop herself, she added, "Be careful driving home."

She had no idea why she tagged that final admonition onto her goodbye the way she did. It was the kind of thing she usually would have said to her daughters. Be careful. Because she cared about what happened to them, obviously.

But, then, why wouldn't she care about Sloan, too? she asked herself. It was only natural. He was a nice man. Not to mention her temporary assistant coach. She needed him. At least for the next month. Of course she cared.

Nevertheless, as she, too, raised her hand in farewell and watched Sloan smile, repeat his good-night, and pass through the front door, closing it behind himself, Naomi knew her caring stemmed from a lot more than anything basketball related. And that, she decided, couldn't possibly be a good thing.

Could it?

That, Sloan thought as he backed his car out of Naomi Carmichael's driveway and into the street, *was a very odd encounter.* And for a variety of reasons, too, he couldn't help thinking further as he maneuvered his way back through her neighborhood and "downtown"—oh, that really was a quaint way to think of it—Wisteria, toward the state road that had brought him here to begin with. Once he left the outskirts of town completely, he was swallowed by the darkness, the black ribbon of two-lane highway bisecting the even blacker night. Clouds obscured whatever light might have shone from the moon and stars, and the headlights of his roadster illuminated nothing but more darkness up ahead.

Sloan felt almost as if he were the last man on earth. A little more than forty-five minutes lay between him and his Buckhead town house, but he was reluctant to turn on the car stereo. Somehow, the silence was much more welcome. And certainly more conducive to thinking, of which, Sloan figured, he had a lot to do. So he drove on in silence and thought about the evening he had just spent with Naomi and her daughters, and how very odd the whole occasion had been.

The first reason why it had been odd was because he didn't normally visit anyone who had children. Especially four of them. Especially ranging in age from four to sixteen. Few members of Sloan's social circle were even married, let alone procreating. He wasn't ever around children, ergo he wasn't ever comfortable with them. Ergo, he should have felt wholly *un*comfortable in the Carmichael home, surrounded as he had been, by such utterly alien creatures. But he hadn't felt uncomfortable at all. On the contrary, all of the Carmichaels had made him feel quite welcome. And it hadn't just been the children who were alien, he thought further. Because Naomi, too, was unlike any other woman he had ever met.

Which brought him to the second reason why his encounter had been so odd. Simply put, Sloan didn't generally spend hours talking to women. Certainly he'd never *lost track* of those hours by talking. No, he spent hours doing other things with women—he'd even lost track of hours doing those other things with women—but never talking. He only talked extensively to women who were his co-workers—though he *didn't* lose track of the time in those cases. And with his women co-workers, he had no desire whatever to do those other things he might spend hours— and losing track of the time—doing with another woman. With Naomi Carmichael, however, who was, in a sense a co-worker...

Well, suffice it to say that, at some point during the evening—Sloan wasn't sure when, exactly—he'd realized that talking wasn't the only thing he wouldn't mind doing with her.

Enter odd reason number three. Sloan just didn't go for women like Naomi. Ever. He dated women who were ultrafeminine, ultra-attentive to their physical appearance, ultrasuccessful in their chosen fields, and ultra-aware of him as a man. He did not go for women who were nearly as tall—and every bit as athletic—as he was, or women who favored a wardrobe of sweats—even when entertaining guests in their homes—or women who worked in less-than-desirable surroundings—like Jackson High School— or women who seemed no more aware of him as a man than they were aware of the living room carpet as a man.

Not once had Naomi Carmichael offered Sloan any sort of come-hither come-on this evening, yet in spite of that, he'd been more than a little aware of her as a woman. In fact, he'd been very aware of her as a woman. Too aware. Even though she didn't seem to be aware of her own womanhood at all herself. Even though she'd been dressed almost identically to him. Even though she pulled in an income that was only a fraction of his own. Even though she was someone's mom. *Four* someones' mom. The realization of such things hadn't swayed him at all in finding her very attractive.

Stranger still was the fact that she had revealed to him such personal things about herself and her past—

and that Sloan had *encouraged* her to reveal such personal things—and he hadn't once felt uncomfortable
during the exchange. Which, he thought, pretty much
amounted to odd reason number four.

Comfort, he reflected again. That was what it all
seemed to come back to. He had just been comfortable in a place, and with people, and in a situation,
where he *should* have felt remarkably *un*comfortable.
But he hadn't felt uncomfortable at all. What was
likewise curious was that now that Sloan had felt the
comfort of the Carmichael home, he realized how
much comfort had been missing in his own. Even his
own home, after years in residence there, hadn't ever
felt as comfortable to him as one evening spent in the
home occupied by Naomi and her daughters.

Wherein lay odd reason number five.

Even after knowing her a matter of hours, Sloan
realized that, simply put, he liked Naomi. He liked
her a lot. He also liked her daughters. He couldn't
imagine what kind of an idiot her husband must have
been to have left such a family behind. Ah, well, he
thought further. Who was he to try to understand the
mysterious behavior of others, when his own was
nothing short of bizarre?

It was going to be an interesting month, he couldn't
help thinking further. And for some reason, he suddenly found himself looking forward to lending a
hand to the Lady Razorbacks. He only hoped he could
stop at a hand. Especially when so many of his other
body parts seemed to be so interested in their coach.

Oh, yes. An interesting month indeed.

Chapter 6

Thursday evening was an almost identical repeat of the previous Tuesday, right down to little Sophie's wanting to introduce Sloan to more very useful engines—which, he had to admit, he enjoyed immensely. He hadn't played with trains—or any other toy, for that matter—since he was a boy, and he'd forgotten how much fun it could be to just lose a little time, a little reality, playing make-believe. Games of pretend were such a big part of little lives, he reminded himself. And it was just too bad that, when their lives got "big," people tended to forget about the importance of things like that. Sophie, though, was remarkably adept at reminding Sloan of a lot of the things he should remember.

All of the Carmichael girls were, really, he realized

very quickly. Evy and Katie's single-minded focus on basketball reminded Sloan of what it was like to choose a goal and pursue it relentlessly until it was achieved. He hadn't done anything like that himself since college. His goals always seemed to change from one day to the next, and he often abandoned one goal before achieving it because another came along that seemed more important. Then he'd abandon that goal, too, for something else that took his fancy. In fact, he couldn't recall the last time one thing had been more important to him than anything else in the world. And Ginny's breathless preoccupation with boys reminded Sloan what it was like to fall in love for the very first time. And the second time. And the third time. And how every single time seemed to be more passionate and unbearable than the time before.

Even by that second night, the Carmichael women were already getting under his skin, he thought, as he watched them all abandon their places at the dinner table to move into what looked like a well-orchestrated evening tradition of cleanup and homework rituals. And as the younger Carmichaels retreated to their respective roles, Sloan and Naomi once more retreated to the living room to enjoy coffee and conversation. In fact, the only difference tonight over Tuesday night was that when Sloan once more found himself seated in Naomi's very comfortable living room with a very comfortable Naomi, *he* was the one who ended up imparting bits of himself and his past to *her*. As the evening wore on and the coffee ran out, they once again forgot about talking basketball strategy and the conversation instead took a turn for the personal. Sloan's personal.

He told her about growing up in Atlanta, but he found himself skirting the subject of his family. It wasn't that he was ashamed of them—on the contrary, he was proud of his parents' and his younger brother's accomplishments and status, and his own, in the community. But somehow, Sloan wasn't comfortable—there was that word again—discussing his family's wealth and prominence with Naomi, who seemed to be struggling, though succeeding fairly well, just to get by. Too, he honestly didn't think his own background and family made for conversation that was all that interesting. So instead he focused vaguely on his childhood and education, less generally on his decision to go into law, and more specifically on the job he performed now.

And, much to his delight, he did uncover a few more things about Naomi, too—but only because he had to consciously turn the topic of conversation to her whenever she seemed intent on steering it back to him. He learned about her own upbringing in a small town in South Carolina, about her three older brothers—no sisters—about how she'd lost her mother to cancer when she was six, and about how she couldn't deny that much of her athleticism had come about not just because she was so surrounded by males while growing up, but also because she wanted to keep herself as healthy as possible—especially now, so that her girls wouldn't experience a loss as deep as her own.

And as Sloan listened to her talk, he realized something very important about Naomi Carmichael. She was a doer. A doer and a get-doner. And she relied on no one—no one but herself—to do and get done. And although he couldn't help but admire the quality, something about it being so present in Naomi bothered him more than he wanted to admit. Because suddenly, he kind of liked the idea of lending a hand, and not just to the Lady Razorbacks.

Which was crazy, he told himself. Not only did Naomi clearly not welcome such things into her personal life, but she wasn't a woman suited to him. And even if she had been a woman suited to him, she had four—*four*—children. No matter which way a man looked at it, there was just no getting around that. Whatever strange attraction he might be feeling for her—and the attraction was, most definitely, strange—it was totally out of character for him, and, he knew, utterly temporary.

He reminded himself that in a month's time, his obligation to Naomi and the Lady Razorbacks would be over. He would have no reason to come to Wisteria, and over time, this strange attraction would go away. If he acted on it, it would only make things more difficult when the time came to tell Naomi goodbye. And it would distract them both from the matter which had brought them together in the first place—coaching a basketball team that was poised for the state championship.

Not that Naomi had offered any strong indication that she would welcome any acting on his part, anyway, Sloan reminded himself further. Still, he couldn't deny that there was *some*thing buzzing in the air between them. He had no idea what, precisely, it was. But he could tell from the way he caught her looking at him sometimes that Naomi felt it, too. Even if she was as unwilling to act upon it as he was.

Which, of course, was good, he told himself. Because he was unwilling to act on it, too. And that was why, in the days and evenings and weeks that followed, Sloan made damned sure he kept his attraction to Naomi to himself. Nevertheless, in the days and evenings and weeks that followed, it somehow became a custom for Sloan to have dinner at the Carmichael home after each Tuesday and Thursday night practice. And also, in the days and evenings and weeks that followed, somehow—and Sloan honestly had no idea how—his attraction to Naomi only multiplied.

He told himself after each of their encounters that he only imagined the magnitude of his fascination with her. And then, just about the time he started believing himself in that regard, he would see Naomi again. And the fascination would be there once more, stronger than ever, mocking him.

It made no sense. Here was a woman he saw primarily during athletic encounters, during which time they were both dressed in ragged workout clothes, and during which time they both did a lot of yelling and sweating, yet every time he saw her, the pull Sloan felt for her grew a little bit stronger, a little bit tighter, a little bit more urgent. She was just so strong, so commanding, so admirable. There was no way a man could ever *not* find her fascinating. But there was no way—no way—Sloan could allow himself to act on that fascination.

No matter how badly he might want to.

Finally, though, on their last night coaching together—the Lady Razorbacks' regular assistant coach would return to his duties the following week, just in time for the start of the state tournament—Sloan felt like he had to do *some*thing. His time with Naomi was almost over, he reminded himself. There would be no reason for him to come back to Wisteria, though he did have every intention of attending the tournament games to see how the girls fared. He had to. Not just because he had a vested interest in their performance, but because he'd become rather attached to several of them. Especially, he couldn't help thinking, the Carmichael girls.

So, as had happened on every previous Tuesday or Thursday night over the past four weeks, on the final Thursday night of Sloan's coaching duties, four weeks after that first Tuesday night, he ended up staying much too late at Naomi's house. Because, as had been the case on all the evenings that had come before it, the conversation and the surroundings—and the company—were just too appealing for him to conjure the desire to leave. Finally, though, reluctantly, he did make himself get up off of the sofa and head for the front door. But not before finalizing plans he felt it necessary for both of them to make.

"So, what are you doing this weekend?" he asked as he pulled open the front door, preparing to leave.

Obviously perplexed by the question, Naomi arrowed her dark eyebrows downward and studied him with much confusion. "This weekend?" she echoed.

He nodded. "Yeah, I thought maybe the two of us could get together this weekend and talk about the team and the tournament," he reminded her. "I mean, I know your regular assistant coach is coming back next week for the tourney, but until then, I still feel like I need to contribute something."

"Oh," she replied, still sounding a little puzzled. Then, before Sloan could suggest a place for them to meet, she hurried on, "I, ah, I—I can't do this weekend. I, um, I have a…uh, a…um, a thing. A thing that I, um…that I need to go to."

Sloan eyed her warily, wondering at her sudden attack of nerves. Over the last four weeks, he'd never seen her anything except cool, calm and collected—except, of course, for those few unguarded moments when he'd caught her gazing at him in a way that was warm, wanton and wistful. Why, suddenly, was she blushing and stammering and looking at everything in the room except him?

"A thing?" he repeated dubiously.

She nodded quickly, and, he couldn't help thinking, not a little anxiously. "Yeah. A, ah…a thing. This weekend. I have a definite, um, thing. To go to, I mean. A really important thing. A thing I can't get out of." Seemingly as an afterthought, she added, "I'm sorry."

Sloan told himself not to take it to heart, the fact that she was so obviously giving him the brush-off. Clearly, she had no *thing*. Clearly, what she *did* have was a reluctance to see him in any capacity other than the one she'd seen him in for the last month. She was trying to tell him politely that she didn't want to see him outside the realm of coaching, even if, ostensibly, the whole point to getting together would be to discuss coaching. He told himself to be big about it and let her off the hook. For some reason, though, he couldn't let it go that easily.

Feeling playful—and boy, before making Naomi's acquaintance, had it been a long time since Sloan had felt playful—he asked, "What kind of thing?"

Her eyes widened in panic at the question. "Um, you know, a…a thing."

"An important thing," he said, recalling her earlier, if vague description, and trying not to smile at how easily he'd cornered her, and at how uncomfortable she became when she was cornered. This could potentially be a lot of fun. And man, it had been a long, long time since Sloan had had a lot of fun. Then again, he reflected, he'd had a lot of fun over this last month, hadn't he? With all the Carmichael women, come to think of it. But before that, he couldn't remember the last time he'd had any *real* fun.

"Right," she told him. "An important thing. A really important thing."

"And where, exactly, is this important thing to be held?" he asked. "Here in Wisteria?"

She seemed to give the question some thought— for a full two or three seconds, at least, Sloan noted— then shook her head quickly. "No, not here in town. Somewhere else."

"Where?" he persisted.

Looking more panicked with every passing second, she told him, "It's, um, it's much too far. It's in, uh… It's in, um… It's ah…Atlanta," she finally told him. "I have a thing in Atlanta."

Immediately after saying it, she must have realized her faux pas, because she squeezed her eyes shut tight in obvious distress. Sloan smiled devilishly, knowing her reaction came about because she realized she had just played right into his hands. And it was with no small effort that he kept himself from laughing outright.

"Really?" he said with much interest. "Atlanta? Well, you'll be right in my backyard. This is perfect. We can meet for dinner with no problem. In fact," he added, hoping he wasn't laying it on too thick, "I just remembered I have a thing this weekend, too. Maybe it's close to where your thing is."

She eyed him *very* suspiciously at that.

"Really," he said. "I have a thing this weekend."

And in that moment, he made definite plans to have a thing that very weekend, just so he wouldn't be lying to her. Unlike *some* people he knew. "What day is your thing?"

She narrowed her eyes some more. "Saturday?" she said.

He expelled a sound of utter incredulity. "Mine, too," he told her, doing his absolute best not to do or say anything that might spoil his total solemnity. "Wow. That really is a coincidence. So where exactly in Atlanta is your thing going to be?" he asked further.

She parted her lips fractionally, as if she wanted to say something, but had no idea what. "Well, where's *your* thing?" she asked, turning the tables.

Sloan pulled a site out of thin air. "At the Four Seasons Hotel," he told her.

She nodded with—dare he say it?—relief. "Oh, see, that'll be a problem, because my thing is on the other side of town, at the San Moritz."

Hoping he *really* wasn't pouring it on too thick now, Sloan opened his hand and smacked his palm resolutely against his forehead. "That's what I meant to say. The San Moritz. I always get that mixed up with the Four Seasons. But what I meant to say was the San Moritz. That's where my thing is, too." He smiled. "We must be going to the same thing."

Naomi continued to eye him with much suspicion, but she didn't say a word. Oh, she opened her mouth to do so—several times, in fact—but no words ever actually emerged.

"So what's your thing?" Sloan asked mischievously.

She smiled—devilishly, if he wasn't mistaken, something that made his own smile fall a bit. "It's a meeting of the Clemson University Alumni, Georgia chapter," she told him smugly. "Guess we're not going to the same thing after all, since you went to Vanderbilt."

Oh, he wasn't going to let her off that easily. "Still," he said, "since we're both going to be at the San Moritz on Saturday, we might as well get together. Do they give you dinner at those things? The San Moritz has a great restaurant. I'll make us a reservation for seven, how will that be?"

Instead of replying to his question or suggestion, Naomi asked, "So what's your thing in Atlanta this weekend? You never did say."

This time it was Sloan's turn to open his mouth and have no words come to his aid. He struggled for several tense seconds, then smiled. "It's a reunion of sorts, too. I'm getting together with some old friends from high school. Future Estate Planners of America. FEPA." Then, before she had a chance to say a word, he hurriedly added, "The San Moritz Hotel, seven o'clock Saturday night. I'll see you then."

And as quickly as he could, Sloan hurried out the door and down the front walk to his car. Before she had a chance to call him on his ruse. Before she had a chance to say no. Before she had a chance to back out.

And before *he* had a chance to change his mind. Not that he would, he quickly realized. Because suddenly, he couldn't wait to see Naomi Carmichael again. Especially since, *this* time, it would be on *his* turf.

Chapter 7

"You look awesome, Mom."

Naomi gazed into the full-length cheval mirror
tucked into the corner of her bedroom and wondered
what on earth had possessed her to do this ridiculous
thing. But when she saw her reflection, she immediately had her answer. Obviously, it wasn't *her* doing
this ridiculous thing. No, the woman doing this ridiculous thing was a total stranger. Because the woman
in the mirror, although she bore a vague resemblance
to Naomi, clearly was *not* Naomi.

Instead of her usual sweats and or blue jeans, she
was dressed in a plain, long-sleeved, knee-length
cocktail dress with a modestly scooped neck, a garment she hadn't removed from her closet for years.
Smoky stockings hugged her legs, and her feet were

tucked into low-heeled black pumps. The only jewelry she wore were the pearl earrings her aunt Margery had given her for her high school graduation.

And it didn't stop there. Ginny had insisted that her mother *had* to wear makeup if she was going to be going someplace so nice, so she had given her mother a complete makeover which, instead of making Naomi look as if she'd just been hit by a Lancôme bomb, made her look as if the beauty fairies had visited her in the night and had smoothed out and perfected each of her facial features without cosmetic enhancement. Her eyes seemed larger and darker, her lashes longer, her mouth fuller, her cheekbones more prominent. Yet somehow Ginny had done it all without making Naomi look like a streetwalker.

Ginny had also acted as her fashion consultant, *tsk-tsk-tsk*ing at every article of clothing Naomi possessed until stumbling on the black dress at the very back of the closet. She'd had to dig for the earrings, too, but had been delighted once she'd discovered them—and not just because she intended to borrow them for the upcoming ninth-grade mixer.

Evelyn, however, was the daughter who had *insisted* that Naomi absolutely *had* to go to Atlanta tonight. She'd overheard the conversation between her mother and Sloan the Thursday before, and the moment the door had closed behind him, she had hurried into the living room to start making plans. Naomi had quickly cut her oldest daughter off, had insisted she was going to call Sloan the next morning and cancel their date, that she never should have agreed to see him in the first place, that he had caught her unawares, and she simply hadn't known what to say. She *had* known, though—and she still did—that going out socially with Sloan Sullivan would be a very bad idea. Because over the course of the last four weeks, she had begun to care about him way too much.

Every Tuesday and Thursday afternoon for the last month, she had found herself feeling as nervous with anticipation as a girl going out on her first date with a boy she'd had a crush on for years. She'd found herself wishing she could wear something other than sweats for their encounter, knowing full well that a little black cocktail dress like the one she wore now simply was not appropriate apparel for basketball practice. And as she'd watched him during practice, noting the fluid movement of his body and the rapt center of his concentration, she had grown more and more attracted to him physically.

Worse, as she'd watched him interact with her family, she'd grown more and more attracted to him emotionally. With every meal he'd shared with her and her daughters, she'd noted an easiness and camaraderie of spirit in him that few people—few men— would be able to manage when confronted by so many women. And she'd seen, too, how attached her daughters were becoming to Sloan. Especially Sophie, who craved attention and so seldom got enough. All of them, she thought now, craved attention from him in one way or another, attention that had been missing in all their lives for much too long.

Naomi also told herself now, as she had told herself all along, that she couldn't allow Sloan into her life—into their lives—any more than she already had. Because he was only a temporary addition. Very temporary. And she didn't want the void he would doubtless leave behind when he went to be any bigger than it already would be.

And although Naomi hadn't been able to tell Evy all of those things, she had assured her daughter that she couldn't—wouldn't—see Sloan socially. Evy, though, had made her promise that she would keep their appointment.

"You need this, Mom," she had told her mother. "You never get to go anywhere. And you and Mr. Sullivan get along so well together."

"But, Evy," Naomi had objected, "I can't drive all the way to Atlanta just to have dinner with a man."

"Why not?" her daughter had demanded. "This is perfect. You'll be in your own car, and you can leave whenever you want to. He's a nice man, Mom. A total hottie. I know you like him. And I can tell he likes you. And you never get to have any fun."

And that, Naomi had thought then, was the kicker. She really didn't ever get to have any fun. And Sloan was a nice man. Not to mention a total hottie. She did like him. And she knew he liked her. She just wasn't sure it was a healthy—or productive—kind of liking. Because it was only a temporary liking. Wasn't it?

Still, Atlanta wasn't that far away, she reminded herself. It might be fun to go out to eat with him, someplace nice. It was only dinner. And she would pay for her share so that she wouldn't feel indebted to him. And she and Sloan did get along well. And this could be a nice kind of conclusion to their— working—relationship.

Of course, there was that other relationship, she reminded herself. The one-sided one she'd created in her besotted brain. The one that had been generated by one fantasy after another over the last month, not all of them sexual in nature, though, certainly, there had been a few where she and Sloan had been—

Well. Involved in something other than coaching.

Oh, for heaven's sake, what was the harm? she asked herself, pushing her annoying thoughts away. There was little chance that Sloan was going to try anything funny. Although there had been one or two times over the last month when she'd looked up to find him watching her in ways that were…questionable…he'd really offered no indication that he was interested in her in any way other than a friendly one. As long as she could keep *herself* from jumping *his* bones and ravishing him shamelessly and doing something she'd regret later—and she was *pretty* sure she could keep herself from doing all those things— then what was the harm?

"Beat it, you guys," Evelyn said now to her sisters, scattering Naomi's thoughts once and for all. "Mom and I need to have a woman-to-woman talk before she goes out."

Well, that certainly sounded ominous, Naomi thought as she gathered up the few things that would fit into the little beaded purse Ginny had loaned her, an accessory that was roughly the size of a carpet fiber.

The other girls protested, but Evy stood firm. "Out, runts," she insisted, pointing at the bedroom door. "Now."

Grumbling, each of her three sisters obeyed. Evy closed the door behind them and leaned back against it, gazing at her mother as if she were about to lay down the law. If it hadn't been for her accelerated height, in her faded blue jeans and massive flannel shirt, her tattered ponytail caught high on the crown of her head, Evy could have passed for a girl much younger than sixteen. However, when she opened her mouth to speak, she sounded every one of her years. And then some.

Meeting her mother's gaze levelly, Evy said, "I hope you've left enough room in that purse for a condom."

Naomi gaped at her. It was, to say the least, not what she had expected to hear from her daughter. *"What?"* she said.

Evy pushed herself away from the door and crossed the room to stand in front of her mother, crossing her arms over her midsection as if she meant business.

"Look, Mom," she said gravely, "things have changed a lot since you were dating before. You have to practice safe sex now. And I also want you to know that if you don't want to come home tonight—"

"Evelyn!" Naomi gasped, jumping up off the bed and straightening to her full height, which was still a couple of inches taller than her daughter. "Of *course* I'll be coming home tonight. And I do *not* need to save room in my purse for a condom."

Boy, had times changed. Naomi remembered her aunt Margery telling her to always save room in her purse for a dime, in case a boy got fresh with her, and she needed to make a phone call for her father to come and get her. Now her daughter—her *daughter*—was telling her to be sure and pack a condom.

In response to Naomi's exclamation, Evy only smiled and shrugged. "Well, if, at some point in the evening, you decide that you *don't* want to come home tonight," she insisted, "just remember that I'll be here to keep an eye on things. Really, Mom. It's *so* not a big deal."

Spoken like a true sixteen-year-old, Naomi thought. A sixteen-year-old who had yet to even date a boy, let alone dabble in anything even remotely resembling sex. Basketball was Evy's passion, Evy's life, right now, and had been for years. She had no interest in dating. Which, of course, was just fine with Naomi. Still, her daughter's lack of socializing with the opposite sex hadn't exactly broadened Evy's horizons. Not that Naomi necessarily wanted them broadened, mind you, but she did worry sometimes that her daughter just didn't have a realistic view of the whole male-female dynamic.

Then again, that might not be such a bad thing, she couldn't help thinking.

"Oh, and just in case," Evy added. She reached behind herself, into her back pocket, and withdrew a small plastic packet, extending it toward her mother. "I really do think you should take a condom with you. You never know. Like I said, it's not a big deal."

Naomi gaped at her daughter again. "Where did you get that?" she demanded.

Evelyn lifted one shoulder and let it drop. "One of the girls at school."

Naomi bit her lower lip thoughtfully. She had known for some time now that this conversation would eventually take place. She'd just been hoping she could put it off for a bit longer, until Evelyn was, say…fifty or so.

"You have friends who are sexually active?" she asked, hoping she kept her voice casual, when in fact she felt like grabbing her daughter and locking her in the closet until she could have her fitted for a reasonably comfortable chastity belt.

"One or two," Evy said.

Well, at least she was being honest, Naomi thought. "And how do you feel about that?" she asked her daughter.

Evy gave her another one of those one-shouldered

shrugs and said, "Personally, I think it's kind of gross."

Oh, thank God, Naomi thought.

"But there is this guy in my chemistry class who's kinda hot," she continued.

Oh, dear…

"And I think he's interested in me," Evy continued.

Oh, no…

"But I don't think I'm near ready for anything physical, you know?" her daughter finished.

Naomi felt some measure of relief, but couldn't quite keep herself from pointing out, "A minute ago, you told me it's not a big deal."

"I meant for you," Evy said with a smile. "You do have four daughters, Mom. I figure you've done it at least four times. Probably more."

Naomi smiled back, then cupped her daughter's face gently in her hand. "It never stops being a big deal, Evy," she said softly. "Remember that. It is *always* a big deal. That's why you want to be in love when it happens. Because it *is* a big deal. Always."

Her daughter smiled back. "I'll remember that."

"I hope you do."

Evy glanced down at the condom she still held in her hand, and Naomi told herself not to panic that her daughter seemed so comfortable with the thing. "Guess you won't be needing this then, huh?" Evy asked.

Naomi smiled at her daughter again, but for some

reason, she couldn't quite bring herself to say no. Still, her lack of a response must have told Evy something, because she tucked the condom into her back pocket again.

"Are you going to give that back to the girl you got it from?" Naomi asked hopefully.

"Maybe I'll keep it as a reminder," Evy said. "I'll hang on to it for a while."

"A long while, I hope," Naomi said pointedly.

Evy laughed. "Yeah. I imagine it'll be a long while. I got basketball to think about."

So she did, Naomi thought. Would that Naomi had been able to keep her own thoughts on basketball for the last month, she wouldn't be in the strange position she was in now—a position she still couldn't believe she'd let herself be talked into.

Because she *had* let herself be talked into it—there was no way she could deny that. *Let* was the operative word here. She could have come clean with Sloan Thursday night and just told him he'd caught her in a lie, and that she'd just wanted to avoid seeing him socially, because it wasn't a good idea. He'd known she was lying anyway—any fool could tell that. And he'd deliberately maneuvered and manipulated the conversation until he had her right where he wanted her. Worse, Naomi had allowed him to maneuver and manipulate, fully knowing what he was trying to do. He'd finagled a way for them to be together, and she'd done nothing to stop him.

Why?

It was a question that had circled through her head for two days, and she was no closer to an answer now than she had been the first time she'd asked herself. She didn't know why she wanted to drive all the way to Atlanta, just to have dinner with Sloan. Even if he was nice and charming and interesting. Even if she did find him profoundly physically attractive. Even if he did make her feel things she hadn't felt for a very long time, things she had begun to think she would never feel again. Even if she hadn't been able to stop thinking about him since their first encounter.

Okay, so maybe she knew why she wanted to drive to Atlanta to have dinner with Sloan. Because she was lonely, and she found him attractive, and it had been a long, long time since she'd felt so comfortable with another human being. She still didn't think it was a very good idea. Because in spite of their attraction to each other, anything the two of them might undertake wasn't going to go anywhere. Sloan was a workaholic who lived in another town, a man who had infinitely more interest in taking on the stock market than he did in taking on a family. He was a man who could commit to nothing except his job. He'd made that totally clear to her that very first night.

But in spite of her little pep talk to herself, Naomi scooped up the little black beaded purse, smoothed a hand over the elegant black dress, and took one final look at herself in the mirror. Because, even knowing everything she did, she wanted to have dinner with Sloan Sullivan. It was only dinner, she promised herself. That was all. Dinner and a little conversation. It would be just like all those Tuesday nights and Thursday nights had been, except that the two of them would be in different surroundings. More romantic surroundings. More intimate surroundings. And they wouldn't be sharing the surroundings with four other people. No, the two of them would be *aaalll aloooone.*

Dinner, Naomi reminded herself forcefully. It was only dinner. And conversation. And then, for sure, she would come home. And then she would never see Sloan again. And then...

She sighed heavily. And then, she had no idea what she would do. She'd just have to take it one step at a time.

Chapter 8

When Sloan first caught sight of Naomi, he almost let his gaze wander right over her, so unexpected was her appearance. And it wasn't unexpected just because he had been fairly certain she would chicken out at the last minute and not come tonight. No, it was also unexpected because, when he finally did register her appearance, he at first didn't think the woman he was looking at was Naomi, because she just didn't look like herself tonight. No, tonight, she looked... She looked... She looked...

Wow. She looked...*wow*. In fact, she looked very, *very* wow.

He couldn't quite say what she had done to herself that made her look so different from the way she usually did, because, in truth, she didn't really look any different from the way she usually did. Except that, somehow, she looked totally different from the way she usually did.

Or something like that.

Her short, dark hair was the same as always—except different, in that she had tucked the curly tresses behind her ears, something that showed off her facial features more prominently than before. And her facial features looked the same as always—except different, in that her sooty eyes seemed larger, darker, sexier, somehow, and her full, lush mouth looked even tastier than it had before. Although she wasn't wearing her standard sweats, what she did have on was by no means revealing or provocative—well, not provocative in the traditional sense of the word, anyway—which shouldn't have made her look all that different from the way she usually looked. Except she did look different. Because the black dress hugged her curves with *much* affection, and due to its lack of decoration, it focused Sloan's attention back on her face, a face he hadn't realized, until this moment, was so beautiful.

Everything about Naomi tonight just seemed to have jumped up and yelled, "Hey, look at me! Do I look fabulous or what?" Because she did look fabulous. Extremely fabulous. In fact, she looked much too fabulous for Sloan's comfort and peace of mind.

But then, that was good, right? he asked himself. Because not only was it going to be a joy to gaze at her from the other side of the table, but now he could finally understand his attraction to her. Underneath all the sweat and sweat suit he'd seen of her so far, there was a woman. A womanly woman. Obviously, somehow, he'd known that all along, and that was why he hadn't been able to stop thinking about her since their initial meeting.

Because he *hadn't* been able to stop thinking about her since their initial meeting. No, she had pretty much consumed his thoughts—both conscious and unconscious—for the last month. And now he understood that that was because Naomi Carmichael was, quite clearly, a womanly—unforgettable—woman. A womanly woman who, he had to admit, seemed all the more feminine now because, over the past four weeks, he had seen her looking, well, not particularly feminine. Not especially womanly.

Tonight, though, she was most definitely womanly. And then some. Before now, he would have considered her a handsome woman with classic, elegant features. But tonight, through God alone knew what magic, she had become a raven-haired beauty. To put it mildly. And, tonight, he had her all to himself, on his own turf, where anything might happen. Anything at all.

Well, well, well.

When he realized how long he had been gazing at her without making an effort to attract her attention, Sloan rose from the table where the hostess had seated him and began to approach the front entrance where Naomi stood. But she must have sensed his motion—

or perhaps she had just sensed *him*—because, immediately, she turned her head toward him. She smiled when she saw him, but he could tell right away that she was nervous. Maybe even as nervous as he was himself.

And then he wondered why *he* was nervous. Sloan Sullivan was never nervous. Never. Especially around women. And Naomi, in particular, was a woman he shouldn't be nervous around. Because, hey, they were only friends, right? And they were only here to talk basketball. And they were only going to have dinner. Dinner and a little conversation. To discuss the strategy for the Lady Razorbacks in their upcoming tournament. Why should that make him feel nervous?

Oh, sure, Sullivan. Basketball. Strategy. Riiight.

That was why he had gone to such lengths to ensure that she would meet him here tonight, he told himself. That was why he had taken two hours to get ready beforehand. That was why he had insisted to the hostess that she seat them at a table well away from the main traffic area, where the lighting was low and romantic. And that was why, before he'd left home tonight, he had impulsively tucked a condom into his wallet.

That last action still had him wondering at himself. How on earth could he be anticipating—even subconsciously—that things between himself and Naomi would go anywhere beyond the dinner and conversation stage tonight? Or any other night, for that matter? She had four children, he reminded himself. She wasn't his type. Nor was she the type to go for some casual sexual encounter. Therefore that last little accessory he had added to his person tonight would be in no way necessary. In spite of that, he had packed it, anyway.

Just in case.

Wishful thinking? he wondered now. And if so, just what was he wishing for? Because he wasn't the kind of man to take advantage of a woman just to quell some physical urge. And even if he was, he wouldn't take advantage of a nice woman like Naomi Carmichael. And that, he reminded himself, was precisely what she was. A nice woman. She was what his grandfather Sullivan had always termed, ''The other kind of girl. The kind you marry.''

So just what, exactly, was Sloan thinking?

He pushed his troubling thoughts away for now, promised himself he *wouldn't* think, and focused instead on the vision of loveliness who approached him. She seemed to grow more nervous with every step she took toward him, which was only fair, Sloan had to conclude, because he grew more nervous with every step she took toward him, too.

''You look absolutely edible…uh, incredible,'' he quickly corrected himself as she came to a halt in front of him.

He saw right away that his slip of the tongue—or slip of the libido…whatever—made her even more nervous than she already was. Of course, it made him more nervous, too, among other things, so they were

still on equal footing—or some other body part—
there. She ran her gaze over him from head to toe,
silently evaluating his dark suit and white dress shirt,
and the discreetly patterned Hermés silk he'd taken a
full fifteen minutes to select from his eclectic—and
ample—assortment of neckties. Then she nodded her
head approvingly and grinned again.

"You look pretty edible...uh, incredible, yourself," she mimicked, smiling. "Is this the real you?"

He narrowed his eyes in puzzlement. "The real
me?" he echoed. "What do you mean?"

"I mean is this the way you usually look?" she
clarified. "Is this the type of thing you usually wear?
For work and—and the rest of your life, I mean."

"Oh. Yes," he said. "I guess it is. Certainly I'm
dressed like this more often than I'm dressed the way
I have been for practices. This is closer to the real me
than the other person you've seen."

She nodded, seeming to give his response much
thought. Then she gestured to her own clothing and
said, "This *isn't* the real me. I *never* dress like this.
I'm far more often dressed the way I am at practices.
That's the real me," she reiterated. "The one you've
seen up till now. This—" with a sweeping hand, she
indicated her apparel again "—is a total aberration."

Somehow Sloan got the impression that she really,
really, *really* wanted to emphasize that point very,
very, *very* strongly. So he nodded back and said, "I
see. Well, *both* versions of you are very nice to my
way of thinking."

The conversation stalled a bit there, and he found himself wondering what she was thinking, what *she* might be anticipating—even subconsciously—from the evening ahead. Had *she* tucked a condom into her purse, for instance? he wondered. Somehow, he thought not. Still, dressed as she was—and nervous as she was—he didn't think she was especially focused on basketball and tournament strategies, either.

It was going to be an interesting evening.

He gestured toward their table, mumbled a few meaningless words, and then turned and led her in that direction. Ever the gentleman, he pulled out the chair beside the one he had been occupying himself— suddenly, he didn't want to be sitting *across* from Naomi, but much rather preferred to sit *beside* her— then, when she was comfortable, he scooted her in. He resumed his seat, as well, then turned to her and realized he had no idea what to say. Fortunately, he was rescued from having to perform a thought process by the prompt appearance of their server, who inquired as to their drink preferences.

When he glanced over at Naomi, he noted that she appeared to be... Hmmm... Well, the word *flummoxed* came to mind most readily. Because she seemed to have no idea what she was supposed to say, in spite of the straightforwardness of the question. She opened her mouth, as if she intended to order, but no words emerged, as if she couldn't conjure what, exactly, it was that she wanted.

So, valiantly, Sloan stepped in and told their server,

"Why don't you bring the lady a champagne cock-tail?" There. That should do it. He hadn't met a woman yet who didn't like a champagne cocktail. "And I'll have a JWB and water with a twist."

The young man made a mental note of the order, nodded obsequiously and, like a good little waitron, promptly disappeared.

"Thank you," Naomi said when he was gone. "It's been so long since I've eaten in a nice restaurant, I couldn't remember what I like to have. Usually, when I go somewhere with friends, or even with the girls, I have a margarita, or an ice-cold bottle of Rolling Rock." She smiled, and something inside Sloan grew warm at seeing it. "Somehow, though, that just doesn't feel right in a place like this."

He smiled back, that warm something inside him spreading now to his every extremity. Wow. That felt really, really good. "Then you're long overdue for a night like this," he said. And somehow, as he said it, even he got the impression that he meant something other than dinner in a nice restaurant.

Naomi seemed to think so, too, because she reacted to the statement by blushing becomingly. She didn't seem offended, though, Sloan noted. So maybe the two of them weren't on *exactly* the same wavelength. Still, he could practically feel that little foil packet in his wallet starting to heat and hum against his chest.

"So," he said suddenly, hoping to quell that heating and humming—at least for now, "should I ask you how your alumni reunion is going, or do you just want to come clean and tell me you were lying about that?''

She expelled an anxious, though good-humored, little sound. "Gee, you didn't believe me?" she asked.

"Should I have?" he countered easily.

She eyed him thoughtfully. "I don't suppose it would do any good to insist I was telling the truth, would it?"

He shook his head. "No. It wouldn't. No more good than me telling you that *I* was being honest about *my* engagement."

She gaped comically. "You mean you weren't? How shocking."

He grinned back. "Yes, isn't it?"

She expelled a soft sigh of resignation, then folded her arms in front of her on the table and leaned forward a bit, as if she were about to impart a kernel of great wisdom. "I'm sorry I wasn't honest with you about that," she said softly.

Sloan mirrored her gesture, leaning in, as well, something that brought their foreheads almost to touching. And he took heart in the fact that she didn't pull back even the slightest bit when he crowded into her space that way. He also noticed that she smelled wonderful, of some faint, floral fragrance that was utterly tantalizing.

"Why weren't you honest?" he asked, just as softly.

She shrugged a little halfheartedly. "I don't know. I guess I just didn't think this was a good idea."

"This?" he echoed. "You don't think it's a good idea for us to get together this way and talk strategy for the team and the upcoming tournament? What kind of coach are you anyway?"

She met his gaze levelly, her dark lashes lowering just the slightest bit, something that lent an air of sultriness to her already seductive appearance. "Gosh, color me presumptuous," she said, "but I just can't quite convince myself that the reason we're here tonight is to talk Lady Razorbacks basketball."

He met her gaze unflinchingly, but felt as if he were being pulled down into dangerous depths the longer he looked at her this way. "Isn't that the reason we're here?" he asked.

She hesitated a moment before replying, "Is it?"

"I don't know," he said, still focusing on her eyes. And as he did, he felt the dangerous depths rising higher around him, virtually enveloping him, making him think how he really wouldn't mind so much drowning, as long as Naomi Carmichael was the one who was flooding him. "Why did *you* come to-night?" he asked further, his voice growing quiet as he posed the question.

She hesitated only a moment before countering deftly, "Why did you?"

He smiled. "I asked you first."

She smiled back. "And I asked you second."

Sloan studied her in silence for a moment more,

then, when he heard the soft strains of one of his favorite Gershwin tunes coming from the next room, he told her, "I came to dance."

Her smile fell some, and she arched her dark brows in surprise. "You what?"

"Dance," he repeated. He tilted his head toward the music, to draw her attention to it, too. "They're playing our song," he said with a playful grin.

"Our song?" she repeated. "I didn't realize we had a song."

"We do now," he told her.

She listened intently for a moment. "'A Foggy Day' is our song?" she asked skeptically.

"Well, it's as good as any," he said. "Come on," he cajoled good-naturedly. "Dance with me, Naomi."

She looked faintly panicked in response. "But…but…but…" she began. Unfortunately, no other words except for that one—rather inelegant one—came to her aid.

Unhampered by her unwillingness, Sloan stood with much purpose. But the moment he did, their waiter returned with their drinks, and Naomi seized on their arrival to negate his intention.

"Our drinks," she said with much relief. Before their server had even settled hers on the tabletop, she snatched it up, grasping it as if it were a lifeline someone had just tossed to her over the side of the *Titanic*. "We just got our drinks. We have to have our drinks." She lifted her lifeline, smiled jarringly and said, "Cheers!"

For a moment, Sloan thought about challenging her, insisting that they enjoy one dance before dinner, to whet their appetites, if nothing else. But Naomi looked so distressed, so frightened, by the prospect of even dancing, that he took pity on her.

For now.

Reluctantly, he seated himself again, and reached for his own drink. "Cheers," he concurred, though with a bit less enthusiasm. Before drinking, however, he vowed, "We'll have that dance after dinner, then, shall we?"

And before Naomi had a chance to reply one way or the other, he lifted his drink to his mouth and sipped. Done deal, he decided. They would dance— or something—after dinner.

Chapter 9

Naomi couldn't remember the last time she'd had such a wonderful meal, in such a wonderful place, with such a wonderful man. Of course, she decided as she watched Sloan surreptitiously from beneath lowered lashes—which was the way she had watched him throughout the evening—that was probably because she'd *never* had such a wonderful meal, in such a wonderful place, with such a wonderful man. Not until tonight, anyway.

She sighed with much feeling as she spooned sugar into her coffee and shifted her attention to the remnants of the chocolate torte she and Sloan had shared for dessert. She really, really, really wished she could finish it. She so hated to see chocolate—especially rich, expensive chocolate—go to waste. But she was so full, she simply could not touch another bite. Between the champagne cocktail, the four—count 'em, *four*—dinner courses, the bottle of, very nice, Pinot Grigio and the very generous serving of torte, she feared that if she consumed one more bite of anything, she would, quite simply, explode. As it was, coffee was probably pushing it.

But she was having such a good time, she wanted to prolong it in any way she could. The evening had been utterly magical, the kind of occasion she'd normally only fantasize about. No, actually, that wasn't quite true. Because Naomi couldn't have even fantasized something as nice as this. Her fantasies over the last few years had run more toward things like, oh, say…going fifteen full minutes without having to hear, "Mom! She's looking at me again!" or "Ms. Carmichael, I just don't understand this whole gerund thing," or "Coach, I can't work out today 'cause I got my period." Yeah, fifteen minutes of uninterrupted silence, fifteen minutes totally lacking in turmoil would definitely be a fantasy in Naomi's normal life. This evening, on the other hand…

This evening had transcended fantasy.

Sloan was just so… She bit back another sigh as she turned her gaze upon him again. So handsome. So sweet. So witty. So kind. So successful. So charming. So… So everything. All month long, she'd been insisting to herself that he wasn't her type, that he was too smooth, too polished, too rich, too successful, too… Too everything. He was a prosperous big-city attorney who'd gone this long without having married, so obviously, he enjoyed his successful, metropolitan, single life-style. He was the kind of man who, she had gathered from their numerous conversations, was used to a string of high-profile, late-night, social commitments, someone who would never be satisfied with the quiet, predictable, home-and-hearth routine that Naomi so dearly embraced.

Nevertheless, after tonight, and thinking back on the previous evenings they had spent together, coaching the girls and sharing dinner and indulging in conversation afterward, all Naomi could think was that Sloan Sullivan was really very...

Perfect. He was perfect. Which, of course, meant he wouldn't be around for long. Certainly no longer than his month-long commitment to the Lady Razorbacks. Which ended, she reminded herself, tonight.

"You owe me a dance," he said suddenly.

And just like that, Naomi's warm contentment exploded into hot confusion. "Uh...what?" she said eloquently.

He smiled. "You owe me a dance," he repeated. "The one we didn't get to have before dinner. We can have it now."

"But...but...but..."

"Come on," he coaxed, standing. "It'll shake off the dinner lethargy before we have to go home."

Naomi stopped herself before she allowed herself to think about other ways to shake off the dinner lethargy—talk about fantasizing. Oh, sure, over the last month, she'd had one or two—hundred—instances of fleeting—or prolonged—fantasies of a questionable nature where Sloan Sullivan was concerned. Fantasies in which the two of them were…strategizing. Naked. But she'd assured herself that such fantasies were perfectly normal for a woman her age who had a healthy sex drive—even if that drive hadn't been driven for a looong time. It was just fantasizing, that was all. Perfectly understandable, considering the circumstances and situation. As long as she didn't insert the key—so to speak—in the ignition of her sex drive, she'd be totally and completely—

"You know you want to," Sloan said, jarring her back to reality. And, man, she hated it when that happened.

"Uh," she began again, as eloquently as before. "I, um, I, uh… What?"

"Dance," he said again, grinning indulgently. "With me."

"Oh. I, um, I'm not sure I can dance after that big meal," she hedged.

"Sure you can," he insisted. "That'll just make it even more enjoyable, because we'll have more energy."

Hmm, Naomi thought. For some reason, he seemed to be talking about something other than dancing when he said that…

"C'mon," he wheedled one last time, extending his hand toward her.

And, God help her, Naomi found that she simply

could not resist the promise—or the temptation—that lit his blue, blue eyes. So, without questioning why she did it—or speculating upon what the ultimate outcome might be—she, too, stood and placed her hand gingerly in his.

The moment she touched him, a warm, wistful sensation suffused her entire body, wandering indolently through her limbs before pooling heavily deep in the pit of her stomach. Wow, she thought. She would have sworn there wasn't room for anything else in there, but somehow, Sloan just slipped right in.

He had already signed the credit card voucher—laughing her off when she'd insisted on paying for her half of the meal—so Naomi looped her little purse over her wrist and allowed him to lead her into the next room, where a small ensemble was playing something languid and lusty and low. A half-dozen or so couples were swaying languorously on the floor, and, without comment, Sloan led her to the center of them all. Then he drew her into the circle of his arms, pulled her *very* close, and tucked her head comfortably against his shoulder.

Never in her life had Naomi been able to lean her head comfortably against a man's shoulder. At best, she had always looked eye to eye with one. At worst, she'd had to keep a straight face while one nestled his head against her breasts—what little she'd had to nestle against when she was in high school, anyway. She'd always felt like such a great, hulking ogre around the boys at school and at college. Even her

ex-husband had only been a scant half-inch taller than
she. With Sloan, though, she felt almost petite.

She smiled at the thought. Talk about a fantasy...

But he was a fantasy, she reminded herself. Because in many ways, he really was too good to be
true. Men like him simply did not come along very
often. And for women like her—women who were
busy being moms and going gray and driving mini-
vans and pushing forty—men like him never stayed
long.

She tried to remind herself of that again as she
gingerly urged her hands over his shoulders and
folded her arms loosely together behind his neck. Really. She did try to remind herself of that. But as he
looped his arms around her waist and urged her
against his long, hard body, Naomi realized she
wasn't really listening to herself—mainly because she
was too busy nestling herself more resolutely against
him. And as she filled her lungs with the spicy, masculine scent of him, as she registered the heat of his
body seeping into her own, as she felt the gentle,
rhythmic thumping of his heart beating in time with
hers, she realized that she wanted to think about the
fantasy instead.

And then somehow, as Naomi was nestling herself
against Sloan, he was suddenly nestling himself
against her, too. As a result, the two of them ended
up with their bodies rubbing flush against each other,
and it felt almost as if he were wrapping himself
around her, enveloping her in all that was him. And

Naomi let herself be absorbed willingly, because she'd found herself in a place that was just too sweet to retreat from.

As the music shifted, so did their bodies and their rhythm, fluidly, as if each were completely in tune with the other. Without planning any of it, they moved gracefully as one, and without ever speaking a word, they expressed quite eloquently their wants and needs and desires. Vaguely, Naomi reminded herself that she was going to have to be going home soon. But every time the realization drifted into her head, she halted it by promising herself, *Just one more song...*

But as one song folded into another, each of the other couples began to leave the floor, leave the room. Eventually, even the band took a break, replacing their live music with taped. Naomi and Sloan scarcely noticed, however. They'd left the real world behind some time ago. They didn't need live music or other couples to enjoy what they'd discovered. They simply needed to draw each other close.

For long moments, they danced without speaking, their bodies swaying gently to and fro, to and fro, to...and...fro... One song segued into another. And then another. And then another. And with each passing tune, they grew more comfortable with each other, moving their hands from shoulder to neck to back to arm and around and about again. Bit by bit, Naomi investigated every polite inch of Sloan she was able to reach, her discovery making her fingers itch to explore those other, less accessible, parts of him, as well. He, in turn, explored her body at his leisure, with deceptively harmless little touches that struck flames wherever they fell.

And the more he touched her, the more Naomi wanted to be touched. And with every caress he stole of her body, the next was a little bolder, a little more curious. Tiny fires erupted along her arms and shoulders and back, then wandered inward, imploding in her midsection with an incandescent heat. For the first time in years, she wanted a man—really *wanted* him. And for the first time in years, she allowed herself to think about what it might be like to have him.

And then suddenly, before she realized what was happening, Sloan was kissing her. Or perhaps, she thought hazily, she had kissed him. In either event, it wasn't a soft, uncertain, solicitous kind of kiss she might have expected for a first-time kiss, but a confident, almost commanding kind of kiss that scorched her from her mouth to her belly. It was the kind of kiss that demanded a response. So what else could she do but respond?

And the moment she did… Oh. Sloan swept her away into a tempest. Their bodies, which had swayed so sublimely for… How long was it now? she wondered hazily. She couldn't quite remember…. But their rhythmic to and fro halted abruptly the moment she returned his kiss, with a fierceness and fire to mirror his own. And then the two of them only stood still in the center of the deserted room, hands tangled in hair, fingers bunching in fabric, mouths locked in heated exploration, bodies on fire with need.

Naomi couldn't think, couldn't form a single, coherent idea in her brain. All she could do was feel—the way her blood was humming in her veins, the way her heart was hammering in her chest, the way heat pooled deep in her pelvis, demanding satisfaction. And heavens, how she never wanted those sensations to stop. Heavens, how she wanted to cling to Sloan Sullivan forever.

"Oh, Naomi, I've wanted to do this for so long," he gasped against her jaw before covering her mouth with his again.

Naomi nodded, not sure she trusted her voice, hoping she conveyed to him her total agreement on that score. She had wanted it, too. For so long. Probably from that first night the two of them had spent chatting in her living room. As he'd left that night, she'd felt as if something were missing, as if there were something she wanted, needed, to do before he left. Kiss him, that was what it had been, she realized now. Kiss him and hold him and maybe even—

"I want you, Naomi," he murmured as he pulled away again. He gazed down into her face, his eyes dark with his wanting, his cheeks flushed with his passion. "I know it sounds crazy, but I want to make love to you. I think I've wanted to make love to you since that first night I met you. Over the past month... Watching you... Talking to you... Spending time with you..."

He seemed incapable of finishing a single thought, and Naomi was completely sympathetic. She couldn't begin *or* finish one herself. She let her eyes flutter closed, hoping that by blocking out the sight of his face, she might retrieve her senses and say the things she knew she should say. But by blocking him out visually, she only sensed him more powerfully in other ways—through his heat, his scent, his touch. And she realized that even though she knew what she *should* say, she doubted very much she could get the words past her throat. Because, to be honest, she didn't want to get them past her throat. She wanted to keep them buried inside.

Sloan dipped his head to hers again, but this time, instead of pressing his lips to hers, he dragged his open mouth along the sensitive column of her throat. "I can get us a room," he rasped as he went. But even through his rough passion, Naomi could sense his uncertainty. "It would only take a minute," he hurried on. "Please, Naomi. Let me get us a room."

Oh, God, she thought. Heaven help her, she wanted to say yes. She wanted to say yes very badly.

"It doesn't have to go any farther than you want it to," he promised her before kissing her hastily again. "Just…we need to be alone. At least for a little while. Now. Please."

Before she could think about what she was doing, and before she could second-guess herself, Naomi nodded quickly.

Sloan, evidently as uncertain about his own reaction as she was of hers, didn't wait around long enough for her to change her mind—or for him to change his mind, either. With another quick, passionate kiss, he murmured, "Stay right here. I'll be right back."

And after what seemed like seconds, but must have been much longer, he *was* back. Brandishing a plastic key card.

Naomi swallowed with much difficulty as she looked at it, but when her gaze flew to his, and she saw that he was as confused and consumed as she was, she nodded silently. He took her hand in his, and with surprising calmness, led her to a bank of elevators off the lobby. She watched the illuminated numbers as they rode up in silence, then let him lead her, their fingers still linked, to a room at the end of a hall. He opened the door for her and bid her enter first, and she preceded him in. Her gaze went immediately to the big king-size bed at the center of the room, already turned down, chocolates on the pillow, as if someone had been expecting them.

And then she heard the door click softly closed behind her.

Chapter 10

When Naomi turned around, she saw Sloan standing with his back pressed against the door, his gaze fixed on her face, as if he couldn't quite believe that they had done what they had done. And he looked at her with some uncertainty, too, as if he couldn't tell for sure if she would stay or she would go.

A thrill of something hot and urgent rocketed through her, and she suddenly felt as if she were a teenager, poised to experience her very first sexual encounter with a boy she'd dreamed about for years. She wasn't sure what to expect, but she couldn't wait to get started. Here was mystery and the unexplored and the promise of something electrifying.

Middle-class, single, working moms didn't do this kind of thing, she told herself. They didn't go to luxury hotel rooms with incredibly handsome, charming men, with nothing but the clothes on their backs. They didn't indulge in passionate, impromptu sexual encounters. They didn't dare.

Did they?

As she argued with herself mentally, Sloan continued to gaze at her in silence, as if he were waiting to take his cue from her. So, banning any and all second thoughts, and without blinking an eye, Naomi tossed her little black beaded purse onto a nearby chair. She was staying, dammit. She did dare.

This was just so exciting, she thought. So thrilling. So fantastic. So unreal. So unlike her. She didn't want to think about the repercussions, didn't want to think about anything at all, except for how she felt in that moment. Good. She felt *good*. Better than she had felt for a long, long time. For so many years, she had been doing for other people, and neglecting herself. For so many years, she had been a mother to her daughters, a teacher to her students, a coach to her team. But she'd never seemed to find the time or opportunity to be just a woman. She'd never done anything for herself.

Tonight, she would do something for herself, she vowed. Tonight, she would be just a woman.

Evidently taking the tossed purse as a positive sign, Sloan reached for his necktie and began to untie it. Naomi watched with fascination—and a dry mouth— as he unlooped the length of silk and tugged it from beneath his collar. He tossed it to the chair beside her purse, then shrugged off his jacket and discarded it, too. Then he went to work on the buttons of his shirt. With each one he freed, he took a step forward, until the garment hung open and he stood mere inches away from Naomi.

Oh, my, she thought. When she saw the rich scattering of dark hair that spanned his broad chest, her throat parched up like paper. Which was strange, seeing as how other parts of her body grew damp in response to the sight. Before she even realized what she was doing, she lifted her hands and tucked them under his shirt, skimming the garment open wide before nudging it over his shoulders and down his arms. He smiled as she performed the gesture, then cupped his hands over her shoulders and pulled her close, covering her mouth with his. Naomi buried her fingers in the soft hair of his chest, marveling at the density of the muscles she encountered beneath her fingertips.

He growled something soft and contented as she pressed her palms more resolutely into his warm flesh, then he shot a hand behind her, to the zipper of her dress. Naomi, too, murmured a low, feral sound as he dragged the zipper down, down, down, past her waist and over her bottom, until the dress gaped open and she felt the cool kiss of air on her bare back. She moved her arms so that he could skim the garment down over them, then the dress pooled in a heap of black at her feet. She stepped out of her shoes, hooked her thumbs into her panty hose, and pushed those down over her legs, as well. And then she stood before Sloan in nothing but a pair of plain white panties and a perfectly functional white bra.

Mom underwear, she couldn't help thinking. Immediately, she wished she'd had the foresight to don a pair of sexy black lace panties and demicup bra instead. Then she remembered she didn't own a pair of sexy black lace panties or a demicup bra. She only owned plain, functional white cotton. She wasn't the sexy black lace type. At least, she hadn't thought she was. Not until now. Sloan, however, seemed not to notice or care. No, he was much too busy unhooking that functional white bra and tossing it, too, to the floor.

Naomi was amazed that she didn't feel one scrap of self-consciousness in being undressed with this exciting, thrilling, passionate man. Instead, she felt emboldened. Because Sloan had ceased kissing her as he undressed her, and now he gazed at her half-naked body with much reverence.

She knew she was in good shape for a woman her age who had borne four children. But she knew wasn't a teenager anymore, either. And for one brief, terrifying moment, she knew that was as obvious to Sloan as it was to her. Then he smiled, an utterly lascivious, salacious smile, and she realized that maybe, just maybe, he didn't want a teenager. Maybe, just maybe, he wanted a woman instead.

He opened his mouth to say something, but for some reason, Naomi didn't want him to talk. She didn't want to talk, either. She only wanted to touch and feel and experience. So before he could speak, she pressed her lips to his, slipping her tongue into his mouth as she moved her hand to his belt.

But she gasped and pulled back some when she felt his hands on her breasts, his fingers closing over her possessively. He palmed her and squeezed her and rolled his thumbs over the swollen peaks, then he bent and filled his mouth with one of them. First he raked her nipple with the tip of his tongue, and then he laved her with the flat of his tongue, and then he sucked her deeply into his mouth. She gasped again at the wantonness of the sensations that shot through her, tangling her fingers in his dark hair. She wasn't sure if she was trying to stop him from doing what he wanted to do, or ensure that he continued forever and ever. She only knew a heat and a passion and a hunger that fired through her body, through her soul, through every last part of her. And she only knew that she wanted more.

"More," she murmured aloud before she even realized she meant to speak. "Oh, Sloan. More. Please. More."

She wasn't sure, but she thought he chuckled seductively against her damp flesh in response to her command. Then, for a moment, she wondered if he had heard her at all. Because he didn't alter what he was doing, only continued to lave her as he filled his hand with her other breast, capturing the tender peak between thumb and forefinger, rolling the stiff bud gently as he suckled its twin. Clearly, he intended to do this at his own pace. And, lucky for her, his pace seemed to be very, *very* leisurely.

Gradually, though, he began to urge her backward, toward the bed. Naomi went willingly, pulling him along, even though she knew he would follow enthusiastically. When her legs bumped against the mattress, they buckled beneath her, and she landed on her fanny. Sloan didn't even break stride as he joined her on the bed, fairly crawling over her as he pressed her backward onto the mattress. At some point she had freed his belt and unfastened his fly, and she felt him pressing hot and urgent against her thigh as he lay down beside her. Immediately, her hand flew to that part of his anatomy, her fingers dipping into his open trousers to curl around his solid length.

"Oh," he said softly in response to her exploration. "Oh, Naomi. Oh, boy…"

She grinned at her command over him, then urged him over onto his back. He lifted his hips long enough for her to tug down his pants and boxers, then kicked them off completely. But her command of him ended there, because he rolled her onto her back then, insinuating one strong thigh between her legs. The pressure of him there was an exquisite torture, and, instinctively, she thrust her hips upward. The rubbing of their bodies struck a spark of heat against that most sensitive part of her, and she moaned softly at the keen pleasure the gesture brought with it. Then she lowered her hips to the bed again, an action that gen-

erated yet another scintillating friction of heat, one
that shot an erotic shudder of delight coursing through
her. Again and again, Naomi bucked against his thigh,
her body growing warm and fluid with every movement she made, until she finally groaned aloud her
frustration at being unable to satisfy herself that way.

Sloan seemed to understand her distress, because
she suddenly felt his hand at the waistband of her
panties, shoving them down over her hips and legs
without ceremony. And then his hand was there,
where his thigh had been before, his fingers moving
deliberately, unhurried, between the damp folds of her
sensitive flesh. She cried out at the invasion, but thrust
her body upward again, and he buried a finger deep
inside her. She bucked again, and he inserted two.
Again, and he penetrated her with three.

Over and over he pleasured her that way, widening
his fingers, driving them deeper, until Naomi cried
out her ecstasy, and her physical response flowed
hotly over his hand. For a moment, she could only
lie there, reveling in the ripples of delight that echoed
through her. Never in her life had she experienced
such an exquisite pleasure. Never before had she been
taken to such heights. Before she returned to earth
entirely, however, Sloan lifted her from the mattress
and, seating himself on the edge of the mattress, he
straddled her over his lap.

Still feeling drugged and dazed by her release, Naomi lifted her hands instinctively to his shoulders,
curling her fingers into his hot, silky flesh. Instinc-

tively, she knew she would have to hold on tight for this ride. When she glanced down between their bodies, she saw that, at some point, Sloan had sheathed his heavy, stiff shaft in a condom. Vaguely, she wondered if she should be concerned about his preparedness, as if he'd been planning what she told herself she'd never seen coming. Then he was situating her over his long member, his hands gripping her hips firmly as he guided her down onto his teeming length.

And then he was inside her—*deep* inside her—penetrating her so fully, so completely, she halfway feared he would split her in two. Soon, though, Naomi ceased to think at all. Because she realized then that, on the contrary, instead of being split in two, she was forged into one—with Sloan. Throwing back her head, she cupped her hands over his shoulders, digging her knees into the mattress and spreading herself wider, so that he could fill her entirely.

And he did fill her entirely. So entirely, she knew in that moment that she would never feel empty again. As he buried himself inside her as deeply as he could, she wove her fingers through his silky hair and pulled him close. He nuzzled her breasts as he drew closer, then opened his mouth over one and drew her inside again. Now she was in him, and he was in her, she thought. There was no way the two of them would ever be separate again after this.

She wasn't sure how long they coupled that way, only knew that with every motion of their bodies, she gave more of herself to Sloan, and took more of him for herself. Eventually, he changed their positions again, so that she lay on her back on the bed with him kneeling before her, circling her ankles with strong fingers as he opened her legs wider, lifted her hips from the bed as he hooked her ankles behind his neck. And then, just when she thought she was about to come apart, he changed their positions again, and she was bent over on the bed, and he was behind her, his hands on her waist as he thrust himself into her again and again and again. Finally, though, they lay side by side, facing each other, and as Sloan kissed her again, he draped her thigh over his, cupped his hands over her bottom, and drove himself into her. Deep.

Gradually, his pace increased, and Naomi met every plunge and every lunge. And then, with one final forward thrust, his body went absolutely still, and he roared his completion, spilled his fulfillment. Naomi was no more able to keep her own joy inside, and she, too, cried out in both anguish and ecstasy.

Then he moved their bodies again, so that she was on her back once more. He kissed her hungrily, ravenously, thoroughly, almost as if this would be the last time he allowed himself the pleasure to do so. She returned his kiss with equal fire, equal furor, until he finally broke the contact. For a moment they only gazed into each others' eyes, gasping for breath, groping for coherent thought, both of them more than a little dazed by what had happened.

Then Sloan smiled a small smile and, very softly, he said, ''I'll be right back.''

And then Naomi was alone in bed, wondering where he had gone. The condom, she recalled immediately. He'd had to dispose of that. That modern safety measure that had prevented the mingling of their physical essences and protected them from both unwanted pregnancy and sexually transmitted dangers.

Would that it had prevented the mingling of their emotional essences, too, she couldn't help thinking. Would that it could protect her, at least, from other, more insidious dangers, too.

Because now, as the warm rosy afterglow of their lovemaking turned into a crisp, stark light of reality, Naomi realized the enormity of what she had just done. She had just made love with a man who had entered her life only temporarily. She, a woman of nearly forty, a woman with four daughters, a woman who had prided herself on being sane and solid, had just done something completely stupid. She, a woman who, until now had only had one lover in her entire life, had just made love with a man who, she was quite certain, had taken infinitely more lovers than that. A man who, she was likewise certain, would have no idea of the significance she attached to what they had just done. A man who did this sort of thing as a pastime. A man who'd had a condom at the ready, and no second thoughts.

Which was just as well, Naomi decided. Because

she was having more than enough second thoughts for both of them.

It never stops being a big deal, Evy. It is always *a big deal.*

The words she had spoken to her daughter only a few short hours ago came back to haunt her like a bad dream, and only then did Naomi realize her fatal mistake. Sex *was* a big deal. To her, at least. It had always been a big deal. That was why she had been a virgin when she'd met the man she ultimately married. And it was why she hadn't been with anyone since her husband had left. So why, suddenly, had she abandoned her conviction and done something like this?

Naomi decided immediately that she didn't want to explore the answer to that question. Not here. Not now. Not until she was alone someplace where she could make sense of everything that had happened tonight. Of everything that had happened over the last month. Because she was fairly certain that once she did make sense of it—if indeed such a thing were even possible—she wasn't going to like what she discovered.

As quickly as she could, she located her discarded clothing and got dressed. She finger-combed her hair, knowing the gesture was futile. She knew she must look exactly like what she was—a woman who had just engaged in a night of hot, unbridled—if casual—sex. Except that it hadn't been a whole night. And it certainly hadn't been casual. Not to Naomi, anyway.

Alone. She needed to be alone right now. Alone and far away from this place where she had just made a gross error in judgment. Perhaps the grossest error—in more ways than one—that she had ever made in her life. Sloan was still in the bathroom, even though he'd had plenty of time to take care of what he'd needed to take care of, and she could only conclude that he hadn't yet emerged because he had no more idea of how to react to what had just happened than she did. He probably wanted to be alone, too, she couldn't help thinking. Alone and far away.

But, hey, he was the one who had gotten the room, so she should be the one to get lost, right? Right. It would be the polite thing to do, right? Right. At least, Naomi thought that would be the polite thing to do. She had no idea how one was supposed to act after having casual sex. She'd never had casual sex before. Not even tonight. Intuitively, though, she suspected that leaving was the way to go here. Because the longer she lingered, the more in danger she became of doing something really stupid. Like crying, maybe. Or worse, like asking Sloan to make love to her again.

Quickly, she snagged her purse and ran a hand through her hair again. Part of her screamed at her that she should stay and see this thing through, that running away would only compound the mistake she had already made. But another part of her—the scared part—told her to flee. And as much as Naomi hated being scared, as much as she told herself to be strong, she couldn't help herself. She didn't know what to do. And in times of distress, she thought, there was just one foolproof method of survival.

Run away.

So Naomi did.

With no small panic coursing through him, Sloan gripped the sink in the hotel bathroom, gazed at the man in the mirror, and wondered who the hell the interloper was. He didn't recognize himself. How could he? He'd just done something totally out of character, something he'd sworn to himself he would never do. He'd just lost control with a woman. Completely and utterly lost control. He'd become so intoxicated with wanting her, needing her, *having* her, that he'd ceased to think, had only acted, and oh... What those actions had made him feel. Feel for the woman with whom he'd been acting. And she wasn't just any woman. No, Naomi was a *nice* woman. A nice woman who deserved infinitely better than a casual one-night stand with a man who lost control.

But had it been casual? Sloan asked himself. And had it only been for one night? It sure hadn't felt casual. It had felt... Incredible. Never in his life had he enjoyed an experience like the one he's just shared with Naomi. From the moment she had stepped into his arms on the dance floor, he'd felt as if the two of them had wandered into some kind of alternate reality. And then, when he'd kissed her—or had she kissed him? he wondered; he couldn't really recall now—when he'd tasted her sweetness and felt her warmth suffusing with his own, he'd simply been swept away.

He grinned wryly at the idea that he, Sloan Sullivan, pragmatic workaholic and confirmed bachelor, could be *swept away* by anything—especially a woman. Especially a woman who had four children, and who lived in a white frame house, and who drove a minivan. Especially a woman who could bring home the bacon and fry it up in the pan. Then again, he thought further, recalling the hot and heavy sensations that had plagued him for the last four weeks, she was also a woman who'd never let him forget he was a man. 'Cause she was most definitely a wo-man, w-o-m-a-n.

Good God, he thought. She'd even moved him to song.

He gazed at his reflection in the mirror again, marveling at how he even seemed to have changed physically since the last time he looked at himself. Maybe it was just good lighting, but his eyes seemed brighter all of a sudden, and the lines bracketing his mouth seemed to have eased. Even his skin appeared to be glowing. Somehow, making love to Naomi made him look and feel as if he had shaved years off of his life. He certainly hadn't felt this good, this vital, this *alive*, in a long, long time.

God, what was he supposed to do now? Unfortunately, no answer was forthcoming from the man in the mirror. Because Sloan had no idea what to do now.

But there was a woman waiting for him on the other side of that door, he reminded himself, and she was most assuredly expecting some kind of a response. Sloan just wished he had a response to give her. One that made sense, anyway. Because all he knew at the moment was that he wanted Naomi again. Badly. And he suspected it was a reaction that wouldn't be subsiding anytime soon. Because right now, in this moment, he couldn't imagine a time in his life when he would stop wanting her. And that pretty much scared the hell out of him.

Afterglow, he told himself quickly. What he was feeling now was simply the result of that uncertain, unreal afterglow that came in the moments after making love. *Of course* he was going to be feeling this way after incredible sex. *Of course* he was going to want to do it again. Lots of times. For the rest of his life. After a day or two, such feelings would subside. After a day or two, his desires and needs would go away. After a day or two, his hunger for Naomi would be nonexistent. Oh, sure, he'd miss her now that their…association…had come to an end. But in a day or two, he'd be fine. Of course, that didn't help him with the right now….

He inhaled a deep breath and told himself to stop being ridiculous. He'd had lots of afterglows to deal with over the years. There had been lots of women with whom he'd dealt—for lack of a better word— after making love. In many ways, Naomi was no different from any of them. Even if, he couldn't help thinking further, she was totally different from all of them.

He shook the thought off and opened the bathroom door, then strode through it as casually as he could manage. Which was no easy feat, seeing as how he was stark naked and utterly confused. But he realized even before looking around that the room was empty. Empty of a lot more than Naomi, too.

But mostly, he noticed that she was gone. Almost as if she'd never been there at all. And she was probably gone in a lot more ways than one, he couldn't help thinking further. And somehow, the realization of that came as no surprise to him at all. And for some reason, too, it settled deep in the pit of his stomach, like a cold, congealed lump of clay, a sensation, he suspected, that wasn't going to go away anytime soon.

Great, he thought. This was just great. What was he supposed to do now?

Chapter 11

The gymnasium of East Central High School in suburban Atlanta was a complete one-eighty from the Jackson High gym to which Naomi and the Lady Razorbacks were so accustomed. This school clearly didn't suffer from underfunding, as evidenced by the bright lights—not a single one of which was broken or burnt out—splashing illumination down over vivid red bleachers that looked as if they'd just been purchased, and a state-of-the-art scoreboard that was flashing in time to the Jackson High School pep band's rendition of "Rock Around the Clock."

And the Razorbacks' opposing team, the Lady Falcons of Dorman High School of Augusta, appeared to be no less well equipped than the school hosting the state finals. The Falcons sported crisp-looking red-

and-gold uniforms that could very well have been designed by a professional, a sharp contrast to the Razorbacks' tattered and faded blue-and-white jerseys and shorts.

The Falcons seemed to be better equipped with school spirit, too, Naomi couldn't help noticing. The bleachers were packed with students and parents and sports writers, the vast majority of whom waved red-and-gold banners for Dorman High. Only a few splashes of blue and white here and there offered any indication that the Lady Razorbacks of Jackson High School weren't—quite—alone, even though their school was much closer to Atlanta than Dorman was. All Naomi could hope was that her Razorbacks would outdo the Falcons in terms of strategy, scrappiness and heart.

Then again, she already knew those superior qualities were pretty much givens. In two weeks' time, the Jackson High team, with the help of Naomi and their returning assistant coach, Lou Melton, had outstrategized, outscrapped and outhearted every school they'd played, until, finally, they had made it to this, the state championship game. If they could just maintain their momentum and their determination—and Naomi was certain that they could—then they'd be taking home the state trophy to Jackson High School in Wisteria for the first time in the town's history.

Naomi braved another glance into the stands, where one particular splash of blue and white had alerted her earlier to the presence of what might very well be the Lady Razorbacks' number one fan. Sloan Sullivan had attended each of the tournament games as a spectator, had shouted louder and longer than even most of the parents had. He'd always managed to work his way down to the bench at some point during the game, to say hello to the girls and offer some unofficial coaching. He'd greeted Naomi with a formal nod or a softly uttered "Hello" each time, but he hadn't approached her to talk. Which was just as well, she always told herself on those occasions. Because she had no idea what to say to him.

There had been times over the last two weeks when she'd assured herself she had only dreamed—or fantasized—the evening she'd spent with him here in Atlanta before. Invariably, though, she'd recall with too much clarity the way they had been when they were together, the ways he had touched her, the ways he had kissed her, the ways he had set her entire body on fire. And she would be forced to remember that what the two of them had done together that night had been all too real. And all too extraordinary. And all too temporary. And much too big a mistake for her to ever repeat it again.

Her face flamed now just to remember that night. The things they'd done to and with each other, the errant, erotic words he'd whispered in her ear at the height of their passion, the way he'd made her feel…

She squeezed her eyes shut tight and spun back around again, before Sloan caught her looking at him. He hadn't called her once since that night. Of course, she reminded herself, she hadn't called him, either. And she was the one who had run out on him that night, she reminded herself further. There was no reason for Sloan to think she really wanted to have any further contact with him. Maybe he was as confused and embarrassed by what had happened as she was. Maybe he found it as difficult to approach her as she found it to approach him.

In which case, both of them were doubtless thinking the same thing: that what had happened was a mistake and an aberration, something that should never, ever have happened in the first place, something that should never, ever happen again.

Naomi told herself she should be relieved that they were on the same wavelength. She told herself she should be happy that they'd come to an unspoken agreement, because it prevented them from having to experience any further awkwardness. So why didn't she feel happy? Why wasn't she relieved? Why, even two weeks after the fact, did she still want Sloan every bit as much as she had wanted him that night? More, even? Worse, why did she miss even more than making love to him those quiet evenings the two of them had spent alone just talking?

Because as breathtaking and incredible as sex with him had been, those nights spent talking over coffee had commanded just as many of her wistful memories and melancholy regrets over the last two weeks. Since Sloan had departed from her life, Naomi's house felt so empty now somehow. Funny, that, seeing as how it had always felt so crowded before.

Or maybe it wasn't so funny, after all, she thought further. Because she knew that the girls, too, felt Sloan's absence rather keenly. Sophie, especially, asked when he would be coming to visit them again. And Naomi, heaven help her, hadn't had any idea what to tell her youngest daughter. Nor had she known what to say to her oldest daughters, even though she suspected that Evy, at least, understood the situation pretty well. Oh, her oldest daughter might not know *exactly* how far things had gone between Naomi and Sloan that night, but Evy was a big girl. She'd known Naomi and Sloan were attracted to each other, had witnessed her mother's apprehension and excitement before going out with him that night. She hadn't pressed Naomi for details when she'd come home so late, but she knew something was up. And Naomi hadn't had any more idea what to tell Evy than she had known what to tell Sophie about why Sloan had so abruptly severed personal ties to all of them.

For now, though, she pushed all those errant thoughts of Sloan away. She had a team to coach, a team that was going to take home a championship trophy tonight. After that...

Well, Naomi wouldn't think about that right now, either. Another nice thing about being in the tournament was that it had given her something to focus on besides Sloan. But once this game was over, and she no longer had game plans and practices on the brain, she knew her mind was going to fill with thoughts of him.

Later, she told herself again. She'd think about all that later. Right now, she—and her girls—had a game to win.

After much sweating, shouting, and nail biting— and after two agonizing overtimes—the Lady Razorbacks squeaked by the Lady Falcons, thanks to Evy's three-pointer in the last two seconds of the game. Like the rest of the team, Naomi was hoarse from yelling and cheering by then, but she didn't care. They'd all worked so hard for so long, and now—finally—they could celebrate. They were the best in the state. And they had a big ol' trophy to prove it.

She was so caught up in the celebration, in fact, that she didn't even notice the visitor to the locker room until Evy walked up with him in tow.

"Hey, Mom, look who I found," she said as she tapped her mother on the shoulder.

Naomi spun around to find her daughter standing beside a very reluctant-looking Sloan, and, just like that, a hot flame ignited in her belly and spread a rapid wildfire throughout her entire system. Although she'd seen him from a distance often enough over the last couple of weeks, she wasn't prepared now for this up close version. Especially since he didn't appear to be either of the Sloans she had come to know and— dare she admit it?—love. Neither sweats nor business suit adorned his form right now. Instead, he wore lovingly faded blue jeans and a tight, long-sleeved, navy polo that strained over his broad chest and shoulders and doubled the intensity of his blue velvet eyes.

Naomi opened her mouth to say something—though heaven only knew what, because her brain felt as empty as a pocket—when Evy saved her the trouble. Sort of.

"I made him promise to join us for the victory celebration," she said. "He hasn't said yes yet, but maybe if you asked him, Mom, coach to coach, I mean…"

She smiled as she let her voice trail off over that last part, as if she knew perfectly well that coaching had nothing to do with it, then she nudged Sloan discreetly forward. And then, pretending she saw something over Naomi's shoulder, she shouted at one of her teammates and abandoned them both.

At first, Naomi couldn't say anything, because she was much too busy reveling in the joy of just being close to Sloan again, at feeling giddy and light-headed with his simple nearness. His eyes really were as blue as she'd recalled them being, she noted. And he really was as tall and as broad as she had remembered. She had thought maybe she was embellishing him in her memories, making him more of a man than he actually was. Now, however, she saw he was every inch the man she had thought him. And then some. And she was nearly overcome by having him close enough to touch again. She just wished she had the nerve to reach out and touch him.

"Of course you should join us for the victory celebration," she finally managed to say, trying not to stammer, doing her best not to blush, but unable to halt the way her heart hammered hard in her chest. Heavens, just looking at him made her dizzy. "You're part of this team, too," she added.

"Not really," he denied good-naturedly. "I was only around for a month."

"Hey, you made quite an impression during that month," she said. "You made a huge difference during that month." Too late, she realized how he might misconstrue the statements. Then again, she thought, maybe, deep down, she hadn't been thinking about the team when she'd uttered them.

His dark brows arched up slightly at her comment, and he offered her a halfhearted smile. "Did I?" he asked.

She hesitated only a moment, then nodded. "Yeah. You did."

He eyed her thoughtfully in return, then, softly, he said, "With the team, you mean."

Naomi hesitated once more, then thought, what the hell? She might as well come clean. "Yeah, with them, too, I guess."

His smiled kicked up a few notches. "I wanted to call you," he said, his voice even softer now. "After that last night, when we…" He gazed past her at the celebrating girls, and even though the members of the team clearly had their minds on something other than their coach and her former, temporary, assistant, he dropped his voice a little more. "After that night, I couldn't stop thinking about you. About how much I wanted to make love to you again. About how much I just wanted to see you, spend time with you." He took a step closer, started to reach for her, then checked himself and dropped his hand back to his side. "I've missed you, Naomi. So much. For the last couple of weeks, I've felt like a part of me has been gone."

Naomi's heart pounded harder with every word he spoke, rushing blood through her veins at a frenzied pace. She told herself not to hope, not to put too much into what he was saying. But when she looked into his eyes and saw the flicker of heat burning there, she knew—she *knew*—his feelings mirrored her own.

"Why didn't you call me?" she asked him.

"Why didn't you call me?" he countered.

She closed her eyes. "If you knew how many times I wanted to…" But she couldn't quite make herself finish the statement.

"Why did you leave that night?" he asked her.

She opened her eyes again, then shook her head slowly. "I panicked. I didn't know what to do. I'd never done anything like that before with anyone, Sloan. And I realized you probably did stuff like that all the time, and—"

"I'd never done anything like that, either, Naomi,"

he assured her fiercely. "That was most definitely a first for me."

She grinned. "You didn't seem like a virgin to me."

"You know what I mean."

"But you're still a lot more experienced than me," she pointed out.

"Am I?"

"I've only been with one man besides you," she confessed.

"And I've *never* been with a woman like you," he assured her. "Never."

She swallowed hard at that. "Then why didn't you call me?" she asked again.

He expelled a soft, frustrated sound. "I wanted to. So badly. But I figured you had too many other things to worry about right now," he said. "I didn't want to distract you from the tournament by making you wade through…stuff…with me."

"Are you kidding?" she replied, feeling a bit bolder now after all of his revelations. "You've been nothing but a distraction to me since the day I met you."

He grinned hopefully. "You mean you won the championship in spite of me?" he asked.

She shook her head. "No. Not in spite of you. We couldn't have made it without you. It's amazing the way you showed up right when we needed you the most."

"We?" he echoed.

"Me," she corrected herself. "You showed up right when *I* needed you most. And *I* couldn't have made it without you." She inhaled a deep, fortifying breath and decided to go for broke. "I still don't think I can make it without you. I know I don't *want* to."

He considered her with much speculation for a moment, then asked, "About this victory celebration...?"

"Ah, yeah," Naomi said. "Lou and I promised the girls we'd go for pizza or burgers or whatever they wanted before we take the bus back to Wisteria tonight."

Sloan nodded thoughtfully. "You're going back to Wisteria tonight, too?" he asked.

"Well, originally, I had planned to, yeah."

"I couldn't maybe talk you into, oh...staying the night?"

Naomi smiled, then turned to look over her shoulder at Evy, who was currently enjoying a traditional, after-championship baptism. "Well, gee, I *guess* I could depend on my oldest to take care of things at home for a night. She's normally very responsible. When she's *not* getting a Gatorade shower, I mean."

"My place?" Sloan said when she turned back around to gaze at him again. "It's not quite as homey as yours, but—" he smiled devilishly "—it's closer."

Naomi smiled back, feeling every bit as devilish as he looked. "You know, maybe that's something we can rectify," she told him.

He looked faintly puzzled. "What do you mean?"

"I mean maybe we can meet halfway on that home thing eventually. Surely we could find *some*thing between Atlanta and Wisteria that has some promise."

His smile grew wider by a mile. "Maybe we can meet halfway," he agreed. "Eventually. So what do you say, Naomi? Tonight? Your place or mine?"

She felt her own smile growing wider as she said, "I have an even better idea. How about *our* place instead?"

As afterglows went, Sloan thought, this was one of his better ones. He pulled Naomi closer and snuggled her damp, warm, naked body against his, tugging the sheet up over them in the king-size bed in the room they had taken at the San Moritz Hotel. *Our place,* he remembered her calling it only a few hours ago. He liked the sound of that. Maybe they should make it a tradition to come here every year, on their wedding anniversary or something, to commemorate the first time they—

He halted himself before finishing the thought. *Every year?* he asked himself. *On their* wedding *anniversary?*

He waited for a shudder of terror to rock him at the very thought of being married to someone. And waited. And waited. And waited. Strangely, though, there was no shudder of terror that even trickled through him. No, all he felt was a warm, wistful sensation of being exactly where he belonged wandering through him instead. The thought of being married to

Naomi, instead of horrifying him, only made him feel wonderfully complete.

"Hey, Naomi," he said absently, letting his fingertips glide slowly over her upper arm and shoulder, then back again.

"Hmmm?" she murmured, nestling her head beneath his chin, draping her thigh over his.

"I've been thinking," he continued.

"Thinking?" she echoed softly. "How could you think during that? My brains were totally scrambled."

He smiled. Good. That was what a man liked to hear after making love to a special woman. And Naomi, he had learned over the last several weeks, was most assuredly special. Among other things.

"I wasn't thinking during *that*," he told her. "You had me way too worked up to do anything as mundane as think."

"Good," she murmured. "That's what a woman likes to hear after making love to a special man."

Sloan narrowed his eyes suspiciously as he gazed down at the dark head snuggling against his chest. Jeez, they weren't even married yet, and already she was reading his mind.

"So what were you thinking about?" she asked him, her voice a quiet purr and warm caress against his throat.

"I was thinking that, you know, the two of us made a good team when we were coaching," he said.

"Well, we *are* responsible for the current state champs," she reminded him unnecessarily.

He nodded. "Yeah, and it made me wonder if we'd be as good doing other things together."

She turned her head to look up at him then, her smile wicked, wanton and wild.

"I mean at something besides what we just did together," he qualified.

She batted her eyelashes at him. "Oh."

"Though, mind you, we are awfully good at that, too," he agreed. "But I had something else in mind. Another game we might play together that we'd be good at."

"What's that?" she asked.

"House," he told her. "I thought me might be good at playing house."

Her dark brows furrowed downward in confusion. "House?" she repeated. "But...I never even played house when I was a little girl. Why would you want to—"

"Okay, then we won't play it," he said. "We'll just do it."

Now her dark brows arched upward in surprise. "What do you mean?"

"I mean I want to live with you, Naomi. With you and your daughters. I want us all to be together. As a family. Because I love you. All of you." When she only continued to gaze at him in massive befuddlement, he hastily added, "As long as that's what you want, too, I mean."

"You want us all to live together?" she said. "You love us? All of us?"

He nodded, feeling nervous for the first time since the two of them had started talking again. Surely this didn't come as a surprise to her, he thought. Surely she saw this coming. Then again, a few hours ago, he'd been worried he would never speak to her again, and she hadn't looked any too certain about the future, herself.

"Gee, I don't know, Sloan," she said gravely. "I don't think I could live with a man unless I was married to him." She punctuated the remark with a dazzling smile, and he knew then that she was only stringing him along. "Of course, seeing as how I love you, too, maybe that won't be a problem?"

"Fine," he said. "Then I'll marry you. I need to make an honest woman out of you, anyway." He hesitated only a moment before reminding her, "We did rather neglect something very important this evening, after all."

She studied him in confusion for a moment, then, suddenly, her eyes widened in obvious concern. "A condom," she said. "We didn't use one."

"No, we didn't," he confirmed. "You, my darling wife-to-be, could, as we speak, also be a mother-to-be."

She shook her head quickly. "Oh, no. No, no, no, no, no."

He smiled and nodded. "Oh, yes. Yes, yes, yes, yes, yes."

She nibbled her lower lip anxiously. "Well, Sophie *did* ask Santa for a baby brother last Christmas...."

Sloan grinned again. "Would she be just as happy with a baby sister?"

"Another girl?" Naomi asked. "Are you serious? Could you handle living in a house with that much estrogen?"

"Are you kidding?" he replied, mimicking her shocked tone. "When Evy and Katie can kick my butt at roundball and Sophie has a train setup like the one I always wanted when I was a kid? Piece of cake."

Naomi smiled, too, then snuggled closer still to Sloan. "As long as you don't mind the family plan, Mr. Sullivan, then yes, I think we could play house very nicely together."

Sloan sighed heavily and with much contentment, then scooted both their bodies down deeper onto the bed. "Then let's get started," he told her. "You be the mommy, and I'll be the daddy. Naomi and Sloan and their daughters." He grinned as he heard her laughter bubble up, then gathered her as close as he could. "You know," he said softly, "I just don't think it can get any better than that."

* * * * *

magazine

♥———————————————————————— **quizzes**

Is he the one? What kind of lover are you? Visit the **Quizzes**
area to find out!

♥———————————— **recipes for romance**

Get scrumptious meal ideas with our **Recipes for Romance**.

♥———————————————— **romantic movies**

Peek at the **Romantic Movies** area to find Top 10 Flicks
about First Love, ten Supersexy Movies, and more.

♥———————————————————— **royal romance**

Get the latest scoop on your favorite royals in **Royal Romance**.

♥——————————————————————————— **games**

Check out the **Games** pages to find a ton of interactive
romantic fun!

♥———————————————— **romantic travel**

In need of a romantic rendezvous? Visit the **Romantic Travel**
section for articles and guides.

♥————————————————————— **lovescopes**

Are you two compatible? Click your way to the **Lovescopes**
area to find out now!

Silhouette® —

where love comes alive—online...

These New York Times *bestselling authors*
have created stories to capture the hearts and minds
of women everywhere.
Here are three classic tales about the power of love—
and the wonder of discovering the place
where you belong....

FINDING HOME

DUNCAN'S BRIDE
by
LINDA HOWARD

CHAIN LIGHTNING
by
ELIZABETH LOWELL

POPCORN AND KISSES
by
KASEY MICHAELS

Available only from Silhouette
at your favorite retail outlet.

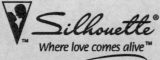

Where love comes alive™

INTIMATE MOMENTS™

presents:

Romancing the Crown

*With the help of their powerful allies,
the royal family of Montebello is
determined to find their missing heir.
But the search for the beloved prince
is not without danger—or passion!*

Available in May 2002:
VIRGIN SEDUCTION
by Kathleen Creighton (IM #1148)

Cade Gallagher went to the royal palace of
Tamir for a wedding—and came home with
a bride of his own. The rugged oilman thought he'd married to
gain a business merger, but his innocent bride made him long
to claim his wife in every way....

*This exciting series continues throughout
the year with these fabulous titles:*

January	(IM #1124)	THE MAN WHO WOULD BE KING by Linda Turner
February	(IM #1130)	THE PRINCESS AND THE MERCENARY by Marilyn Pappano
March	(IM #1136)	THE DISENCHANTED DUKE by Marie Ferrarella
April	(IM #1142)	SECRET-AGENT SHEIK by Linda Winstead Jones
May	(IM #1148)	VIRGIN SEDUCTION by Kathleen Creighton
June	(IM #1154)	ROYAL SPY by Valerie Parv
July	(IM #1160)	HER LORD PROTECTOR by Eileen Wilks
August	(IM #1166)	SECRETS OF A PREGNANT PRINCESS by Carla Cassidy
September	(IM #1172)	A ROYAL MURDER by Lyn Stone
October	(IM #1178)	SARAH'S KNIGHT by Mary McBride
November	(IM #1184)	UNDER THE KING'S COMMAND by Ingrid Weaver
December	(IM #1190)	THE PRINCE'S WEDDING by Justine Davis

*Available only from Silhouette Intimate Moments
at your favorite retail outlet.*

  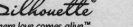

Silhouette®

Where love comes alive™

Visit Silhouette at www.eHarlequin.com

SIMRC5

Award-winning author

SHARON DE VITA

brings her special brand of romance to

V. *Silhouette*

SPECIAL EDITION™

and

SILHOUETTE **Romance**™

in her new cross-line miniseries

SADDLE

FALLS

This small Western town was rocked by scandal when the youngest son of the prominent Ryan family was kidnapped. Watch as clues about the mysterious disappearance are unveiled—and meet the sexy Ryan brothers...along with the women destined to lasso their hearts.

Don't miss:

WITH FAMILY IN MIND
February 2002, Silhouette Special Edition #1450

ANYTHING FOR HER FAMILY
March 2002, Silhouette Romance #1580

A FAMILY TO BE
April 2002, Silhouette Romance #1586

A FAMILY TO COME HOME TO
May 2002, Silhouette Special Edition #1468

Available at your favorite retail outlet.

Silhouette®

Where love comes alive™

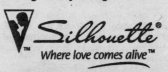